8/1/15

BURN

Also by Walter Jury and Sarah Fine

SCAN

BURN

WALTER JURY | SARAH FINE

G. P. PUTNAM'S SONS
An Imprint of Penguin Group (USA)

G. P. PUTNAM'S SONS
Published by the Penguin Group
Penguin Group (USA) LLC
375 Hudson Street, New York, NY 10014

USA | Canada | UK | Ireland | Australia
New Zealand | India | South Africa | China
penguin.com
A Penguin Random House Company

Library of Congress Cataloging-in-Publication Data
Jury, Walter, author.
Burn / Walter Jury and Sarah Fine.
pages cm
Sequel to: Scan.
Summary: "Tate learns quickly that the H2 are the least of his problems
when a new alien race begins to threaten the planet"—Provided by publisher.
[1. Adventure and adventurers—Fiction. 2. Fathers and sons—Fiction. 3. Inventors and
inventions—Fiction. 4. Extraterrestrial beings—Fiction. 5. Science fiction.] I. Fine, Sarah. II. Title.
PZ7.J965Bur 2015 [Fic]—dc23 2014031200

Printed in the United States of America.
ISBN 978-0-399-16068-4
1 3 5 7 9 10 8 6 4 2

Design by Ryan Thomann.
Text set in Maxime Std.

For Mom and Dad—Nana and Babba,
as their grandkids call them!
—W.J.

ONE

IN MY WORLD, THINGS ARE COMPLICATED. AT LEAST, they are right now. I've just destroyed a Walmart. At any moment, my worst enemy is going to come charging out of its front entrance, determined to hunt me down. I'm standing, exposed and vulnerable, at the side of the road not a quarter mile away, so it wouldn't take him long. And the thing I've been fighting for is *gone*.

The past three days have rearranged my understanding of myself and this planet so drastically that I'm not sure I can cram another hard truth into my head. The things I do know tumble over one another in my mind:

My mother is in surgery. For a bullet wound. She can't help me.

Race Lavin, the guy she was trying to protect me from— who also happens to be part of an alien race called the H2—is probably regaining consciousness right now in the hardware section.

His men have taken my father's invention, the scanner that tells the difference between H2 and human, the device my dad said was the key to our survival, the thing he died for. And his best friend, George, the guy I was trusting to help me put the pieces of this puzzle together, is a few feet away from me, slumped over the wheel of his car. His blood is smeared across the seat. Another life lost in our secret war.

"Tate, I think we have to go." Christina's slender fingers encircle my wrist. "I hear sirens."

I blink. Wisps of her dark blond hair blow around her face, which is pale with fear but set with determination.

"I don't know where . . ." I have no idea where to go. My mom said I should meet her at the hospital, but it doesn't seem safe.

Nothing seems safe.

Christina's grip tightens. "We need to move, though. I'm not sure it matters where right now. As long as we're away from here."

I take one last look into George's bullet-riddled car. I would have expected it to be armored, seeing as he works for Black Box, a private weapons manufacturer. But even if it was, it was no match for the large-caliber ammo Race's agents were firing from their shiny black helicopter. Which means they could tear through our current ride—a sedan borrowed from Rufus

Bishop and his inbred clan of human supremacists—like paper. There's already a bullet hole in the thing's rear panel, a farewell gift from the Bishops in return for the accidental death of Aaron, Rufus's oldest son.

I've made a lot of enemies this week. Alien *and* human.

My only ally is tugging me back toward our car. I have so many things to figure out, so many things to do, but as her hand slips into mine, I realize I need to prioritize. And protecting her is at the top of the list. I put my feet in motion and jog beside her. We jump into the car, and I swing us onto the road, heading north.

"Are we going back to New York?" she asks.

"I don't know," I say hoarsely. "I need to get into my father's lab and dig up what he was working on, but I have a feeling Core agents will be waiting for me to show up." The H2 central leadership has a history of brutally suppressing any threat to their secrets, and I am most definitely that, even without the scanner. Just before I choked him out, Race made it clear that the device wasn't the only thing he was after. He wanted me to help him get into my father's lab. As. If.

"Your dad's phone."

Her voice yanks me out of my churning thoughts. "What?"

Christina touches the side of my face. "It's buzzing in your pocket, Tate," she says quietly. "Why don't you let me drive? You need to think things through, and I can manage this part."

I pull off the state highway into a subdivision, parking in

front of the community pool. We switch places, and I lean over and kiss her cheek. "I'd be in serious trouble without you," I say, and then instantly regret it. She shouldn't even be here with me. Her biggest worry should be passing the chemistry final tomorrow, but right now, missing an entire week of school is the least of her problems.

I stare down at my hands, using my thumbnail to scrape off a few red smudges. This is the third time in as many days that I am wearing the blood of someone I care about. This time it's from George, but last time . . . I look over at my girlfriend. The white bandage is visible beneath her thick, wavy hair. It covers the stitched-up graze wound given to her by Core agents. She's not even recovered from the concussion she sustained two days ago. She hasn't had a chance, because we've been running and fighting nearly every moment since it happened. "Christina . . . you really need to see a doctor about your head—remember what David Bishop told you? You need a CT scan. Maybe you should—"

"Don't even, Tate. I feel fine. And I can tell by the look on your face that you're about to try to be noble and send me home, but it's not going to happen. I'm in this with you, and that's it. Save your head space for something else, like seeing who's trying to reach you." She frowns. "Or who's trying to reach your dad, I guess," she murmurs.

I pull my dad's sleek, untraceable phone from my pocket. "Someone texted."

"Who is it?"

I stare at the icon, a black envelope on the screen. And the name next to it is—"Raymond A. Spruance." I touch the black envelope, and a box pops up, requesting a password.

"Is that one of The Fifty?" she asks, sounding nervous. The Fifty are a group of human families who understand the threat from the Core very well—they've been defending themselves from this alien elite ever since the H2 crashed their ships into the oceans four hundred years ago, refugees fleeing from something pretty bad, if I'm to trust Race Lavin. Which I won't. But my father, who sat on the board of The Fifty, warned me to be careful with them, and he was totally right. So far, two of their number—Rufus Bishop and my dad's former boss, Brayton Alexander—have tried to kill us.

"I don't know, but the name . . ." I stare at it, sifting through my memories. "This isn't about The Fifty. Raymond A. Spruance was a famous admiral during World War II." My heart picks up its pace. An encrypted, secret text from a long-dead admiral— one my dad made me study in depth. "What if this message is from my dad?" I whisper.

"Tate . . ."

I can tell by the way she says my name that she's worried I might be losing my mind. "No, listen. This is exactly like something he would do." For years, he made me study military history. Along with chemistry, physics, ballistics, jiu-jitsu, and a host of other things. I thought he was just a hard-ass, but he was preparing me for this, and now I need to use what I know. "What if he set up some sort of messaging system in case something happened to him?"

"Sent to his own phone?"

"Who knows where else this message went?"

"But, Tate, how would it know something had happened to him? And . . . he died on Monday. It's Thursday now. Though it feels a lot longer than that," she adds quietly.

"I know. Something could have triggered it, though. Maybe because he hasn't logged in in the last seventy-two hours. Or there was an intrusion in his systems, or someone unauthorized tried to enter his lab? Race straight up told me that the Core want to get in there." I stare at the password box. "It will only open for people who know the password."

"Do you know it?"

"No, but that's kind of the point. I'll bet he didn't tell anyone."

Or maybe he did. His last words to me were *When the time comes . . . it's Josephus.* There are eight little sections in the password box—that's how long the password must be. My fingers shake a little as I type *Josephus.*

The screen flashes red, and the upper left quadrant goes black. "Shit." I bow my head and try to get my heart to slow down. I need to think. He didn't send a message under the name "Spruance" randomly. I type *07031886*—the birth date of Admiral Raymond A. Spruance.

The screen flashes red again, and the lower left quadrant goes black. I'm guessing I'm running out of chances. If I don't figure this out, this message might disappear, and it's important. It has to be.

I blow a long breath from between pursed lips, thinking about Spruance. His nickname was Electric Brain. I slowly type *electric*. Another red flash, and the upper right quadrant goes dark. "Damn!"

What is wrong with me? I've burned through three of four shots at getting this message, all in less than a minute. I'm supposed to be thinking like my dad, but instead I'm thinking like . . . me. My dad made me study at least a hundred major battles that took place throughout the centuries; he was a fan of Spruance in particular because the guy stayed cool in the midst of chaos, and my dad valued that highly. Spruance was involved in the Battle of Midway and won a Distinguished Service Medal afterward, and Dad actually made me memorize the citation, because he said that those qualities would help a man get through anything. It had commended Spruance on his *endurance* and *tenacity*. And this password is eight characters long.

I hold my breath and type *tenacity*.

The screen flashes green. A message appears:

BROKEN BY IT, I, TOO, MAY BE; BOW TO IT I NEVER WILL.
AND, JUST IN CASE: MARGARET DEAN, I HAVE LOVED YOU ALWAYS.

"What does it say?" Christina asks, and her brow furrows as I tell her. "Are you sure that's from your dad?"

I swallow the lump in my throat. "Yeah. The first part is a quote. Abraham Lincoln said it." And God, it's like my dad was predicting his own death. Especially because—"Margaret Dean was Raymond Spruance's wife. I think my dad is referring to my mom. I wonder if she got the message, too." It'll tear her heart out if she gets access to it, and she's so smart that I bet she could figure it out.

"What's he trying to tell you?"

Dad always planned ahead. *Four steps ahead,* Rufus Bishop had told me. "Christina, I think we need to go to Kentucky."

She laughs. "What?"

"Whenever Dad had me study a specific person, like a general or a president or whomever, he told me to go back to the very beginning, because if I understood where a man came from, I could understand what shaped his thoughts."

"And Spruance was born in Kentucky?"

"No. He was born in Maryland. But this quote is from Lincoln, and Dad never did stuff by accident. He's trying to tell me—and maybe my mom—to meet him . . ." I clench my fists. "He's trying to tell us to go to Lincoln's birthplace. Which happens to be Hodgenville, Kentucky." I program it into the GPS on his phone. "It should take us about eight hours to get there."

"We'll have to get gas."

I curse. "We can't use my debit card. It'll tell the Core exactly where we are."

She smiles grimly. "Good thing I stole some cash from the professor." She pulls his wallet from the pocket of her sweatpants and hands it to me. It's an expensive-looking leather thing with cw on it. Charles Willetts. A friend of my mother's who turned out to be an enemy, though I'm still not sure what side he was on. He never scanned himself, and thinking back, I wonder if he avoided it on purpose. He was supposedly H2, but he wanted to keep the scanner away from them. He wanted to get it to George instead, even though they were seemingly on opposite sides.

I peek inside the wallet. "There's at least a hundred. It'll get us there." I raise my head. "Did he hurt you?"

Her mouth tightens. "Only a little. He . . . he got really weird after you left, Tate." She shudders. "He was pulling at the neck of my shirt, saying he needed to touch my skin . . ."

I take her hand, wishing I could find Willetts and *kill* the creepy old guy. She squeezes my fingers as she says, "He got distracted when someone started banging on the door, and I grabbed the gun and hit him with it. I took his wallet and keys and ran."

"How did you get out?"

"Same way you did, judging by the dent you put in the roof

of that SUV in the parking lot. It was crazy, all these ambulances and stuff, a helicopter landing on the lawn in front of that university Rotunda, so I slipped away in the chaos."

And she could have gone anywhere. She could be halfway to New York by now. Yet she came straight to me. I stroke her hand. "You're amazing." And I love her. I told her as much last night, but it turns out she was dead asleep. I want to tell her again, but I also want it to be the right time. Preferably when we're not running for our lives.

Christina turns on the radio and sets the station when she finds some of her cherry-flavored pop music. I sit back and allow myself the luxury of staring at her while she sings along. We motor down the road, heading for a tiny town in central Kentucky that is, I hope, the location of one of my dad's safe houses. If I really understand who my dad was, though, it won't be just a place to lie low. There's a reason he'd send us that kind of message, a reason he'd direct us to that place specifically. It's not New York, and it's not his lab, but I'm hoping that once we get there, some answers will be waiting.

TWO

SWEAT PRICKS AT THE BACK OF MY NECK AS THE LATE- afternoon sun beats down on us. Christina shifts slightly, trying not to make any noise. We're squatting behind one of the many chokeberry bushes in this large yard, having walked here from the gravel road about a half mile away.

In front of us is a shack. Like, really, a shack. Rotting clapboard, cracked and broken windows, front door hanging off its hinges. No sign of life anywhere, but that doesn't mean we're not being cautious. When we rolled into town, we went straight to the birthplace of Lincoln, but as soon as I saw the National Park sign, I knew it wasn't a place my dad would locate a safe house or any kind of meeting place. So we headed to the Hodgenville town hall and looked at property records. My dad's name wasn't anywhere to be found. Neither was my mom's. Or mine. But there was one name I recognized:

Raymond A. Spruance bought a property on the outskirts of town about two years ago, and here we are.

"Are you sure this is the right place?" Christina whispers.

I glance over at her. She looks dead tired, and I'm sure she's craving a hot shower, a nice meal, and a long sleep. I know I am. "If this isn't it, we'll go back to that hotel we passed in town, okay? But let's investigate first. Come on. I don't think anyone's here."

We come out from behind the bushes and cross the yard, then carefully mount the rickety stairs to the shade of the porch. I lead the way as we edge around the door and into the shack. The floor is dusty and bare . . . except for an old sock lying in the corner. I walk over to it, and when I see the musical note stitched on the ankle, I start to laugh.

"What's up?" Christina asks, coming over to me.

I point at the musical note on the sock. "Did you know there was a famous composer named Frederic Archer?"

Her arms slide around my waist. "So this is definitely your dad's place, then?"

"Yeah, has to be," I say, my voice strained. I stand right on top of the sock and look around to see what this vantage point shows me. There's no furniture in this place, which is an open room with two closed doors at the back, maybe leading to a bedroom and a kitchen. Nothing's written on the walls, and the ceiling—wait. There's a rusty nail hammered into the wooden board right above my head. I reach up and twist it, pulling it out, my breath coming faster.

Nothing happens. I look down at the bent nail, which has turned my fingers orange with iron oxide. It was right above my head. Right above the sock. I kick the ragged thing aside, uncovering a small hole in the floor. I kneel next to it and then, following my instincts, insert the nail into the hole. It catches, and a deep vibration thrums up my arm. Christina clutches at my shoulder while the house shakes and the door behind me unlatches, opening a crack. I push it ajar in time to see the floor of the room sliding open, revealing a metal staircase descending into darkness.

I stand up, stick the nail back in its hole in the ceiling for future use, and take Christina's hand. "Definitely my dad's place." And it's both awesome and gut wrenching. "Come on."

Together, we descend the stairs, our palms skimming along the cool concrete walls. I feel another vibration before I hear it, and I look up to see the floor sliding across the opening to the staircase, plunging us into total darkness. Christina touches my shoulder, and I put my arm around her. "It's okay. Just keep a hand in front of you so you don't hit a wall."

Groping in the inky murk, we walk down a few more steps and reach the bottom. My hand brushes a metal door, and I feel my way to a keypad, which lights up as soon as I touch it.

"Please say you know the password," Christina says.

"I might." My heart beats a jittery rhythm in my chest as I punch in *Josephus*.

It buzzes and lets out a tiny electric shock. I yank my hand back with a yelp and shake the pain from my fingers. "I guess that wasn't it," I mutter, frustration prickling along my limbs. *Goddamn.* Another dead end. Dad wouldn't have wasted his final breath on that name, on that message, if it wasn't important. So what the hell did he mean? I grit my teeth. It barely matters right now, because I've trapped myself—and my girlfriend—in the basement of a shack in the middle of freaking nowhere. What matters now is finding out what the password actually is.

I try *tenacity*. Shock. *Spruance*. Shock. *Scanner*—"Shit!" I step back, the painful tingles coursing up my fingers.

Christina's breath is warm in my ear. "Slow down. Take a few minutes and think about it. We're okay. No one's chasing us at the moment. It's all right." Her arms are tight around my waist, like she's trying to hold me up. "Have you tried passwords he used in the past?"

I blink down at the obnoxious keypad. I can almost hear my dad's grim chuckle. The shock isn't damaging, just annoyingly painful. Like my dad's criticisms. I blow out a breath, and then I slowly type my mother's middle name, one of his favorites despite the obvious security risk. And . . . no shock. The door clicks and swings open. Several lamps and overhead lights illuminate the space, motion-activated, I guess.

"Whoa," Christina mutters as we walk into an apartment, echoing my sentiments perfectly.

This place looks exactly like our apartment in New York, minus the windows. Same furniture. Same layout. Even a few of the same family photos. All that's missing is my stuff, strewn all over the coffee table. I close the metal door behind us and head for the kitchen. And sure enough, when I pull open the refrigerator, I see several Meal Number Tens. Eight ounces pinto bean soup with lean ham. Four wheat crackers. Two ounces dried pineapple, banana, and mango. Two ounces mixed nuts. "Hungry?" I say to Christina, pulling two of them out.

"Thanks," she says, taking them. "Are you going to tell me how you're doing with this? It's so strange."

I shrug. "Not for my dad. If I'm right, he'll have a lab here, too. I need to go take a look at it, but let's eat first. You look like you're about to fall over."

We sit at the table, and as I take my usual seat, I think of the last time I did. The last time I saw my dad as he was supposed to be, combed and pressed and ticked off at me. We'd been eating breakfast with George, and they'd been talking about population estimates, and how my dad's calculations showed the numbers shifting more quickly than anticipated. Now I know he meant there are more H2 every day, and fewer humans. But there were also anomalies—fourteen of them. And, thinking about how George's skin flashed orange under the light of the scanner instead of red or blue like everyone else, I have to wonder if he was one of those anomalies. I wish I knew what that meant.

After we're finished, I try to call my mom, but her phone goes straight to voicemail. I send her a text: *SAFE. Call soon?* I hope she'll understand my meaning. And if she got Dad's message, too, she might even know where we are. Still, I really want to hear her voice right now, and I need to know she's okay. I can only hope she's safe in the hospital, sleeping off the anesthesia, and not in the hands of the Core. Maybe Angus McClaren flew from Chicago to help her out. She said they were friends. I don't like thinking of her alone and vulnerable—especially because I left her that way. After a few minutes of waiting for a response, I start to poke around the apartment. It's precisely like my home in New York, but there's no sign my dad was ever here, save the fact that the fridge is stocked.

Finally, we make our way down yet another set of stairs and find a door that looks exactly like the one leading to my dad's lab. Except: I don't have my dad's fingerprint. It's sitting in a plastic case in my room in New York. Exhausted, I lean against the wall. Another freaking puzzle to solve.

"Tate, it feels late," Christina murmurs.

I'm about to argue when I notice the shadows beneath her eyes. I pull out my dad's phone. It's only eight, though it feels way past midnight. "I know what you mean. This can wait until tomorrow. Let's go get some sleep." We've been up since four, and I barely got two hours of rest last night.

We take showers, and I find some clothes for us in the drawers of the bedroom—clothes that fit me, like he knew I'd come. With wet hair and heavy limbs, we settle onto my bed. I'm relieved that Christina doesn't ask to sleep somewhere else, because I need her here beside me. She rests her head in the crook of my shoulder, slides her arm over my chest, and settles in. "Thank you," I whisper. *For so many things. For being all I have in the world right now. For sticking by me.*

She squeezes me like she hears every thought, and then we drift into sleep.

I awake with a gasp, yanking myself out of a dream of my dad tossing ice water on my face. I grab for his phone and see that it's four in the morning—the time he usually woke me up to work out. Wincing at the memory, I inch out from under Christina, resting her head on the pillow and allowing myself to stroke her cheek before tiptoeing out of the room. I need to get into his lab. Maybe he left something for me. He had food in the fridge, clothes for me in the drawers. He was prepared for me to come. I pad down the stairs to the lab and stare at the entry mechanism. A fingerprint scanner. On impulse, I press my thumb to it.

And to my shock, the screen flashes green and says: *Welcome, Tate. Password?*

"I have no idea what the password is," I mumble. But . . . my dad *wanted* me to get in here. He programmed it to accept my thumbprint, and not just his own. And then it occurs to me—what if I wasn't the only one who could hack? He had no idea I'd invaded his systems, but what if he'd been invading mine? With shaky eagerness, I punch in the last password I used to access my server at home. It works. "You wily asshole," I whisper, chuckling to myself. "You must think you're pretty clever." It comes out strained. I never could have anticipated missing him this much.

The cool interior of the lab raises goose bumps on my arms for more reasons than the temperature. Once again, it's a replica of my father's lab in New York. Some of the same weaponry lines the walls. It's chillingly familiar—right down to the screen across the room, black with three numbers in the center:

2,943,287,999
4,122,239,861
12 (?)

That bottom number . . . It used to read: 14. Two fewer anomalies now. Once again, I think back to George and how he flashed orange. Everyone else had flashed either red for H2 or blue for human. Was he one of the two who are gone now? Does my dad have some satellite orbiting Earth, scanning the population? I'm betting he does. I just don't know why he wanted to do that. Population numbers aren't that interesting.

It only told him what he already knew, that the H2 outnumber us by more every day. But most H2 think they're human, and the Core want to keep it that way. My dad seemed pretty eager to keep this technology a secret, too. So why was he scanning everyone? And what do those anomalies represent? It can't be hybrids, because when humans and H2s reproduce, the result is another H2, which is why the population numbers are the way they are. So . . . is it some next step in our evolution?

"I thought I might find you down here," Christina says as she peeks through the door I left open. Her hair spills over her shoulders. She looks amazing in my clothes. Or maybe it's the fact that she's here at all.

"Morning," I say, pulling my gaze from her body and peering around the room. And as soon as I do, I see it, something that wasn't in the lab at home. On the desk in the corner is a notebook. I stride over to it, swallowing back hope. It's a simple Steno, full of scrawled calculations and diagrams, none of which make sense to me. That's saying something, since I was studying some pretty advanced mathematics before everything went to hell. I turn page after page, looking for something familiar and finding nothing. And finally, I get to the last page with writing on it—the rest of the pages are blank. But on that page, it says *Find it in 20204* scribbled in unusually sloppy handwriting, like my dad was in a hurry. And at the bottom of the page, it says *Race: "Sicarii."*

"What's a Sicarii?" Christina asks, appearing at my shoulder.

"It's Latin for 'assassin,'" I say, thinking back to my language lessons. "Probably the perfect word to describe Race Lavin." He was, after all, responsible for my dad's death.

"And the number?"

"I don't know. Maybe it's a zip code?" I punch it into my dad's GPS, and sure enough—20204 is a zip code located within Washington, DC, containing a few major government departments. "I wonder if this is where the Core is headquartered or something."

"Please don't tell me you want to go there." She sounds frightened.

"Yeah, you and I are going to wage an assault on the US Department of Health and Human Services." I gesture at the rack of weapons along the wall. "That doesn't sound fun to you?"

She smacks my arm. "You're so obnoxious." But she doesn't seem as scared now, which makes me smile.

"My priority is to find whatever my dad wanted me to, and if I have to go to DC, I will. But first I need to see what else he left for me here."

"Are those security cameras?" Christina points over my shoulder.

I turn to a set of screens to the left of Dad's desk. "Yeah, probably. That's what he had set up at home."

She laughs. "Is that your room?"

I glance up to the screen in the top row and see my

room . . . but it's not the room we slept in last night. It's my room at home. I recognize the spill of dirty laundry off the edge of the bed, the sneakers on the floor, the clutter of papers and books on the bedside table. "Yeah . . ." I take a closer look at the screens. "These are from all over. Look—" I point to a screen in the middle row, where bright sunshine glares from a window in a living room that looks like the one upstairs. "It's only five in the morning on the East Coast. This must be in a safe house that's somewhere else entirely. And look at that one." I point to the bottom row, where security cameras show our backs as we gaze at the screen. "These are from here, obviously."

Christina's hand closes over my forearm. "And that?"

The bottom left screen shows a yard filled with weeds. In the distance is a field. It's the front of this house. And the sight of it sends adrenaline exploding through my system. Because there's a blond guy climbing the rickety porch stairs.

We've been found.

THREE

"STAY HERE," I SAY TO CHRISTINA AS I STRIDE OVER TO
the wall rack and pull a semi-auto pistol from one of the pegs.
Like all things my father made, it's black, sleek, and dangerous.
Once I've got it cocked and locked, I glance over to see my
girlfriend staring at me with wide eyes.

"He's in the house," she whispers, pointing to a screen next
to the one that displays the yard—and this one shows the interior of the shack. I can't believe I didn't notice the camera
when I came in, but this guy doesn't, either. He's skinny and
young-looking. More like a boy than a man. Younger even than
I am. His eyes are focused on the two doors at the back of the
main room, just like mine were.

"He won't get in," I assure her. "There's no way—" My
mouth snaps shut as he pulls the rusty nail from the ceiling
and sticks it in the hole in the floor. We hear the machinery

working above us, the floor moving aside, the stairway to the basement being revealed. "Okay, take this," I say, walking toward her and holding out the gun. "You see this little thing?" I touch the thumb safety. "If he comes in here, you point this at him, and if he threatens you, slide this down and start pulling the trigger. Do not mess around."

She gingerly takes the pistol, and I curl my hands around hers, showing her how to hold it. "Tate, he looks like a harmless kid."

I meet her dark blue gaze. "So do I."

She swallows hard and nods. I head over to the rack, grab myself another, and jog out the door, shutting it behind me. I take the stairs to the main level two at a time, knowing the kid is probably already at the door, wondering if he could possibly know the code to get in, wondering who the hell he is. I reach the top of the steps and pause, pressing myself against the wall and listening.

From the kitchen comes the crinkling of plastic wrap. *What the fuck. He's already inside.* I creep silently through the living room and peek around the wall, into the kitchen. The kid has his back to me and is shoving crackers from a Number Ten into his mouth. I raise the weapon, aim it at the back of his head, and thumb the safety off. At the muted click, the kid freezes.

"Tell me who you are, or I'm going to ruin your meal permanently," I say.

The meal falls from his grasp, sending soup and dried fruit

and nuts spattering across the floor. "D-don't, please," the kid whispers, raising his hands in the air. "I'm just looking for Uncle George."

I frown. "Who the hell are you?"

The kid looks over his shoulder at me. He's a few inches shorter than I am, wearing wire-framed glasses over bright green eyes now glazed with anxiety. His blond hair flops over his forehead. "Leo Thomas. Can I turn around?"

I step back. "Go ahead, but keep those hands up."

He obeys. His Adam's apple bobs as he stares into the barrel of my weapon. "If you're not Tate Archer, I'm going to be very disappointed."

I step forward and press the weapon to his forehead. "I'm not playing, Leo. How did you know how to get in here?"

His eyes are round and slightly crossed as he peers up at the black snout of the gun. "Um. Having trouble thinking straight. Imminent death on the brain."

I roll my eyes and move away, but only a little. And I wait.

He draws in a shaky breath. "I'm looking for my uncle George. He was supposed to be here if something ever went wrong."

I arch an eyebrow.

Leo's fingers twitch nervously. "I think something went wrong."

"And if I told you my name was Tate?"

He smiles. "I'd be really relieved."

"Why?"

"Because it means I'm in good hands."

"How would you know?"

"Because your dad told me so. And it didn't take much to know he'd use your mom's middle name as his password."

I grit my teeth and take a few more steps back. "Dude. I need you to tell me your story. Now."

"Do I have to stand here with my hands in the air while I do it? I mean, I could, but—"

I flick the safety on and lower the weapon. "How did you know my dad?"

He grins. "I *knew* you were Tate. I've always wanted to meet you. I've known your dad for as long as I can remember." His smile falters when I don't return his enthusiasm. "He'd come for Fifty board meetings, and he'd visit me whenever he was in town."

"How do you know about The Fifty?" This kid can't be older than fourteen, and my mom told me that members of The Fifty didn't tell their kids about the H2 or anything until they were at least sixteen. It was certainly a shock when I found out, though the circumstances had something to do with it.

"My parents were members. The Thomases. But . . ." His glasses slip a little on the bridge of his nose. "They died. About eight years ago. Car accident. My dad was the only Thomas left, except for me. So The Fifty raised me at the headquarters in Chicago, and I've been allowed to sit in on board meetings. I can't vote, though. Not until I'm sixteen."

So this kid can probably tell me a lot. And he looks fairly harmless. I relax a bit. "You said you thought something went wrong. What have you heard?"

"What happened to your dad, for one." He shakes his head. "I want you to know I don't believe anything they're saying about him on the news. I know it's a big lie made up by the Core."

My stomach feels hollow. "He's really dead, Leo. I was there when it happened."

"I know. I mean . . . the rest of it."

"What are you talking about?"

"How he's a terrorist, how he was going to blow up that school in Manhattan."

"What?" I say with a laugh, though it comes out strangled.

He looks over my shoulder at the television in the living room. "It's all over the networks. You can see for yourself."

I pivot on my heel, keeping him in my periphery in case he makes a move. I grab the remote and flip channels until I find CNN, and after a minute of staring, I see it scrolling across the news ticker at the bottom of the screen: *Frederick Archer's body to be released by Secaucus medical examiner's office . . . NYPD's quick action averted yet another school tragedy . . . would have been the largest domestic terrorist attack since Oklahoma City . . .*

"Oh my God," I breathe, rage crackling in my chest. "This is bullshit." And that's what Leo meant about the Core's lies. Race kept everything quiet while he was chasing me, but now that he's lost me, he's probably spreading this story to get me to do something rash and stupid, to lure me out.

"Well, not everyone buys it," Leo says. "Especially because of her." He points to the screen, a bemused smile on his face. They're showing a clip of an interview with a spindly older woman who looks really familiar. Helen Kuipers is her name. I turn up the volume.

"—telling you, it was some kind of radiation device. Or a laser. I don't know, but the kid was waving it over everyone, and when it got to me, it changed color, from red to blue."

It's the lunch lady from the cafeteria that day, one of the few who flashed blue—*human*—beneath the light of the scanner my best friend, Will, had snatched from me.

"She's been everywhere over the last two days," Leo comments. "Making the most of her three minutes of fame, I guess. She thinks she was marked or irradiated or something, and she's insisting it was linked to some government conspiracy . . . Really, she comes off as crazy. She's one of the only witnesses willing to talk about what they saw, though, so she's gotten a lot of play. I'm assuming the Core were able to intimidate the rest. But this lady thinks the whole blowup was about that glorified flashlight thing."

So Leo knows about The Fifty and the Core and my dad,

but apparently he doesn't know about the scanner. He's looking at me like he's hoping I'll explain, but I'm distracted as the clip ends and a somber anchorwoman appears on-screen. "Authorities have confirmed that Helen Kuipers, one of the witnesses to the events in the cafeteria of Beacon High School on Monday, has been missing since yesterday morning. Her daughter says Ms. Kuipers never arrived home after taping an interview in the WABC studio. Police are investigating."

So the lunch lady talked, and now she's missing. Just like the Core, silencing any human who poses a threat to their secret. "They got to her," I say.

"Who?" It's Christina. She's got the gun in her hand, and she's cautiously watching me and Leo from the hallway. Her gaze flicks to the screen as they show my dad's driver's license photo. Beneath his photo, it says "Frederick Archer, suspected terrorist." Her eyes get wide. "Oh no . . ."

"Who are you?" asks Leo.

She tears her eyes from the TV. "Christina. I'm Tate's girlfriend. Who are you?"

His brow furrows as he looks her over. "Which family are you from?"

"This is Leo," I tell her, pointedly ignoring his question, especially since he ignored hers. "He was raised at The Fifty's headquarters, so he knows almost everything."

She nods at me, and something silent passes between us.

We're not going to mention that she's H2. Some of The Fifty, most notably the Bishop family, are distinctly homicidal when it comes to the planet's dominant species.

"Sit down," I say to Leo. "And keep your hands where I can see them."

He settles himself on the couch. "Are we going to get past this at some point? I'm on your side, and I was hoping you could be on mine. Uncle Angus left in a hurry after Uncle George disappeared, and I—"

"What do you mean, 'George disappeared'?" I ask.

"About three days ago. Right after the board meeting. Angus lost touch with him. No one knows where he went."

Christina bites her lip and comes to stand next to me, looking down at Leo with curiosity. I glance at her out of the corner of my eye and then say, "George is dead, too, Leo. He was killed by the Core yesterday morning."

All the blood drains from Leo's face. "What?" he whispers, his eyes going shiny.

When she registers the pain on his face, Christina shoves her weapon at me and then goes to sit next to Leo on the couch. She takes his hand as tears streak down his face. "It was quick," she says quietly. "He probably didn't have time to be scared or in pain." Leo curls in on himself, and she pats his back while my own eyes burn. I miss George, too. I was depending on him to help me. He was a good man, and—

"Wait. He was missing for three days?" I ask. He was killed only twenty-four hours ago. "Angus didn't know he was coming to Charlottesville?"

Leo wipes his face with his sleeve and peers up at me. "What's in Charlottesville?" he asks in a raspy voice.

Christina's brow furrows as she meets my eyes. "Maybe your mom asked him to keep it secret?"

"She didn't ask him to go to Charlottesville until Tuesday morning at the earliest."

"But today's Friday, and the last time anyone heard from him was Monday night," Leo says, sniffling. "He was supposed to come to headquarters for a meeting on Tuesday, but he never showed."

"It could fit," Christina says. "By that time, your mom had called him."

"Angus and a few of George's family members went to his hotel room in the afternoon, and it was a mess." He grimaces, and his voice cracks as he says, "They said it looked like there had been a struggle. They thought maybe the Core had taken him away. But I hoped he'd escaped and come here."

His face crumples again, and he covers it with his hands, his shoulders shaking. Christina puts her arm around him and scoots closer, whispering comforting words to this stranger, this boy who understands my world better than I do. The last ten minutes has added yet another dimension of mystery to this whole thing, and I can't take it. "I'm going back down to the lab,"

I say, clicking off the television to suppress my urge to throw it across the room. "You're going to come so I can keep an eye on you. And if you turn on us, Leo, please believe that I'll kill you, okay?"

Christina shoots me a look that says *Is the asshole act really necessary?* I clench my teeth. Enough people have violated my trust in the last few days to make me permanently wary, and I'd think she would understand that. This kid is playing on her sympathies, and that's pissing me off, too. Not to mention the fact that my dad is being framed as a freaking *terrorist.* Leo's lucky I don't kick his ass right now just to work off the sheer, blinding frustration of it all.

The three of us head down to the lab, and I hunch over the keypad and enter my code, not wanting him to see it. Once we're in, I grab a stool and settle Leo in the corner by the door. "Are those vibracoustic probes?" he asks, pointing at a set of wands on a rack across the room. "Uncle Fred let me help him on that design, and—"

"We're not here to reminisce," I snap, not wanting to hear how this kid had a better relationship with my dad than I did. "Just . . . be quiet, okay? I need to finish searching this place, and then we'll decide our next move."

His mouth shuts, but his chin trembles as he nods. Christina stands close to him, her arm over his scrawny shoulders. Her scowl tells me she no longer believes my behavior is an act. She's just thinking I'm an asshole. And I don't really have the energy to explain myself to her, so I head over to the population counter screen. When I touched the display in the other lab, it had showed some plans, like a blueprint for something. It might be for the satellite, or it might be for the scanner itself. And since my dad said the scanner was the key to our survival, I need to find out as much about it as possible. If I can do that here and now, so much the better, because the Core is probably—

"Tate." Christina's voice is like a whip, sharp and sudden. "Look at the surveillance screens."

I do. And my heart just about stops. There are people in the New York apartment. In the middle row of screens, the ones that show the place where I've lived for my entire life, black-suited men are milling about in the living room. Core agents. In my home.

I lunge for the display, seeking a volume switch, anything to activate some sound so I can hear what they're saying, but there's nothing. So I squint at the screens, trying to read lips. I don't recognize any of the men. Race isn't there. But one of them, a guy with a hook nose and hair the color of a storm cloud, seems to be in charge. He partially covers his mouth as he points around the apartment, directing the men where to search. It's like he knows there are cameras on him, and knows exactly where they are.

I watch helplessly as they ransack my living room. Something dark streaks across the floor at the agents' feet, and with a pang, I realize it's Johnny Knoxville, my cat.

"What are they looking for?" Christina asks.

I have a sinking feeling I know. Somewhere, probably in his lab, my dad is storing wreckage of an H2 spaceship, the alien technology he used to make the scanner. Race told me he wanted to get to my dad's stuff, and now they're trying to take it by force. I'm willing to bet that they tried something yesterday—whether it was attempting to hack his system remotely or trying to enter one of his other safe houses or labs—that triggered that text message that was sent to his phone. "They're trying to get their flying saucer back."

Leo bolts up from his stool. "Are you serious? An actual spaceship—in your dad's lab?"

"If they try to get in my dad's lab," I continue as I search for a remote in my dad's desk drawer, "they'll be in for some nasty surprises. He has lethal security measures in place." I've seen the plans in his files. He probably had the same setup outside the lab in this safe house. Hydrogen cyanide, which boils at just over room temperature. If the keypad registers three fails within ten minutes, wall panels open to reveal vents, within which are blowers motion-activated by movement in the hallway. As the door to the first floor closes and locks, heating elements beneath the eight cyanide canisters hidden in the walls melt the cap-seals and turn liquid to gas. No one in the basement would survive. I hope they give it a try.

I turn around to expand my search for the volume control. I need to hear what those agents are saying. Leo's drifted over to the monitors. He still looks like he hopes I'll tell him the only thing about my dad he doesn't seem to know. Christina frowns as she watches the Core agents in my living room. And then her expression fills with horror, and she starts to scream. I whirl back toward the screens to see what's making her freak out, and my blood turns to ice. The hook-nosed agent is standing right in front of the surveillance camera hidden in the heating vent above the trophy case. And he has a pretty blond woman by the throat, a gun to her head.

It's Christina's mom. The agent inclines his head at the camera, and Mrs. Scolina stares up at us with a terrified, pleading expression. The agent smiles. And then he speaks, the movements of his mouth exaggerated. I can almost hear his voice in my head as he says, "It's time to come home, Tate. We'll be waiting at your girlfriend's place. You have until eight p.m."

FOUR

I MANAGE TO CATCH CHRISTINA IN MY ARMS WITHOUT
taking my eyes from the screen. As she cries, the screen goes
dark. Then it begins to play again, on a loop, the whole thing
unraveling before our eyes, letting us relive the horror.

Leo's voice cracks as he curses. "That's her mom, isn't it?
It's her mom."

I lock eyes with him as I hold Christina against my chest.
And I nod. This is my fault. All my fault. I bow my head and
whisper into her hair. "They won't hurt her. I'll give myself up.
We'll figure this out."

Christina only sobs harder. My fingers burrow in her hair,
and I wish I could draw the fear and the sorrow out of her
head and carry it for her. My own eyes are stinging as she
shudders against me. "They said we have until eight, which

gives us thirteen hours. It takes about twelve to drive to New York. We have to get out of here." I glance at Leo, who's staring down at the Steno notebook where my dad wrote "Race: 'Sicarii'" and "Find it in 20204." I snatch the notebook out of his reach and flip it shut. "Can you make it back to Chicago by yourself?"

"I'm going with you."

"I can't take care of you, too."

Leo stands up straight, his eyes at the level of my chin, all skinny and defiant. He reminds me of me in a way, not yet realizing how small he is, and maybe stronger than he looks. "I can help you guys. You're not the only one with skills."

"Ballistics?" I ask.

He nods. "And self-defense. Chemistry, too. Strategy."

"And tactics," we say together. Because my dad taught him. All those trips to Chicago, and some of that time away from home was spent on this kid. I shouldn't feel jealous. But I do.

Maybe he senses it. "Uncle Angus and Uncle George taught me a lot, too," he offers.

"The moment you get in my way, I'm putting you on a bus back to Chicago. Do you understand me?"

He shoves his hands into his pockets and bobs his head. His jaw is tense—he's clenching his teeth. Determined to prove himself. Fine. I'll let him. "We need cash. Where do you think my dad would have kept it?"

He smiles. "Maybe in the underground garage out behind this shack?"

My mouth drops open. "What?"

"You didn't notice it when you came in?"

I muscle down the urge to flip him off. "Let's go see what he left me, then."

He left me a lot. As I explore the underground garage, Leo sits with Christina on the grass at the top of the ramp. Through the open doors, I hear snatches of their conversation, enough to know that the kid is actually trying to distract her, telling her some story about a time he made a red cabbage pH indicator for a chemistry experiment and ended up accidentally dyeing both his hands red. When I hear her let out a raspy chuckle, I'm amazed. And, okay, a bit grateful. It makes it easier to focus, knowing she's all right for the moment.

Until I hear shots fired, which sends my blood pressure so high that my vision spots. My heart in my throat, I scramble up the ramp and realize Leo's moved on to teaching Christina how to handle a gun. She looks angry and determined as she squeezes the trigger. He's not only made her laugh, he's given her something to focus on, something that makes her feel a little less helpless. Now I'm both annoyed and grateful. I can't get a bead on my feelings about this kid, and I don't have time to worry about it—we've got bigger problems.

"Hey," I say between shots, "people will hear that for miles. Pretty sure it's not deer season." Most major hunting seasons are in the fall and winter, and it's freaking May. This property is in the middle of nowhere, but gunshots carry.

Leo shrugs. "In Kentucky, you can hunt wild pigs, ground-hogs, and several species of bird year-round." He holds up his phone. "I looked it up before we fired a shot."

Christina hands Leo the weapon. "It's okay," she says quietly, then looks at me. "Can we go soon?"

"Almost ready." I can tell by the tension in her posture that every minute of waiting is agony. I jog back down the ramp. This space is neat, three vehicles parked at the base of the ramp, boxes of tools, stacks of building supplies, almost enough to build another shack. I've already chosen our vehicle, so I make my way to a worktable in the corner and go through the drawers. My heart skips when I see my father's face peering up at me from a Kentucky driver's license for someone named Ray Spruance. I pick it up, staring at his steely gray eyes while my own burn.

He'd planned to be here with us.

I force myself to set the license aside and flip through the other fake IDs in the top drawer. There are a few more for him, several for my mom under the name of Margaret Dean . . . and several for me, all under the name of Edward Spruance— Admiral Spruance's only son. I put our pictures side by side. Me and my dad. We have the same eyes and same dark brown hair, except his was always combed and mine is always a mess. Our cheekbones are high, our chins rounded, but maybe we're saved from looking soft by our square jaw. The similarities make my throat tighten. He should have been here with me, helping me figure this out. If it hadn't been for the Core, he would be. Well, that's not quite true. I'm the one who brought the scanner to school. I'm the one who started this whole thing—and now Christina could lose her parents because of it.

I shove my fake driver's license into my pocket, grab a wallet full of cash I find in one of the drawers, and snag the keys for our ride. "Let's go, guys!" I shout up the ramp.

Less than ten minutes later, we're pulling out of the garage bunker in a nondescript forest-green sedan that has some major horsepower under the hood. Christina's in the passenger seat, and now that she's not all purposeful movement, the horror of what's happened seems to have caught up with her again. Her eyes are closed, and she's leaning against the window. "Does your head hurt?" I ask her, and she barely nods. It was a stupid question anyway. Of course it hurts. I put my hand on her thigh and am relieved when she doesn't brush me off. "I'm so sorry. About everything."

She squeezes my fingers. Her skin is cold. "I can't talk about it now. Can we just . . . let it be?"

I guess funny stories about cabbage dye worked better for her. I swallow hard and nod. I'd talk about stupid stuff if I could, but I don't have it in me right now. This is a no-win situation if I've ever seen one. If I don't give myself up, I have no doubt the Core will take it out on Christina's parents—and her little sister. God, I want to kill every member of the Core with my bare hands. If I do give myself up, I have no idea what they'll do to me. And I hate to admit it, but it scares me. They want to get into my dad's lab, and they're willing to do awful things to get what they want. Can I withstand torture? I'll try, but I've studied enough to know that every man has a breaking point. I'm not arrogant enough to think I'm different.

"You're not just going to walk in there, are you?" Leo asks.

"Shut up," I say, sighing. I'm so fucking tired. "Here's what's going to happen. I'm going in, and when they let her parents out, you and Christina will go to The Fifty and—"

"That's stupid. You could fight. You could figure something out."

"Leo, there's a bus ticket to Chicago with your name on it." I hand Christina the phone. "What's the next major town on the route? We'll drop him off."

"Tate," she says wearily, "calm down. He wants to help."

"He's doing the opposite," I snap.

"You're nothing like your dad described," Leo blurts out. "He made you sound like some kind of prodigy with balls of steel. I freaking idolized you for years, and you turn out to be a total coward!"

"She has a little sister!" I shout, slamming on the brakes.

Christina's hand shoots out, and she braces herself against the dash as I pull to the side of the road, fields on either side of us. "Her name's Livia! Am I a coward for wanting her to get out of this alive?"

"You can get her out and not let them take you!" Leo's face is red, and his green eyes are bright with fury. "You can't just lie down and let the Core get what they want! It's not about you, either. It's about your dad's invention. I heard him telling George how crucial the device was, and how that was only one part of his plan. That's the thing the lunch lady was talking about, wasn't she?"

"Yeah, but the Core already have it, Leo."

"And now they want you to help them get to the rest—a freaking spaceship that they could use to do God-knows-what—and you're willing to let them do that?" His reedy voice fills the car.

I'm about to reach back there and toss him into a ditch when Christina whispers, "He's right."

It freezes me in place. "What?"

She looks over at me. "If anyone can get my family out alive, it would be you. I trust you. And I don't want to lose you." A tear slides down her face.

I slump in the seat. Can I do this? And what happens if I can't? "Christina, it's your mom and dad. It's Livia."

"I know. And I believe you can make a plan to get them out safely."

I take the phone from her and text my mom again. *Have to go back to NY. Please call when you can.*

After a few moments spent staring at the screen, waiting for a reply that doesn't come, I put the phone away and pull back onto the road. "I want complete silence for the next hour, please," I say when Leo starts to ask questions. "Not a single fucking word."

He respects that request, and I let the gears in my brain turn, running through scenarios, remembering everything I can about Christina's place, a fourth-floor condo across from Morningside Park. Fire escape along the back of the building, connecting to her bedroom. Narrow courtyard between units, parking lot at the back. Quiet neighborhood, and—

"Will," I say. He lives only six blocks away from her. The memories of our exploits are enough to inspire me. "I think we might have a chance."

Christina falls into a restless doze just before we reach the border of West Virginia. I glance into the rearview mirror to see Leo's eyes on me. "What?"

He shrugs. "You look like him."

"Considering that he contributed fifty percent of my DNA—"

"Just an observation. You asked."

I did. "Sorry." I check the mirrors for the millionth time to make sure we aren't being followed. "Not at my best today."

"Do you want me to drive?"

I laugh. "You've got to be kidding."

"I know how. And Christina obviously needs to rest."

"It's okay. I can think and drive simultaneously." I lean back against the headrest. "I just wish I had more time to do it."

"A good plan, violently executed now, is better than a perfect plan next week."

"You're quoting Patton now?" He sounds like my dad.

"If it fits," he says defensively. We pass a Greyhound as it slows to exit the highway, and Leo sighs. "Uncle Angus is going to be mad when he gets back to Chicago and realizes I'm gone."

"When will that happen?"

"I don't know. He's always busy. I'm on my own a lot. The Fifty headquarters is a big estate on the north shore, with lots of people going in and out."

"But you're a kid. Nobody looks after you?"

"I'm fourteen. It's not like I have a sitter." He shifts in his seat. "Not anymore, anyway," he mumbles.

"Don't you go to school?"

"No. I think they were afraid I'd spill their secrets. After my parents died, they brought me to the estate, and I've had tutors ever since."

"How often did you see my dad?" I clear my throat after hearing the jealous edge in my voice.

"Once a month. When he came for board meetings, he'd

stay at a hotel nearby, and he'd spend time with me, reviewing my schoolwork, giving me extra assignments. He took me to the Museum of Science and Industry a few times." He's quiet for a moment. "I think he felt sorry for me."

Maybe. But my dad wasn't the most sympathetic of guys. "I'm sure he enjoyed your company."

"I think he was just lonely. He talked about you and your mom sometimes."

I wish he'd talked *to* us. "In that case, I'm surprised you wanted to meet me. I was a constant disappointment to him."

The silence rolls in waves from the backseat, and after a while, I wonder if he's falling asleep. But then I hear him say, very quietly, "You didn't know him very well at all."

I stare at the road in front of me. I could argue with him, but that would be pointless.

Especially because I'm afraid he's right.

I don't call Will. I know his schedule anyway. Eleven and a half hours after we leave Kentucky, after two quick stops for gas—one in which I raided the nearby convenience store—and one lightning round at a hardware store in West Virginia, we're pulling up to the curb a block away from his building. And sure enough, about five minutes later, he hops off the bus at the corner, lugging his duffel. His head is bowed, showing off his Mohawk, which is already starting to grow out. His shoulders are slumped. I cram a baseball cap over my hair and get out of the car. "Hey, loser," I say.

His head jerks up at the sound of my voice. "Tate? Oh my God, dude."

"Let me start by saying that my dad's not a terrorist."

"Wasn't even tempted to believe it. I'm sorry about what happened to him, man." He gives me a quick hug, whacking his hand against my back. "Really sorry."

"Thanks," I mumble as we step away from each other.

"Where the hell have you been?"

"Long story."

"You have no idea how weird it's been here. These FBI guys crawling all over the school, confiscating and erasing anything on our phones, warning us not to talk about what happened because it's a national security threat, and then that crazy lunch lady goes and tells everyone that I lasered her—"

I glance around. "Listen—can we get off the street? Are your parents home yet?"

"Not yet." He leans around me as the car door opens and Christina steps out. "Christina! Your mom called me yesterday—" He pauses as her expression crumples.

"I need your help," I say to him.

He arches an inky black eyebrow. "Are you about to get me in trouble?"

"Possibly."

He grins, white teeth contrasting with his dark skin. "Cool."

It never did take much to get Will to go along with my pranks. I grab my supplies from the trunk, introduce Leo as my cousin, and lead Christina by the hand as we enter Will's building. I keep my head down until we're in his apartment. He tosses his keys into a little basket on the counter and turns to us. "You seriously need to tell me what's up."

I concocted my lie on the way here, and Christina's prepared to back me up. As much as I hate to keep the truth from Will, it'll be better and safer for him if he doesn't know everything. I offer my explanation as I pull out his mom's huge soup pot and empty potassium nitrate and sugar into it, then switch the heat to low. I want to do this quickly, but there are some things you just can't rush.

"My dad made some important scientific discoveries, and he's being framed by people who are desperate to get ahold of them. It's like a corporate espionage thing, but they've got some corrupt cops on their side. Now they're at Christina's apartment. They want me in exchange for her parents, because they know I can get into my dad's lab."

"Fuckers," he says.

"My thoughts exactly," Leo replies, peeking into the pot. He's been quiet for the most part, but when he saw me picking up stump remover and sugar at the store, he couldn't wipe the smile from his face.

As the sugar melts, and the mixture in the pot begins to look like caramel, we start to cut up a bunch of water bottles to use for casings. I explain my plan as Christina watches from the doorway. I'd pay a lot to know what she's thinking, but it's almost eight, and we have no time for a heart-to-heart. All of that will have to wait until her family is safe. I was hoping my mom would have been in touch by now, but she hasn't been. I even tried calling her again, but it went straight to voicemail. And, seeing as I have no idea if she's still in control of that phone, I didn't leave a message.

We create eight mounds of the caramel mixture and load them into the plastic casings. It's kind of like working with larger versions of those plastic Easter eggs. Christina makes sure they stay closed with rubber bands. Will has the fuses— he's been the guardian of my contraband for years. As Will and Leo pack up and get ready to head out, already joking like old friends, I slide my arm around Christina's waist.

"How are you?" I ask.

"Everybody I love is in danger right now. I've been better."

I brush her hair away from her face. "I know the feeling."

"Then you know how much I need you to make it through this okay," she whispers, leaning into me, her fingers curling into my shirt.

Her eyes meet mine, gorgeous and stormy blue. I'm caught in that gaze, unable to look away. "If it's anywhere near as much as I need you to be safe and have your family back, then I guess I do." I pull my dad's phone from my pocket. "Keep this for me? I don't want them to have it."

She takes it, cradles it in her hands. "And I'll be giving this back to you . . ."

I kiss her forehead. "In an hour."

A few minutes later, I'm climbing the steps to Christina's building. My heart is beating a furious rhythm in my chest. There were a bunch of agents searching my apartment, so I don't know how many will be in the Scolinas' condo. As much as I hate going in there without knowing exactly what I'm facing, at least I know the layout—I've been hanging out with Christina there for years. Her room is a haven for me, the place where I've spent some of the best moments of my life, and her parents are cool. I hate that they're being put through this.

The place is quiet, but I'm sure Hooknose and his agents know I'm here. I walk the steps to the fourth floor and stop in front of number 401. In all my years of knowing Christina, I've never been so nervous about knocking on her door, and that's really saying something. Before, only my heart was at stake. What's on the line right now is more precious than that.

And as it turns out, I don't have to knock. The door opens, and I find myself face-to-face with Hooknose. He's an inch or so taller than I am, clean-shaven with razor burn along his jaw and deep wrinkles around his mouth. His tone is clipped as he says, "Tate Archer. You cut it rather close," and opens the door wide to allow me inside. "I'm FBI Special Agent Bill Congers. It's nice to meet you." He offers me his hand.

"Don't bother."

He gives me an amused look and motions for me to raise my arms. While he pats me down, I size him up, noting the gun at his hip. Once he's confirmed that I'm unarmed, we walk down the short hallway to enter the living room. Two agents are positioned within, one covering the hall to the front door and one at the entrance to the dining room and the hallway that leads to the bedrooms. Mrs. Scolina, her light blond hair in a bedraggled ponytail, is sitting on the chaise in the corner of the large room, Livia in her lap. The little girl's skinny fingers are balled in the loose sleeves of her mom's shirt. Christina's dad is standing next to Mrs. Scolina's chair. Lean and fit, still a fierce soccer player, he looks younger than his graying hair suggests. His arm is resting on his wife's shoulders, but he looks like he'd love to slam his fist into my face.

"I'm sorry," I say to him. "I wasn't in town. But I came immediately."

"That was wise," Congers comments, running his finger over the bump on the narrow bridge of his nose.

"And now that he's finally decided to show up, he can tell you we're not involved in Frederick Archer's plot," Mr. Scolina growls, his blue eyes cold as he talks about my dad. "I never even met the man!"

I close my eyes and remind myself that now is not the time to defend my father's rep. "Are you guys okay?" I ask Christina's parents. They don't look hurt. They look like they could run. And they're going to have to.

"No thanks to you," says Mr. Scolina. "We're being held under suspicion of aiding a *terrorist*—"

"If Tate cooperates, the charges might go away, Mr. Scolina," Congers says smoothly.

"Where's my daughter?" Mr. Scolina takes a step toward me. "If you've hurt her—"

"Yes, where *is* Ms. Scolina?" Congers asks. "We'll find her, you know. It's such a shame you involved her in your criminal activities. She had such a bright future."

"The threats aren't necessary." I meet his cold gray-green eyes. "I'm here, so stop wasting time."

He doesn't blink. "We'll see. Let's go in the back and talk."

"I'm not going to cooperate until I know they're safe," I snap. "If you want anything from me, you need to let Mrs. Scolina and Livia go, at least."

He shakes his head. "Given the stakes, I'm not willing to lose my leverage until I have access to the information I need."

Mrs. Scolina buries her face against her husband's side to muffle her sob. He strokes her hair and gives me another death glare.

The barrel of a gun nudges at my spine. There's an agent behind me. I glance over my shoulder and see his round head, red hair buzzed short. I raise my hands from my sides. The guy scowls. "Get moving."

"It's all right, Mack. I'm sure Tate will be happy to—" Congers is interrupted by a knock at the door.

Here we go.

Congers cuts his gaze to Mr. Scolina. "Are you expecting someone?" Christina's dad shakes his head, and Congers turns to me. "Are *you*?"

"You guys killed my dad. You shot my mom. *And* my girl-friend." I hate that I have to say that in front of her parents, who go pale at the words. "Who would I be expecting?" I ask in a hard voice, letting my anger show through.

"You bastard," Mr. Scolina says. I assume he's talking to Congers until his fist collides with my jaw.

Mack wrestles him away from me as I stagger to the side. "They're the ones who did it, and you're attacking *me*?" My fingers probe my aching face.

"If you cared about her, you never would have involved her in any of this!" Mrs. Scolina says shrilly.

Her words hit me as hard as Mr. Scolina did, and I'm still re-covering as there's another knock on the door. The third agent, a guy who looks like a younger version of Congers himself, dis-appears into the entryway. "Two kids in soccer uniforms," he says to Congers as he returns. "Selling candy bars, looks like."

"Graham," Congers says to the young agent, "take Tate in the dining room, and we'll let the little girl open the door."

He gestures for Livia to stand up. She watches him with wide blue eyes. Graham motions me toward the dining room. I walk as slowly as possible.

Mrs. Scolina strokes the little girl's back. "Just tell them we're not interested, sweetheart. That's all you have to do." Livia hops off her mom's lap, still looking uncertain.

Red-haired Mack gives her a five. "Get me one. I'm hungry." He leads Livia to the entryway and presses himself against the wall, his gun in his hand.

She heads for the door with the bill clutched in her little fist. My heart is beating so fast I can barely breathe. I'm too far away to help her if this doesn't go well. The door squeaks as she opens it, and then I hear Will's voice.

"Hey, kiddo. Is your mom home? Soccer fund-raiser. We got some good candy." The crinkling of a wrapper punctuates his words. From where he's standing, he'll only be able to see her, and not the armed agents listening to the conversation. I pray he sticks to the plan—we've done enough pranks together for me to know that's not a guarantee, even though I stressed the life-or-deathness of this particular situation to him before we set out.

"We have caramel, too," Leo offers. I picture him, shuffling his feet and sliding a pack off his shoulder. He's got on one of Will's soccer jerseys, and it's hanging from his scrawny frame. I hope the agents don't catch sight of him and notice the overlarge soccer cleats tied to his feet.

But based on the sounds coming from the entryway, all is well. They both seem harmless, just two high school kids trying to raise some cash for their team. Livia asks for one bar, and when Will tells her she's got enough money for two, she shyly asks for a caramel. It's perfect. Mack has holstered his weapon now. From his concealed position next to the Scolinas, Congers rolls his eyes and looks at his watch, probably annoyed by the frivolous distraction.

I hear Will's cleats on the hardwood floor of the entryway and the *thunk* of his bag as he sets it down and digs inside. "Let's see. I have change somewhere."

"I've got some," Leo says, unzipping his pack.

Livia gasps, and a hissing noise fills the entryway. The agents' eyes go wide, but they move too slowly. I shove Graham hard and jump between the Scolinas and Congers as a flaming object whizzes down the hall, trailed by a plume of smoke. The room descends into chaos.

FIVE

WILL HURLS HIS ENTIRE DUFFEL DOWN THE HALL NEXT.
Smoke billows from it as it lands in the middle of the living
room, several feet from the first smoke bomb. A fraction of a
second later, two smaller smoke bombs bounce off the walls,
spewing white-gray clouds. I lunge for Congers as he opens his
mouth to shout an order. Gulping in one last lungful of clean
air, I elbow him in the throat, knocking him backward before
jerking his head down and kneeing him in the face. He slides
to the floor as the fire alarms begin to shriek.

"Fire!" I hear Will shout from the hallway. "Call 9-1-1!"
Hopefully the Scolinas' neighbors are home and will do just
that. We need as much confusion as possible.

Leo helps. His backpack comes hurtling down the hallway
and lands near Will's duffel, doubling the smoke and adding a

bit of fire when the fabric ignites—the chemical reaction must have melted through the plastic casing.

My eyes burning, I yank my shirt over my mouth and nose. Mrs. Scolina screams, and I look up to see two figures wrestling in the living room—Mr. Scolina and Graham. Leo is on the floor with Mack, both of them coughing and gasping. As I run for the hallway to make sure Livia got out, Leo disarms the much larger man and pistol-whips his round head. Leo might be small, but he's dead fast and knows what he's doing.

Still standing in the doorway, Will meets my eyes, and I nod.

"Come on, baby girl," he says, coiling an arm around Livia, who's been huddled against the wall near the front door. He yanks her out of the apartment, heading for the stairwell. With any luck, he'll be three blocks away before anyone notices she's gone. I charge back into the living room, yank Graham's gun from his holster as he struggles with Mr. Scolina, and press it against the young agent's head. Clenching his teeth, Graham puts his hands up, and Mr. Scolina staggers back, coughing up a lung. His wife wraps her arms around him, and I smack Graham hard on the back of the head, dropping him to his knees.

"The fire escape!" I bark, but Leo's already moving, taking Mrs. Scolina by the arm and dragging her through the dining room toward the hallway that leads to the bedrooms. Christina's there, waiting to get them down the metal stairs and out onto the street, ready to throw some smoke of her own if she needs to. I put my arm around Mr. Scolina's back and guide him to the hallway, my lungs raging and stinging.

"My daughter," he rasps.

"Will's got Livia," I say as I hustle him along. I can't see anything now—I'm working by feel. My eyes don't want to stay open—they're streaming, blurring my vision. "And Christina's right outside."

I shove him into the dining room, groping for the wall, praying for some fresh air, dying to see Christina and know she's there and okay and—

A hand grabs at my ankle and lurches me back, away from Mr. Scolina, who blunders through the dining room like a bull, knocking pictures to the floor with his shoulder. "Rachel!" he shouts to his wife as Graham plows into me from behind, knocking the weapon from my hand. I try to pivot around and meet the challenge, but steely fingers are still gripping my ankle, digging in. It's Congers, on the floor where I left him, but very much conscious—and dangerous.

Graham punches me in the stomach, and I gasp, inhaling the smoke. My body goes into full-on rejection mode, doubling me over as my lungs try to turn themselves inside out. The other agents are hacking and stumbling, too, but Graham throws himself on top of me, knocking me to the floor. I land on my stomach. I can't breathe. I can't move. Mack, bleeding from a gash in his freckled forehead, flings himself across the back of my legs before I can plant my foot in Congers's face. I want to call for help . . . but who would I call? I need all of them to be safe. I don't want them here in this smoky apartment, going down with me.

Meaty hands shove my face into the floor, grinding my skull against hardwood while someone grabs my arms and wrenches them behind my back. Before I can jerk myself away, handcuffs enclose my wrists.

"You bastards!" Leo shouts, crashing into one of the dark shapes hovering above me.

"We'll take him, too," says Congers, who's gotten to his feet and is covering his nose and mouth with his suit jacket. "The fire alarms will draw the neighbors. We need to get out of here."

I am rolled onto my back. They don't give me a chance to make a move. There's a hand on my throat and two bodies on mine, smashing my fingers between my ass and the floor. My ears ring.

Leo hits the ground next to me. "Sorry," he huffs. I glance to the side. My eyes are the only thing I can move, and through the spots that crowd my vision, I see the blood flowing from his nose. His wire-framed glasses lie between us, lenses cracked.

He should have escaped when he had the chance. I'd roll my eyes, but I'm still fighting to breathe. Graham is sitting on my chest. I stare at the ceiling, though I can't really see it through the haze. *Be okay, Christina,* I think. *Be safe.*

"We'll take them out through the basement," Congers orders.

"And the others?" Mack asks before he starts to cough again, his face as red as his hair.

"Should we go after them?" Graham continues for him.

"No. We have what we want. Prepare these two for transport." Congers wipes blood from his lips and prods Leo with his toe while Mack clamps a set of handcuffs on the kid. Leo clenches his teeth as he's jerked onto his back and manages to stay silent even when his head cracks against the floor. Congers looks down at us. "Nap time, children."

And that's the last thing I hear before there's a needle-sharp jab of pain in my thigh and a seeping heaviness unfurls within my body, sucking me down into the black.

The first thing that returns is the pain. Raw, hot, throbbing. My wrists, my ankle, my head. I stay very still and surf the rolling waves of nausea. Eyes closed, I listen, focusing on one sound at a time. The low hum of conversation. The deep vibration that tells me I'm in a moving vehicle. Somewhere in front of me, someone's gasping, frightened.

"When did he say he'd arrive?" asks a male voice. Graham, I think.

"Twenty-three hundred hours," replies Congers from right next to me. "The helo's already left Charlottesville. We'll go back into the city once we're sure what we're dealing with. Maybe this detour will end up working to our benefit."

"Why bring the body here instead of DC? What can that scanner tell us that we don't already know?" Graham asks.

My gut clenches. Congers must have the scanner. I wonder if it's in this SUV.

Congers shifts in his seat, and I can almost feel his gaze on me. "Focus on the road, Graham."

My eyes snap open. I'm staring at my legs, my head bowed. A seat belt keeps me upright. I'm sitting between two men in dark suits. Their jackets cover the bulges at their waists, but as I shift, my elbow bumps against the butt of Congers's weapon. My wrists are shackled behind me. My shoulder muscles are screaming.

I slowly raise my head. A narrow two-lane road, headlights shining on the dotted white lines. Someone in this car isn't wearing enough deodorant. The odor is coming from the squirming figure in front of me. Leo. He's between two agents, too, in the middle row of this SUV. There are two more in the front—Graham and Mack. Somewhere along the way, we picked up three more agents. I have no idea how long I've been out, or what time it is, or where we are.

"Welcome back," says Congers. He's sitting on my right. "We're getting close. We'll get you two something to eat soon, as long as you're cooperative."

"Fuck you," I whisper, staring straight ahead.

"Silly, immature words from a silly, immature boy," he replies, sounding bored.

"How's your buddy Race doing? My silliness worked pretty well against the last agents who came after me."

"He's been busy cleaning up the mess you made in Virginia. You'll see him soon."

Great. "I'm not going to help you get into my dad's lab." Now that Christina and her family are safe, it's about withstanding what they do to me, not people I care about. Except, unfortunately, Leo tried to help me, like an idiot, and so I have to decide what's more important—him, or my father's discoveries.

"I would think," Congers says slowly, "that your father would have taught you to evaluate a situation thoroughly before shooting off your mouth. And yet that seems to be one of your most consistent characteristics."

He's right. My dad did teach me that. It was a quality he prized. And being reminded of that only pisses me off more. Then Congers slaps my thigh in a condescending way that makes me wish my hands were free so I could beat the shit out of him.

"We don't have to be enemies, Tate, though I will be if you need one," he says. "But please believe that you will regret it."

"You're the one who framed my dad as a terrorist, aren't you?"

He looks me right in the eyes. "It was necessary."

"Ruining a good man's name was *necessary*?"

"Unfortunately, yes, seeing as his son set off a catastrophic incident that required extensive and decisive damage control. We kept it quiet for as long as we could, but information was leaking. The public required an overarching narrative to pacify them, and so we offered one that fit."

I look away from his cold gaze and swallow hard. I still blame him for smearing my dad's name . . . but I also blame myself. I force the thought down and look outside again. "Where are we going?"

"Your ridiculous rescue attempt drew a great deal of attention, and people were already on edge after what happened at your school on Monday. We decided to exit the city until our agents based there can assure us the scene has quieted down."

He still hasn't answered my question. Judging by the shadowy outlines of trees on either side of the road, we're nowhere near Manhattan. I expected them to take me straight to my dad's lab, but I guess I made that impossible, which seems like a good thing at the moment. I squint at the license plate of a minivan in front of us as Graham comes up on it hard and swerves into the oncoming lane to pass. Garden State. "Are we in Jersey?"

"We have a lab of our own," says Congers with a smile. "Conveniently, it's also a place where no one will hear you scream if I decide to make that happen. Or maybe I should just work on this one and let you watch?" He abruptly grabs a handful of Leo's hair and jerks his head back. Leo's wide eyes stare at the ceiling, but again, he doesn't cry out. "He won't tell us who he is, but you seem to be important to him." Congers lets him go.

"It doesn't matter who he is. It matters what he is. A clueless kid. Just some science club wannabe from my school." As I say it, Leo's shoulders tense.

"Then maybe I should kill him and have one less clueless kid to deal with today," suggests Congers. "But I think his pain will motivate you."

"To do what? My dad's stuff can't be accessed remotely."

"We'll return to New York as soon as we—"

The SUV lurches forward as something crashes into us from behind. Congers and the dark-haired agent on my other side brace themselves against the seat in front, and Graham hits the gas. Congers twists in his seat, as do I, trying to see what hit us, but all I register is headlights closing fast.

It's the minivan we just passed.

"Goddamn idiot road rager!" shouts Graham.

"Don't bet on it!" Congers snaps, then grabs my hair. "Who is it?" he hisses in my ear.

"No idea!"

He releases my hair and glares out the rear window. "It looks like there's only one, but there might be more ahead to box us in. We need to take this one out now."

The van smashes into us again, honking, staying hard on our tail. Graham slams on the brakes, and the driver of the minivan slows accordingly, narrowly avoiding another collision.

The van careens around us and speeds ahead. Its brake lights flash. "What the hell is he doing?" Graham asks.

"Stop the vehicle!" shouts Congers as he peers out the windshield. "Now! Now!" The note of panic in his voice startles me. The minivan is pulling to the side of the road, so it would be easy enough to pass it.

Instead, Graham stomps on the brakes, and we all jerk forward. "Open the back!" Congers calls, throwing himself over our rear seat and leaping out as the hatch swings up. I twist to see him lugging an honest-to-God shoulder-mounted RPG launcher from a case on the floor of the trunk. "Get out! Get the prisoners out! Get behind me!"

I turn back around and look up ahead to see what's got him so freaked. My heart stops.

It's my mom. She emerges from the driver's side of the minivan, which is parked about ten yards ahead. One of her arms is in a sling, but in her other hand is a semi-automatic, and she raises it and fires at the grille of the SUV, looking more pissed than I've ever seen her. And to my horror, Christina jumps out of the passenger seat, holding a gun of her own, her eyes blazing with fury and fear as she joins my mom. She raises her weapon, but my mom shoves her behind their vehicle as Mack opens fire.

"Move aside!" Congers calls. "I'll take care of it!"

With a freaking *rocket launcher*? "No!" I shout, flipping onto my back and kicking the dark-haired agent next to me in the face. His head *thunks* against the frame of the passenger door he just opened. I kick him again and again, and he stumbles onto the road. I dimly register Leo struggling with an agent in the middle seat, but I can't worry about him right now. I hook my ankles over the seat and drag myself toward the open door, desperate to stop Congers, who's about to blow my mom and Christina to bits. My wrists still cuffed behind me, I heave myself out of the SUV.

The agents are wide-eyed and shouting as they fire on my mom and Christina. But I don't slow down to look at the minivan—instead I spin and lunge toward Congers, who's already put the grenade into the barrel and is hefting the green-gray launcher onto his shoulder. "Lovell and Warner, get over here. We'll need your fire!" he calls as I charge at him.

Before I reach him, another agent tackles me from behind, and I fall. Knees-hips-chest . . . I turn my head, and my skull hits pavement. Breath explodes from me in a strangled cry as my bones rattle. Graham was the one who hit me; he's on my back, but I buck my hips and jam my foot back, gritting my teeth at the impact of my heel against flesh and bone. He wheezes, telling me I probably got him in the balls. I raise my head to see Congers peering through the launcher's sight. "Please!" I cry. "No!"

He pulls the trigger. A helpless noise winds from my throat as I curl onto my side to follow the projectile. The grenade rockets toward the minivan—

Holy shit what the hell what the fuck is that

A silvery, blurred thing rises above my mom's vehicle, silent and slick. The grenade flies straight toward the thing, but it tilts lightning quick, and the grenade shoots into the forest across the road and explodes. I stare at the obelisk-shaped object hovering about fifty yards ahead of us, maybe thirty yards above the ground. *That* is what Congers and the other agents were firing at, but I've never seen anything like it. It shimmers like mercury in the light of the burning forest, moving like a helicopter even though it doesn't have rotors. Or wings.

A black dot appears on its lower front, swirling and sparkling and growing. Like some sort of hatch. Or torpedo bay.

"Grab the boy!" Congers cries. "Get him off the road!"

Movement near my mom's van draws my eyes back to the ground in time to watch both her and Christina dive down the embankment—right as the obelisk thing gives off a low, throbbing *whomp*. The minivan explodes, flying into the air like a Matchbox car. One of the agents wrenches me to my feet and tosses me to the side of the road, where I roll and crash through thorny underbrush. My head thumps against a rock. Blood fills my mouth as I bite my tongue. I land in a trickling stream at the bottom of a shallow hill, on my back, smoke and flames spurting from the mayhem above me.

I open my mouth, but I can't manage to draw in air. My eyes are riveted on the obelisk, which shoots backward suddenly as three more RPGs are launched. Congers and his men are shouting, calling to one another to reload, to fire. The obelisk, its hellish spire pointing at the sky, spins, but only dodges two of the grenades this time. The other glances its side and detonates. Before the smoke clears, the obelisk tilts backward, aiming that sharp nose at the horizon. I wait for it to fall from the sky, but instead, it darts away, moving too fast to track. A moment later, it's like it was never there.

Except for the carnage it left behind.

Two agents plunge down the embankment and grab me while Congers barks orders, instructing the others to mount up. My voice returns to me as they lift me from the ground. "Mom! Christina!" They should be nearby. I saw them roll down the embankment. They couldn't be more than a hundred feet away.

But they don't answer me.

No. I can't have lost both of them. I shout until the only sounds that come from me are hoarse croaks. I curse at the agents; I kick and struggle; I rage and thrash. The minivan is a twisted husk, overturned in the road, not two feet from the spot where I was lying when that *thing* fired on us. I spew question after question, but no one speaks to me. They're focused on getting me contained, on getting me into the SUV. As they do, I see Leo, strapped into the seat in front of me, pale and scared as he watches me lose my shit. I'm wedged between Congers and Mack, the red-haired agent. The men on either side of me are sweating, tense, their movements abrupt and hard.

"Mute him," growls Congers, and Mack pulls a black case from the seat pocket in front of him. "He's panicking." Congers loops his steely arm around my throat and cuts off my air supply. "You have to calm down. Calm down now, or you give me no choice."

I gulp for air and come up dry. Vision spotting, I buck and elbow until a spike of pain pierces my thigh, and once again, that heaviness swirls in my veins. I fight it, slamming my head back, trying to hit Congers, but he only squeezes tighter. "When you wake up, we'll talk again."

SIX

MY DREAMS ARE MADE OF FIRE. I LOSE MY MOM AND dad in a hundred hellish conflagrations. Mom always calls my name, and her longing and terror is like a language of its own. Dad is silent and grim, but before the flames devour him, his eyes tell me that he doesn't want to go, that he'd stay if he could, that he's sorry I have to do this without him. I am always bound, unable to move or change things no matter how much I fight. I watch helplessly as the obelisk rises high, moving like a whisper, and opens its sparkling, swirling portal.

Everything after that is death and defeat. And even though the inferno never touches me, it burns all the same.

"Give him another shot. I need him alert."

"Don't touch me," I slur, my defiance hardwired even though it feels like I'm swimming in a sea of motor oil and rebar, everything sharp and jagged, the air too thick to breathe. I'm upright, but only because I'm bound to a chair.

Congers is squatting in front of me as I open my eyes. His expression is stern, and his face is paler than it was before. "Cooperate, and I won't."

It takes effort, but I raise my head. I'm in a windowless box of a room. Buzzing fluorescent lighting above me. Old radiator against the wall. Not a new building, nothing high-tech. I glance at the door, painted metal, covered in nicks and scrapes. I blink, trying to gather my wits.

"I expected your lab facility to be a little swankier," I say, my consonants a bit more defined this time.

Congers slides his finger along the bridge of his nose. "We thought it best not to flee straight to a top-secret facility."

"And what exactly would constitute 'cooperating'?" My hands are cuffed behind the office chair I'm sitting on. My ankles are shackled to its legs. Graham is standing near the door, his gray-green eyes on me. His posture straightens as I size him up.

Congers glances at the young agent before returning his attention to me. "As you are aware, your father had something that belongs to us. We need to reacquire it immediately, especially given this evening's unfortunate series of events. Even more unfortunate, we need your help."

Fuck you. Those are the words on the tip of my tongue. But instead, I stay quiet and simply stare at him. Memories are slipping into place like puzzle pieces. We were being taken somewhere for questioning because I'd called too much attention to us in the city. My mom and Christina showed up. And then . . . "Where are they?" I ask.

Congers's expression doesn't change. He's probably an excellent poker player. "They mean a lot to you."

I try to keep my face as blank as his, but between the pain and the images of Christina and my mom flying down that embankment as that *whatever it was* blew their van to hell, I must give something away.

Congers's eyebrow arches. "I thought so." He stands up. "We have them. All of them. And their survival is very much dependent on whether you give me the information I need to access Frederick Archer's private laboratory."

My heart is starting to speed. He could be lying. My mom and Christina could have escaped. Or they could already be dead. And if I give the Core access to my dad's lab, they won't just have whatever H2 artifacts his ancestor might have found—they'll have designs for all his weapons. They'd have access to that satellite controller. They'd have everything they needed to shut down The Fifty permanently, not to mention the rest of the dwindling human population. "I need to see them. Leo. And my . . . Christina." They would have recognized Christina on the road—but they might not have recognized my mom. And if they don't have her—

"Dr. Shirazi is in our custody, Tate. I don't bluff."

Shit. "If you want me to believe you, I need to see them."

"We believe your mother knows how to access the lab, too," he says. "I wonder which of you will break first."

Heat spreads over my skin, my anger rising to the surface. He's playing a game. Keeping us isolated from each other, each blind to how the other is doing, hoping one of us will crack out of concern for the other. But I know my mom. If she really is alive, she'll know what's at stake if the H2 get access to Dad's lab. They could hurt her over and over again, and she wouldn't give them what they want. "Probably me. Why don't you give it a try?"

"But your mother came for you. A foolhardy rescue attempt fueled by the same emotion that might lead her to help us if we apply the right kind of pressure. If you don't want that to happen, I suggest you give us what we need sooner rather than later."

"First tell me about that thing on the road. The ship that attacked us. You knew what it was."

For the first time, his expression changes, fury hardening every feature. "Distraction techniques won't work, not on me. Tell me how to get into the lab without triggering the countermeasures."

It's not just distraction. The questions are piling up in my brain, crowding one another as they try to escape my mouth. "Are you guys in some kind of covert civil war? Is that why you need my dad's stuff?"

He crosses his arms over his chest. "Tell me how to get into the lab. It has a self-destruct mechanism as well, doesn't it?"

"Was that H2 technology? Who was flying it?"

His voice takes on a razor edge as he says, "How many chances does the entry mechanism give before lethal measures are activated?"

"Where's Willetts?" The professor may be H2, but he's no friend of the Core—he wanted to keep the scanner away from them and was working with George to do it. "Does he have something to do with this?"

"Enough." Congers clenches his jaw. "Graham, go ahead." He nods at the agent, whose mouth is tight as he slams his fist into my stomach. Breath explodes from my lungs, and I pitch forward. Congers catches my chair before I topple to the ground. He wrenches me upright.

"Let's consider that a hard reset," Congers says. "Please stop wasting my time." While Graham rubs his knuckles and waits for his boss to acknowledge him again, Congers repeats his demands for information to access my dad's lab. I keep firing questions at him, trying to find out what the hell is going on, what attacked us on the road, and what it means for the scanner and the rest of my dad's inventions. Every time I evade his demands, Congers's face gets more mottled. He's angry. Maybe a little desperate. But I don't give in.

The third time Congers gives Graham the go-ahead, the guy punches me in the head. He seems determined to pound information out of me—and also to show Congers how tough he is. The impact of the blow turns my vision white. The iron-salt tang of blood fills my mouth.

"I'm going to go speak to your lovely girlfriend." Congers's voice rolls through the thick haze of pain in which I'm float-ing. "Think about what's at stake for you, Tate. You've already lost your father. How much more can you stand to lose?" I hear the door opening. "Come on, Graham."

The door slams shut. The sound of footsteps fades. Even blinking hurts. But I force myself to do exactly that, trying to organize a few coherent thoughts. I focus hard on any sounds that come to me, but apart from the hum of the light over-head, I've got nothing. From the painted cinder-block walls and lack of windows, I gather that I'm probably in a basement, maybe of some old warehouse or office building.

And if that's true, it's possible that I can get out. Maybe wreak enough havoc to escape. The idea jolts adrenaline through my veins, and I raise my head, moving my jaw to make sure nothing's broken in there. I wiggle my hands—standard metal cuffs. Same around my ankles. My eyes scan the floor, searching for a paper clip or an old ballpoint pen, anything I might be able to use to pick the cuffs. But this chamber's been swept, and they probably expected me to try something like that. I grit my teeth and scoot my chair backward toward the radiator against the wall. Leaning back, I search for loose wires or metal fixtures with the right shape . . . nothing. I'm going to have to find my means of escape outside this room, and I know one place to do it, but I need more information first.

Leo. Christina. Mom. I have no idea where they're being kept or what condition they're in. Or if they're even here. But Congers said he was going to go work on Christina, and the idea makes bile rise in my throat. She was supposed to be safe. But I'm guessing she used my dad's phone and finally reached my mom, and together they figured out where I was. I think hard, trying to determine how they could have done that—and then I remember Leo's phone. He had it when we were captured. Maybe they used Dad's phone to trace Leo's, which is now probably in the pocket of one of the Core agents. Christina could have told my mom he was with us. And then Mom and Christina came after me. I wish they hadn't. My fingernails scrape across the radiator, making an echoing *tink* in the silence.

I freeze. Then I tap—three quick, three slow, three quick. SOS. It's just an impulse, a shot in the dark, but when your hands are cuffed behind you and you're in a windowless room, even the most primitive means of communication are better than nothing.

As I'm musing about this, tapping away, I realize that the sounds I'm hearing aren't echoes of my own taps. I curl my fingers against my palm and close my eyes, focusing on the faint sounds. Quick-slow-quick-quick . . . quick . . . slow-slow-slow.

L-E-O.

I guess I shouldn't be surprised he knows Morse code. Somewhere in this building, he's heard my SOS. He taps out two quick, two slow, two quick. A question mark. He's wondering who he's talking to. I start to type out the first letter of my name . . . and then I wonder if I'm talking to Leo at all. I pause.

I-T-S-M-E, he taps out. *It's me.* I almost laugh. I tap out my name, and his response comes immediately: *knew it.*

Where? I tap.

Basement. Next to stairs.

And then he taps out something that makes the breath whoosh from my lungs. *With C.*

My fingers are unsteady as I tap *hurt?*

No, comes his response. I hunch over in my chair, the relief heavy.

My mom, I tap.

Unknown, he replies.

My relief is gone. *H2? How many.*

Six. Suddenly his taps come so quickly I can barely make them out. *Outside*, he taps. Then it's a jumble of noise and I lose the thread and all I can make out is the final words: *more here.* He's maybe trying to tell me something or someone is approaching.

I have to get out of here. I have to get *them* out of here.

I scoot my chair back to the middle of the room. "Hey!" I call out. "Hey!" Each word hurts as my aching stomach muscles tighten.

After a few moments, the door squeaks open, and Graham pokes his head in. "What?"

"I need to use the facilities."

He stares at me. "Hold it."

"Seriously, dude? I'm not joking. Whatever you guys shot me up with is hell on my stomach. Oh, and I probably swallowed a lot of blood when you rearranged my face."

He rolls his eyes, then disappears for a second, but his fingers stay curled around the door. And I smile. He's most likely been left alone to guard me, and he's looking up and down the hall to see if anyone can help him figure out what the hell he's supposed to do. He looks only a few years older than me. I'd bet good money he's related to Congers, too. Maybe his son, because he was looking at Congers in a way that was all too familiar. He's eager to prove himself and doesn't want to mess up. Which means I can mess with *him*.

"Please? I swear. I'm going to shit my pants if you don't help me out."

From the hallway, there's a sigh. Then Graham walks in briskly, pulling the handcuff key from his pocket. He unlocks my feet first, then quickly unlatches my cuffs—but re-cuffs my hands in front of me when I stand up. He pulls his gun and presses it into my back.

"To the right," he says in a clipped voice. "And, Tate, I can't kill you, but there are at least five places I could shoot that are nonfatal but extremely painful. Please don't fuck around."

My muscles go tight. He might be green, but he kind of reminds me of . . . me. "Got it."

I'm a very good prisoner as he escorts me down the hall to the bathroom. For the first several steps, I'm testing my balance, trying to rid my head of the wooziness that comes along with being pounded upside the skull. I'm not at my best, but I can do damage. And I'm going to have to if I want to get out of this. I use my next few seconds to assess my surroundings. Sprinkler system, stairwell six doors from the bathroom. Leo and Christina might be in one of the rooms between here and there. I look over my shoulder at Graham, noting a stairwell far behind him. "Eyes front," he snaps.

I comply. But now I know there are two points of exit. I wonder if they're locked.

And I wonder if Graham has the key.

He keeps his weapon nestled against my side—probably one of the five places he could nail that would leave me bleeding and broken but not dying—and swings the bathroom door open. It's a dingy little space, and he shoves me inside. "You have five minutes."

I groan. "It might take a little longer than that."

"You have five minutes." He slams the door.

I flick the light on with my elbow and am thrilled when the blower fan comes on as well. I need every bit of cover for the noise I might make. As quick as I can, I shift the lid off the tank and moan loudly as I reach into the water and fumble with the chain and hook that lift the seal cap when the toilet is flushed. Closing my eyes to focus, I operate by touch, using the S-shaped hook to pick my cuffs and blowing quiet relief through my pursed lips when I feel them give. I only want them loose, so that's good enough. I replace the hook and groan again, hoping Graham is too grossed out to hover close. After another minute, I flush the toilet and run the faucet, then dry my hands. I make sure my cuffs look locked, and then I kick at the closed door. "I'm done!"

A moment later, the door opens, and Graham ushers me into the hall, pausing to look into the bathroom to see if anything's out of place, but not looking *too* close because he thinks it would stink to high hell. His weapon is holstered, so I guess I've convinced him I'm not a threat. While he does his cursory inspection, I peer up and down the hall to confirm we're pretty much alone in this corridor full of closed office doors and stairs on either end. Leo said he was next to the stairs, but that doesn't help me too much.

All it tells me is that I need to move fast. "So," I say. "What's it like to work for your dad?"

Graham doesn't answer, which tells me that I'm totally right. He's Congers's son.

"I bet he's a hard-ass. Difficult to please. Maybe impossible to please."

No answer. But he does press his weapon against my ribs, a warning. I'm getting to him.

"Seemed like you were trying to impress him earlier. Especially with that roundhouse shot to my head. Did it earn Daddy's approval?" I glance back to see Graham's jaw become rigid with tension. "I guess not."

I'm braced and ready when he swings at me, and I duck beneath his arm and jerk my right wrist free of the cuff, leaving the other hanging from my left wrist. I strip him of his weapon before he has a chance to fire a warning shot. It clatters to the floor as I elbow him across the jaw. As he staggers, I spin behind him and loop the short handcuff chain around his neck, then pull it tight. With me on his back, he slides to the floor, his knees hitting hard. He tries to arch and knock me backward, but I use all my strength to push him facedown on the ground. Saliva shoots from between his lips as he tries to gasp for air. He struggles like a wild man, but I press my chest to his back and flatten his cheek to the linoleum while his face turns purple.

I totally get it, I almost say to him. *I wanted to impress my dad, too.*

That's going to make this doubly painful for Graham, who made one simple mistake, the same one his dad did when he left only his son to guard me—he underestimated me. As soon as he loses consciousness, I drag him into my interrogation room. It doesn't take more than a few seconds to cuff him to the chair. I rip a wad of fabric from my T-shirt and shove it in his mouth to muffle the sound of his shouts when he wakes up. I only have a few minutes before that happens, so I steal Graham's keys and scramble into the hallway, where I scoop up the gun and lope in the opposite direction of the bathroom. "Leo," I call softly, the weapon at the ready.

Just before I reach the stairwell, there's a scraping sound from behind one of the closed doors, and I pause. "Tate?" Christina's voice calls from inside.

My hands are against the door in the next second. "Here," I say, touching my forehead to it as I begin to check the keys. I've just found my first likely candidate when Leo's voice interrupts my thoughts.

"Get away from here!"

"What?"

"They're coming! I can hear them on the stairs!"

I freeze, halting the jangling of my keys in time to hear the footsteps and voices echoing in the stairwell. For a moment, I'm paralyzed—Leo and Christina are still locked inside, and I'm out in the open.

Then I realize what I have to do. My heart simultaneously pounding and aching, I slide the handcuff key under the door, knowing the two of them will be able to find a way to help each other out. And then I back a few steps down the hall, seeking partial cover against another closed office door, and aim. It's a Glock 19, so assuming Graham is operating with a full magazine, I have fifteen shots plus the one in the chamber.

If this is it, I'll take as many out as I can and hope that Christina and Leo can take it from there.

My finger closes over the trigger as my first target swings the door wide.

Race Lavin, his face severe and cleanly shaven but bruised, his eyes bloodred, jerks to a stop when he sees me there. The corner of his mouth twitches. "I told you," he calls over his shoulder.

My mother appears behind him. "So did I," she says to the man at her side.

Congers frowns. "So you did."

SEVEN

I DON'T LOWER MY WEAPON AS MY MOM EMERGES from the stairwell, flanked by Congers and Race. I look her over for signs of injury. Her arm is in a sling and she's streaked with soot and dirt, but she seems okay otherwise. Except she looks really unhappy.

"There is research to show that physical abuse and torture is an ineffective means of interrogation," she says, glaring at Congers.

He doesn't answer. He's got something behind his back, maybe a weapon, and he starts to bring it out but freezes as soon as my finger tightens on the trigger. I'm sorely tempted to shoot him out of sheer aggravation and hatred.

Race raises his hands. "We've come to negotiate."

I ignore him and look at my mom, waiting for a signal.

Her gaze is steady on mine. "Tate, we have new information. Things have changed."

I'm still aiming at Congers's head. "You'll have to be more specific than that."

"We need to help one another," Race says. "And if we don't, the outcome will be catastrophic."

Congers's nostrils flare. "You are, for the time being, no longer our prisoners. We need you as allies." Each word seems to heighten the bad taste in his mouth. "If you'll permit me to move, you'll see I am holding the scanner, not a weapon."

"Show me."

Slowly, he brings his arm out to the side, revealing the sleek, black scanner, which he switches on. It reflects red off his leg, then blue as he angles it toward my mother, then red as the light crosses Race's chest. I move my finger off the trigger.

From behind me comes a muffled shout. Graham's awake. Congers's eyes flick toward the closed door where his son is shackled, and then back to me. He gestures toward the room where Leo and Christina are being kept. "I assume you'll want to free your friends before we talk."

Leo pounds on the door. "Already done. Just let us out."

I lower the gun and pull the keys from my pocket. As I unlock the door, I say, "You might want to let your son out. He's probably uncomfortable."

Race looks down the hallway, concern shadowing his features.

"He deserves whatever you've done to him," says Congers in a clipped voice, and for a minute, I feel bad for Graham. Then I remember how many times he punched me.

As soon as I open the door, Christina flies into my arms, knocking me back against the wall. Her face is pressed to my neck as she says, "I didn't know what they were going to do to you," in a strained whisper.

"I'm fine," I say, trying to keep my focus on Race and Congers even as her scent fills me up. I wrap my arm around Christina's waist and edge her to the side, keeping my body between her and the agents. "You?"

She's pale, and her eyes are red. So are her wrists, which makes my skin heat with rage. She's been through so goddamn much, and it's my fault. She touches my face. "I'm all right, Tate."

There are so many things I want to say to her. *You shouldn't have come after me* is the first one. But this is not the time, especially because Congers is moving forward, scanner raised. Race steps away from my mother, his hand near his waist, where his weapon is holstered. I tense, but as soon as the scanner's light flashes blue over me and red over Christina, both agents relax. I give my mom a questioning look, but her focus is on Christina.

Leo is standing in the doorway of the room, and he winces

as Congers waves the scanner over him, making him look cyanotic for a moment. Behind him are two chairs, cuffs hanging from the sides and legs. His wrists are red, too—and swollen. The too-big soccer jersey is dotted with blood, though he doesn't look badly hurt. He squints at the agents and my mom; he must need those glasses pretty badly.

My mother takes a step forward. "We need to talk."

Leo backs up and sinks onto one of the chairs in the room where he and Christina were being held. I keep my weapon ready as I back into the room, and Christina sticks close by my side. Race and Congers come in and stand against the wall, and my mom enters and closes the door behind her.

"I've just come from Virginia," Race says, confirming what I'd heard from Congers earlier—he came on a helicopter from Charlottesville . . . accompanied by a body. He was supposed to arrive around eleven p.m. The whites of his eyes are a creepy scarlet. I choked him so hard yesterday morning that the blood vessels burst. "I brought the corpse of Charles Willetts."

"When did he die?" I ask.

"About five minutes before I boarded a helicopter to the Walmart," he replies. "He fired on my agents as they came through the door of his apartment."

Next to me, Christina shudders. She'd escaped from Willetts only moments before.

"When did you guys become enemies?" I remember how determined Willetts was to keep the scanner out of H2 hands.

"Was he human?" Was that why he was working with George? Why wouldn't he have told my mom?

"He was neither human nor H2," Congers says. "We've just scanned him."

Neither . . . My stomach tightens. He'd avoided scanning himself. "He scanned orange, didn't he?"

Congers and Race both nod. Neither looks all that surprised at my question.

My mom does, though. "How did you know?"

I'm not ready to give that away yet. "What does scanning orange mean?"

Race glances at Congers. "Bill?"

Congers nods, though he looks pretty pissed. "Tell them."

"It means this planet is going to be invaded," Race continues. "It means the process has already begun."

"And it means that if we don't work together, the same thing that happened to our planet four hundred years ago will happen to Earth," Congers adds.

"Then you'd better tell us what happened," my mother says. She looks tired and angry, but also . . . scared. Her petite frame is practically vibrating with tension as she stands with her injured left arm folded against her body.

Congers looks down at the scanner in his hand. He switches it off and lets his arm fall to his side. "The H2 planet was peaceful, somewhat similar to this one in terms of climate and resources, but much more advanced, even hundreds of years ago. They were engaging in deep-space exploration." He stares steadily at my mother. "They'd discovered Earth but had not made contact because it was so primitive. They'd started studying humans, though."

"But I bet humans weren't the only thing they discovered," Leo comments.

Congers doesn't even look at him. "The leaders of the unified world government announced that they'd made contact with another advanced race within our galaxy, one that had endured a serious environmental disaster on its own planet. Our leaders decided that this race of beings would be sheltered on our planet. Permanently."

My mouth drops open. "They *invited* another race to invade?"

"It wasn't framed like that, of course. These aliens were supposedly refugees. The unified government cleared all airspace to let the Sicarii in and granted them legal status as well."

"Sicarii?" I ask, remembering my dad's hastily scrawled note in his safe house—*Race: "Sicarii."* He must have heard Race say it at some point, maybe during one of the multiple interrogation sessions Race put him through. Or maybe he had some surveillance set up that no one else knew about. But did he know what "Sicarii" meant?

"That's what we call them now," Congers says. "Just like you call us H2." The bitter twist to his mouth has returned. "But they were called something else, just as we were, in a language that is now known and spoken only by a few—because of what they did to our people."

"But you just told us you guys laid out a welcome mat," Leo says.

Race rubs at his temple. "The H2 planet was not like Earth, a patchwork of barely developed nations, chaotic leadership, and constantly shifting power bases and conflicts. It was peaceful and unified—but that made it vulnerable to a centralized infiltration. Here, they may not try to get to world leaders until they control those with power and weapons."

The Core. The Fifty. My stomach drops. Mom gives me an uneasy look.

Leo scowls. "I still don't think—"

"The process has already started." Race's voice is like a whip, and Christina flinches.

"That ship that attacked us on the road—" I begin.

"Was not H2 technology. It was a Sicarii scout ship."

"Why would they need to scout if we were just going to invite them in?" Leo asks, folding his arms over his bony chest.

"Because everything that happened on our planet was orchestrated from the inside," says Congers, "probably by scouts who arrived to pave the way for the rest. When the government announced that all citizens worldwide were to open their homes to the incoming refugees, there were protests, but it was all moving so quickly, because the infiltration had already happened. The laws were changed overnight. The Sicarii mass-transport ships arrived a short time after that, though we have no record of what the exact timetable was. We only know that by that time, few were resisting, because all formal communication structures on the planet were consistently broadcasting support for the arrival of our new 'friends.'"

"No one put up a fight?" I ask.

"Some did," Race replies. "But the loudest and most prominent voices of opposition fell silent—then came out in support of the Sicarii."

I think back to Willetts, who my mother had said was H2, but who seemed to have turned against them. And to George, who scanned orange and in those last moments cared more about the scanner than he cared about me, which wasn't like him at all. "You just said these Sicarii took over from the inside," I say, my heart pounding as I look at Christina. As a terrible thought occurs to me, my gaze roams her face, her body. She was so close to Willetts. "Do you mean that literally?"

"We do," Race says in a flat voice.

"That's why you scanned us just now."

Christina folds her arms over her middle. "You thought one of those Sicarii had . . . what, gotten inside one of us?" She glances at Race's holstered weapon. "Were you going to shoot whoever scanned orange?"

Race doesn't hesitate. "Yes."

"You believe this alien race is parasitic," Mom says. "Do you know what kind? What's the method of invasion?"

"Is it instant, or does it . . . take a while?" Christina asks in a tiny voice. Her breaths are shallow and sharp now. "Because Willetts was—he was trying to touch me. He wanted to touch my bare skin."

"Did he succeed?" Race asks.

"No," she whispers. "At least, I don't think so." Her eyes shine with tears, and I pull her close.

"It's been nearly two days since we were with Charles," Mom says in a gentle voice. "It seems unlikely that whatever these Sicarii do would be that delayed." She turns to Congers and Race for confirmation, but they don't look like they have many answers.

"The Sicarii are insidious," Congers says, eyeing Christina. "They're very difficult to detect. It helps to know touch may be part of how they take over a host."

Christina shivers against me. "Like . . . germs? I was really close to him."

"It's one possibility, but not the only one. But however the Sicarii take over, our ancestors discovered what they were doing too late to organize escape for more than a few."

"How did they discover it?"

Congers holds up the scanner. "I am a direct descendant of the man who invented the technology used in this device. He had a position in the government's space-exploration program, working on a team identifying other sentient life in the universe. It was his job to analyze all samples and data transmitted from the explorers' ships and probes, and he was able to differentiate the species on a molecular level."

Race stares at the device. "By that time, the Sicarii were arriving en masse. Many welcomed them, expecting peace. But that was only because the Sicarii themselves had somehow taken over the bodies of our leaders, and they were spinning that lie."

"My ancestor surreptitiously scanned some of the government ministers when they came to inspect his lab," says Congers. "They scanned orange, not red. He told some of his team members what was happening, that this peaceful cohabitation was actually an invasion, facilitated by leaders who had been taken over by alien entities. He said he had a plan to stop those leaders in a meeting he'd been called to in order to discuss the team's technology and discoveries. Something happened in that meeting, though, and that triggered a contingency plan—the members of his team escaped the planet using the space-exploration vehicles."

"Did the Sicarii discover your ancestor had scanned them?" my mother asks.

"He may have tried to do more than that. There were rumors that he had weaponized the scanning device itself."

Leo leans forward, rapt. "Did he try to assassinate them or something?"

"Possibly. He never made it out of the meeting, but he had anticipated he might not survive. When he did not make contact at the designated time, his team knew something had gone wrong, and they fled with their families and anyone else who could be persuaded to come."

"Which means no one who escaped the planet knew what actually went down," says Leo.

Race nods. "Someone else flew the ship Bill's ancestor had intended to pilot, the one on which he'd uploaded the means to construct a defense system against future invasions," he says. "But after the small fleet entered Earth's atmosphere, that ship disappeared. The others could only assume it had crashed. We've been looking for that ship for a very long time." His eyes meet mine. "And earlier this week, for the first time in four hundred years, that technology surfaced."

"You weren't after it merely to prevent it from being used to reveal the presence of the H2," my mother says.

"That is an important objective," Race replies. "But you are correct—it wasn't the only one. Until last night, however, we were unaware of how urgent the situation had become. And now that we've scanned the body of Charles Willetts, we know it's dire."

My mother looks stricken. "What did the Sicarii do to him?"

"As I said, they are parasites," says Congers. "We don't know how they move from host to host, or even if they can exist outside of the bodies of their hosts. We do know that they crawl inside a person and take over."

"But when they landed on the H2 planet, what did they look like? Wouldn't they have had to look humanoid?" Mom asks.

"Or they'd already obtained humanoid hosts," says Race. "We don't know that the H2 planet was the first to be invaded."

"But how exactly do you know that they're parasites?" I ask. "Have you seen one invade a host? Have you done an autopsy on Willetts? Did you find something inside him?"

"Now that we've confirmed he had been taken over by a Sicarii, we will autopsy the body as soon as we are in an appropriate facility." Congers once again rubs his finger along the ridge of his beaky nose, the only nervous mannerism I've seen from him. "Right now, we only have what we witnessed in the last few days, the information recovered from the ship wreckage of our ancestors, and the stories passed down through generations. We've already told you most of what we know to this point."

I squint at him. "Sounds like most of what you know is based on a multigenerational game of telephone."

"We're constructing plausible hypotheses from the information we have," says Race. "We know the leaders of the government on our home planet turned on their own people. We know they paved the way for the full invasion force and that they scanned orange, which means we know they were Sicarii, because of the technology developed by Bill's ancestor."

"And we know they're here," Congers continues. "And that this is only the beginning of something much worse."

"Why do they need to sneak around, though?" asks Leo. "That scout ship thing destroyed Mitra's van like nothing. If they were so much more advanced hundreds of years ago than we are now, it seems like they could come in and blow us all away without breaking a sweat."

"Then we should conclude that they don't want to blow us away. They want to invade peacefully because we have something they need," says my mother. "That's it, isn't it? They need the *people* on the planet."

"Like . . . for food?" Christina asks, her voice breaking.

"Or for a hospitable biological environment that enables them to adapt to the microorganisms here," says my mother.

"Their behavior is consistent with either hypothesis," says Race.

"No, it's not," blurts Leo. "They came right out in the open a few hours ago. If their strategy really is stealthy infiltration, why fly a spaceship over Jersey?"

"Because *we* have something they want, too. Enough for them to risk being seen," I say, looking to Congers for confirmation. "The scanner. You had it in the SUV, didn't you?"

He nods. "The events of the last week have not only made us aware that the technology exists and is being used—it may have alerted the Sicarii to it as well. And this device is one thing standing between them and their ability to secretly take over."

"How did they know it existed, though?" asks my mom, leaning against the wall like she needs to sit down. Her olive-toned skin is paler than usual, save for the dark, puffy circles beneath her eyes, and I'm reminded that she was in surgery only a day and a half ago. "And why would they be so threatened by it?"

"We have no idea what occurred in that final meeting with my ancestor who invented the scanning technology," says Congers. "My guess is that event made the Sicarii aware of what the technology can do. Even if we haven't figured it out yet."

"But you suppressed information about what happened at Tate's school." Mom bows her head, probably thinking of my dad. I wonder if she knows he's been branded a terrorist. "Even if the Sicarii knew the technology once existed, how would they know where to look now?"

"The lunch lady," I say. "Helen Kuipers. She was on TV. Everyone else might have dismissed her as crazy, but maybe the Sicarii didn't."

Leo grimaces. "And she disappeared a few days ago. Didn't you guys silence her?"

Congers shakes his head. "But the Sicarii may have, after they questioned her about what she saw."

"So we think the Sicarii want to destroy the scanner?" Christina asks. "They could have done that on the road a few hours ago. Problem solved."

My mother shakes her head. "They could have, but they

destroyed our vehicle instead, right as we attacked the vehicle carrying the scanner. And when the Core agents put up a fight, they backed off."

"Maybe they don't want to destroy it," I say. "Maybe they want it."

"If so, they'll try again," says Congers. "It's only a matter of time. And strategy."

I swallow hard. "And of who they get to next." I look at Leo, and then at my mom again, hating to drop this bomb. "George scanned orange when he came to take the scanner from me at the Walmart."

Some of the blood drains from Congers's face. "They've infiltrated both sides. They must have been watching us already. And when they discovered the existence of the scanner, they moved quickly to intercept it, using what they'd already learned about who was connected to whom. Somehow, they knew of our movements tonight."

"We don't know how many of them might be here," Race says to him. "Or whether there are already more within our ranks."

"I think I know how many there are," I say quietly. "My dad scaled up the technology and was scanning the planet using a satellite." I tell them about the population counter and the anomalies—along with the question mark that indicated Dad didn't know what they were. "There were fourteen, but when I checked it again yesterday morning, there were only twelve."

"Because George and Willetts were killed," Leo says. "They probably got George in Chicago—that's why there were signs of a struggle in his room."

I remember being on the phone with George on Tuesday morning. I remember hearing someone bang at his door. My hand is sweating in Christina's grip. "If they were in Chicago . . . that's where all The Fifty were meeting."

My mom pushes herself off the wall. "If there are twelve Sicarii on this planet and we know they're after the scanner, we need to protect it."

"We need to do a lot more than that," Race says. "We need to scan our people."

"And ours," Mom adds. "We also need a controlled environment. Defensible but contained, so that we can establish security and maintain it. Black Box Enterprises."

"You're not suggesting we invite the Core into our weapons factory," I say quietly.

"What if I am, Tate? After all you've heard tonight, surely you understand we have to work together. Black Box is a self-sufficient fortress. It's invisible to satellites, unlike official government agencies. And it has highly advanced perimeter defenses. It would allow us to prevent infiltration while we plan how to eliminate the Sicarii scout force, and, if possible, prevent the mass invasion they're trying to facilitate." Her brown eyes are intense and commanding. "There is no better place than Black Box."

Race and Congers don't disagree, but it's not like I expect them to suggest we head to the Pentagon or Quantico. This is like killing two birds with one stone for them. They can maybe defend against the Sicarii, but also learn all the secrets of The Fifty.

"We also need immediate access to Frederick Archer's lab," Congers says. "We know he must have the wreckage we've been looking for. If there ever was a defense system to protect against Sicarii invasion, even if it simply alerts us to their presence and gives us a chance to fight, we need to find a way to make it work. We believe the technology can be weaponized." He looks down at the scanner as if it's going to tell him the answer. And part of me wonders if it can, in the right hands.

"We know Dad had at least one scanner satellite in orbit," I said. "I could take a look at his stuff and—"

"Our team will investigate," says Congers. "And I hope you've heard enough now to cooperate."

"If you'd told me all of this earlier, instead of having your son beat on me, asshole, maybe I would have cooperated *then*."

Congers merely stares at me, unapologetic. But he only started playing nice when he knew the Sicarii had gotten to the H2, and his decision to keep me in the dark has cost us valuable time.

Race clears his throat, looking at my mom first, then me. "We've all lost people in this fight," he says. "We've all made mistakes, and the toll has been high. I know that will make it hard to trust each other."

I stare at him. *I will* never *trust you,* I think. *And I will never forgive you.* But as I squeeze Christina's hand, as I picture some creepy parasite crawling out of Willetts and taking her over, a chill rides across my skin. "What are you proposing? I'm not helping you get into my dad's lab unless I go in, too, and unless I have a say in what happens to whatever we find."

Congers's eyes light with frustration. "Have you even graduated from high school?" he shouts. "You have no idea what we're facing, and we don't have time to waste like this!"

"Exactly," I yell, releasing Christina, my hand clenched around the grip of my gun. "Which is why you need *me*. And I'm not just going to hand over my dad's inventions and technology to the same people who killed him!"

Race steps between us, his hands up. "He has to be included, Bill. He's proven himself more capable than the average teenager, and he knows more about the lab than we do." He sighs. "And he has a habit of causing enormous destruction when not properly informed or contained."

Mom lifts her chin as she speaks to Congers. "The Core is not the only group that prepares its youth to carry the torch. You should not underestimate my son. Or any of us, for that matter."

Her words lower my blood pressure, especially when she

looks my way. Only a few days ago, she was the one trying to protect me, trying to make plans without me. But now she's realized just how well Dad prepared me. As I think about what lies ahead of us, though, what's coming for us—an enemy that wears our skin and disables us from the inside out . . . I can only hope he prepared me well enough.

EIGHT

AS THE DRIVER PARKS ON THE STREET OUTSIDE THE
Upper West Side building where I've lived my entire life, Mom
turns to me. "Are you ready for this?" she asks me in a low
voice.

"No," I say honestly. "But that doesn't mean I can't do it."

She gives me a pained smile and gets out of the vehicle. The
others disembark, too. Race and Congers stand stiffly near the
front stoop while the other agents remain near the two SUVs
and one truck, scanning the sidewalk warily. It's Saturday, four
in the morning, but our neighbors are mostly middle-aged pro-
fessionals. Not a lot of night owls, so the street is pretty quiet.

The last few hours have been a flurry of phone calls and
planning.

I'm still not happy about taking Core agents into Dad's
lab. But I know what I saw on that road in Jersey. I know

the avarice I saw on the faces of Willetts and George as they worked in concert to steal the scanner. I know how I feel when I think of a parasitic alien trying to take over the body of the girl standing next to me, or anybody, for that matter. And I believe the Sicarii are already in the early stages of an invasion that could come as soon as they disable the threats to their plan. Including us.

For all those reasons, I want to find out what my dad was doing, and why he called the scanner the key to our survival. The Sicarii wanted it, and that makes me wonder more than ever what the device can do, what might happen if they turned it against us, and what we could do to them if we could figure it out.

Leo touches my arm as everyone else gathers on the sidewalk. "Can I go in with you?" he asks, his voice just above a whisper. He gives Graham a nervous glance as the guy glowers at us.

I return Graham's glare. I'm hoping he's decided we're even, but I know the last few hours have been rough for him. "Absolutely, Leo. I need you."

Leo's eyebrows rise, and I see the question there. "You knew my dad, Leo. And you notice things others don't."

His eyes brighten. "I do?"

"Yeah. So keep an eye out, and speak up. I need people I trust in there." I reach for Christina's hand as she joins us near the steps.

"Thanks," Leo says, scuffing the toe of his oversized soccer cleat against the sidewalk.

We all file into the building. My body aches as we climb the stairs to the apartment, but I grit my teeth and resist the urge to lean against the banister and catch my breath. Standing behind me are Race, Congers, Graham, and another young agent named Daniel Sung, an Asian guy with black hair buzzed high and tight—the only Core member thus far who has politely introduced himself. My mom, Christina, and Leo follow them cautiously. All are tight-lipped and tense as I stride to the keypad and type in the entry code. The door swings open. "You guys really made yourselves at home last time you were here," I growl at Congers, striding into my living room and taking in the disarray. "Where's my cat?"

"Agents delivered the cat to a kennel under your name," Congers responds.

I squint at him. "They did?"

He shrugs. "It was going to starve if it was left here."

I should say "thanks," but instead I say, "I hope you didn't destroy the one thing that's gonna get us into his lab."

"You keep talking to me like you expect an apology," says Congers, following me back to my room with the others trailing behind. "Stopping an invasion of this planet far outweighs the invasion of your home."

"Dude, shut up," I grumble, eyeing the mess they made of my space. I mean, it was always messy, but now it's total chaos.

I don't know what they thought they were looking for, since the lab is in the basement, but they tossed my shit all over the place. Congers and Race stand in the hall. My mother peeks in and makes a noise that tells me she can probably smell my dirty socks. I go over to a pile of laundry and kick it aside, then pull up the loose corner of carpet. My dad—and the Core agents, apparently—never thought to look under it because of the pile of stinky workout clothes that was always there. Beneath the loose carpet is the little compartment I dug into the floorboards, and out of it, I pull the small plastic case containing my dad's fingerprint. "Let's go downstairs," I say.

A few minutes later, I'm doing what I've done so many times before: slipping the film containing the fingerprint onto my finger and pressing it to the tab while typing in my dad's password. It makes my chest ache. The last time I did this, he was alive.

The door opens, and it feels like we're unsealing a tomb. Congers tells Sung and Graham to stay in the hallway, and both look unhappy but obey without arguing. The rest of them file in behind me, looking around as I flick on the lights. "Don't touch anything," I tell them. "Trust me. Some of this stuff looks harmless, but none of it is." Race appears at my shoulder, and even though his face doesn't give much away, I can tell he's impressed by the eager sweep of his eyes across the weapons racks. "Look at this," I say, walking over to the black screen that shows the population count. "This is what I was telling you guys about."

The numbers on the screen read:

$$2,943,287,964$$
$$4,122,239,895$$
$$12 \ (?)$$

"So you think the bottom number denotes the Sicarii scouts," Race says.

"I do. Like I told you, it was fourteen before George and Willetts were killed," I reply as Congers and my mother join us while Christina hovers near the door.

Race peers at the screen. "I'd say that's a preponderance of the evidence."

"It's a good hypothesis," my mother replies, always the scientist.

I touch the screen, and it flashes with a bunch of blueprints and plans before going red and asking for the password, just as it did before. I take a deep breath. *Please let this be right.* I've tried it in other places, and I'm scared to hope that it's going to work now, especially because I'm not alone in that hope—everyone else is tense and silent with anticipation. My fingers shake as I type. *When the time comes, it's Josephus . . .* As soon as I type that name, the red dissolves, and I let out a shaky, relieved laugh as the plans are revealed. For what, I have no idea, but since that password was the last thing my dad ever said, I know I'm looking at something important. And relentlessly complicated. The agents and my mother narrow their eyes as they try to read the tiny words and equations. "Do you guys have any idea what it is?"

"I might," says Race. "And if I'm right, your father was much further along than we anticipated—we thought he'd just made a single device, but he seems to have built his own system. Bill, look at this."

Congers leans in, and he might have a good poker face, but he can't hide his surprise. His eyes get wider as he zooms in on the lower left quadrant of the plans. "This . . . could be it." He tears his gaze from the screen to look at me. "You mentioned that your father had scaled up the technology. Did he utilize its full potential?"

"You're gonna have to rewind and tell me what you're thinking."

"The scanner technology differentiates the species. Human. H2. Sicarii. And if those numbers you showed us are indeed from a population counter, he's scaled up the technology using a satellite, as you said. But these plans are for a *network* of satellites."

Race points to a list of names, all pharaohs—Amenhotep, Thutmose, Hatshepsut, and so on. "These designate each one."

"You might be right." I walk over to the shelf and grab the

mobile satellite controller, the size of a small cell phone, the one I found the same day I stole the scanner from this lab. I enter the password—Mom's middle name—and show them the display. "This one is for Ramses." We look back at the screen's listing of pharaoh names designating each satellite. Ramses is the only name listed in red. The others are white. "Maybe Ramses is the only one in the air?"

"Or the only one scanning," suggests my mom. "If all of these are activated and working in concert, they'll form a field. Anything passing through the field will be scanned."

"Like incoming Sicarii," I say. "So it's like an early warning system? How much good will that do us?"

"Look at that," says Leo from behind me, reaching around to poke the screen.

I stare at the small diagram of the satellite. "Is that a . . . laser?" If so, it's more complex and advanced than any kind of laser tech I'm aware of.

"Sounds like the satellites can do more than scan," Leo comments.

"These are like giant weaponized scanners," I say. Some-how, my dad knew we were under threat. He'd already planned ahead. I nudge my mom's shoulder. "Why do you think he hadn't activated the entire satellite shield yet? He'd figured out so much."

Her brow furrows, and she presses her lips together for a moment, then says, "He assumed he'd be alive, Tate. He may have wanted to consult with The Fifty once he was certain there was a threat, or once he'd confirmed what it was. We'll never know."

Congers clears his throat in the heavy silence that follows. "We need to transfer these schematics so we can examine them," he says. "As much as Archer built and discovered, we don't even know if the additional satellites are aloft or what it would take to construct them."

I shake my head. "You're not transferring plans to an unknown machine."

"Tate." Mom touches my arm. "We could manage all of this at Black Box. In fact, it's likely that Black Box actually supplied the Ramses satellite. They may have the information about the others, even if they didn't know how they were being used."

I chuckle. "Knowing Dad, that's entirely possible." We spend a few minutes preparing the plans for remote retrieval. It involves removing a few layers of security, but now that I'm inside, it's nothing I haven't done before. The others wait quietly; it's clear they took my warnings about Dad's weapons seriously, though Leo is eyeing the seizure bags and Race is watching my computer maneuvers with interest. When I'm finished, we search the other computers for any sign of where Dad hid the actual H2 wreckage.

What I find instead is his weapon design files—and specifically a set marked "SIC." Race respectfully stands back as

I explore. There are plans here for the lasers on the satellites, but also for a combat vehicle. It resembles the eight-wheeled Stryker used by the US Army, but with a ton of modifications, including double autocannons—along with additional plans for the custom artillery shells—and a giant lens on the roof of the vehicle. I look back at Race. "I have no idea what that lens is for, but I kind of wish we'd had these when we met the Sicarii on the road."

Race looks at the plans and nods. "Does Black Box have these schematics?"

"No idea."

"Perhaps we should take them."

I smile grimly. "Definitely."

He glances around us. "Any idea where your dad kept the actual wreckage? He wouldn't have placed it in storage elsewhere, would he?"

"Unlikely," mutters Leo before I can say the same thing. My dad didn't trust anyone but himself.

"But we don't know whether we're looking for plane-sized wreckage or shoe-box-type wreckage," I say. "Mom, did he ever talk about it?"

She wraps her arms around her slender body and stares at his desk, the only place in the room that's even a little bit cluttered. And by "cluttered," I mean there are three pencils, a ream of printer paper, and his old black Princeton Tigers mug sitting on its otherwise clean surface. "No," she says quietly.

"He showed me files, but never the artifacts themselves." And I can tell it hurts her.

Leo looks back and forth from my mom to the desk. He walks slowly across the room and looks down into the mug. I shake my head—I didn't really *see* it, because it's always been there. I join him as he squats in front of it. "He didn't drink tea," Leo says quietly.

"Or coffee," I add, glancing at my mom.

She frowns, and I can tell she's realizing how odd it is, too. Now that I really think about it, I've never seen him with it up-stairs, never seen it in the dishwasher, never seen it anywhere but *right there*. "Maybe we should—"

Before I can finish my thought, Leo snatches it from the desk. As soon as he does, there's a soft click that I hear like cannon fire. I brace, expecting some kind of lethal onslaught . . . but all I feel is a hum beneath the soles of my shoes.

A panel in the floor slides away smoothly, forcing Leo—who's holding the mug and grinning like an idiot—to jump aside. What's revealed is a small chamber beneath the lab, with a set of rungs set into the wall. White cloths cover several irregularly shaped objects sitting on the floor. I stare at Leo for a moment, trying to suppress a smile and failing because his is contagious. "You could have gotten us all killed, dude."

He bounces on his heels. "But I didn't."

I catch Race's eye. He's shown respect, and it's time for me to do the same. "Let's take a look."

He looks mildly surprised at the invitation. I descend the rungs and wait for him at the bottom while my mom and the others watch from above. With my heart thumping heavily, I slowly pull the cloth off the largest object, which is about the size of a bicycle. It's a twisted, charred jumble of metal and wire and circuitry, with smooth panels and cracked display screens. And it happens to be over four hundred years old. It's traveled countless light-years. It came from another planet. Another galaxy.

"Where did he get this?" Congers asks in a hushed voice, leaning over the edge.

"His ancestor witnessed the crash. It's been in the Archer family for centuries. But my dad was the one to figure out the technology, and he used it to make the scanner."

Race tears his gaze away from the wreckage. For the first time, I see true regret in his eyes. "I'm sorry he's not here. I'm sorry for the part I played in that. If I could bring him back, I would."

"Me too," I say. Because I played a part in it, too. I haven't forgiven myself, and I probably never will. "He'd want us to focus on the task at hand, though."

Race nods. "Let's do it, then."

"Hey, Tate?" Christina calls in an oddly quavering voice. "Sorry to interrupt, but I think you should see this."

Race and I climb out of the chamber to see her staring at the screen that a minute ago contained the plans for the satellite shield. Now it's back to the screen saver—the population counter. Except now the numbers read:

2,943,287,962
4,122,239,896
16 (?)

Sometime in the last ten minutes, four more Sicarii have arrived on our planet.

NINE

WE CAREFULLY PACK THE WRECKAGE WHILE CONGERS
and Racc call for additional security. By seven a.m., the block
is crowded with black SUVs and dark-suited agents. A small
group of them, including Agent Sung, gather in a cluster near
Congers as he loads the box containing the scanner into the
back of his SUV. Congers actually cracks a smile when one of
his subordinates, a muscular dude named Devon with a weak
chin and jug ears, jokes about finally discovering where the
mythic Black Box factory is hidden.

I can't help but notice Graham standing near the back of the
truck where the H2 spaceship wreckage is being stowed, a few
vehicles down from his dad and the entourage around him. The
younger Congers wipes sweat from his brow as he tosses furtive
glances toward his dad, like he wants to be in that group. Like
he wants his dad to *see* him, working hard while the others slack

off. For a second, I'm actually tempted to go over there and talk to Graham, but then Sung beats me to it. He hands Graham a bottle of water, and the two of them get to work loading the final crates of wreckage into the truck.

By the time we pull away from the curb and head for the highway, the sun is hanging over the rooftops and we've got a convoy of over a dozen vehicles weaving through mercifully light Manhattan traffic. When we get on the thruway, we pick up another several dozen, transforming into a jointed black caterpillar, following close as we move along the road toward the Catskills. It's not like we're keeping a low profile, but seeing as the Sicarii somehow knew where to find our one SUV last night, I think Congers is hoping to find safety in numbers—and decoys. Every few exits, chunks of the convoy peel off, each with a truck that looks exactly like the one that holds the wreckage. And when we exit, heading west toward the mountains with at least thirty vehicles trailing us, another part of the convoy continues, heading north.

In our vehicle, Leo, Christina, and I ride in the middle row. My mom's in the back, with armed agents on either side, scanning the sky for Sicarii scout ships. Daniel Sung's driving, and Graham's looking sullen in the front passenger seat, his collar pulled high in a failed attempt to conceal the bruising I left on his throat. His eyes are on the clouds, as if one of them might be a threat. Our vehicle is armored and we've got ridiculous amounts of ammo in the back, but we're vulnerable, and anyone who witnessed what happened last night knows it full well. Sung's been pushing ninety miles per hour, and the other SUVs are keeping up.

As we take another turn and begin to trundle along the two-lane road that will take us deep into the Catskills, I'm tempted to drift, to pretend I'm here with just Christina, and we're going camping or something stupid and normal like that. She's nestled against my shoulder. Every time I think about what Willetts was trying to do to her—or, correction, what the Sicarii inside Willetts was trying to do—I have to muscle down a shudder.

I put my arm around her and hold her head to my chest as I watch fields and distant mountains pass in a blur of green. "My parents are so pissed," she says quietly.

I bow my head. "Why did you come after me? You were supposed to stay with them."

"Tate . . ." She looks up at me. "I knew you were in trouble. And when you didn't come out of our apartment . . ." She shakes her head. "Don't tell me you expected me to walk away from that."

"You used my dad's phone to call my mom, didn't you?"

She nods. "She'd just gotten into the city. She'd gotten your message."

"But you could have just told her what had happened."

She bites her lip. "I know. It wasn't enough."

She wanted to save me. The feeling is so huge that it can't fit inside me. It squeezes my lungs, making it hard to breathe.

"You could have been killed. She shouldn't have let you go with her."

"I wouldn't tell her what had happened until she agreed to let me go."

"But your parents—"

"I'm an adult," she says firmly. "They couldn't stop me. Oh, and your mom told them she'd keep me safe. Tate, don't you think what we've been through in the past week goes beyond whether we can get a hotel room for prom or whether I can pass a stupid chemistry exam? All of that feels petty and stupid now. All I care about is going through this with you." She presses her cheek to my shoulder. "If those Core agents are right, it might be the only time we have left, and I'm not going to give that up."

I want to promise her we'll be okay, but she's too smart for those words to give her comfort. So I kiss the top of her head and let my lips linger there as we reach a single-lane road marked with a simple "Authorized Personnel Only" sign. We're entering a heavily wooded area, the foliage so dense that the late-morning sunshine barely pokes through. There's no sign of buildings or any kind of development.

"This is the entrance to the grounds of Black Box," my mother says to Sung. "They know you're here, so proceed slowly."

Graham peers through the trees.

"You won't see the cameras," Leo says. "Don't bother."

Graham rolls his eyes. "I've been to secure facilities before.

You expect me to be impressed?" He squints as we roll along at ten miles per hour, and his jaw tenses as we pass another set of signs.

"DANGER: No Trespassing"

I look behind us to see dozens of vehicles snaking along the narrow road, so many that I can't see the end of the convoy even though we're headed down a long hill, giving me a good view of each SUV as it crests the peak. Congers and Race are near the rear, surrounded by even more heavily armed vehicles, with the scanner and the truck transporting the wreckage.

I meet my mom's gaze. There's something in her expression that catches me, but I can't quite read it. Maybe it's just being here again, for the first time since my dad's death. He's certainly on my mind, too. I face forward again, taking Christina's hand as she sits up and tucks a lock of her dark blond hair behind her ear. The trees are sparser now, and we're approaching a sheer cliff face, a gigantic wall of stone that juts up a few hundred feet above the trees and has a smooth, even rim. It looks like a man-made plateau with a perfectly flat top. The signs around this spot are a little more specific.

"Trespassers Beyond This Point Will Be Met with Lethal Force"

"That's it," says my mom.

Christina leans forward, her gaze skimming up the gray and craggy cliff. "Black Box is inside a mountain?"

Graham and Sung stare at the rocky fortress. It's so huge

that we can't see around or over it. We can't even see where it ends on either side. Neither agent looks eager to go in.

Congers's voice splits the silence. There's desperation in every word as he shouts over the radio: "Clear the road; bogie at our six—"

His voice cuts off abruptly as a deep boom echoes behind us. Leo, who's squinting out the back, yelps, "The Sicarii!" at the same time Graham shouts, "How did they know?"

Probably out of reflex and panic, Sung slams on the brakes, bringing us to a grinding halt about a hundred yards from the cliff face. The vehicle behind us nearly slams into our bumper. The rest of the convoy is pulling to the side of the road, making way for the rear vehicle and the truck containing the wreckage, which are racing down the hill, honking nonstop—right as a Sicarii scout ship rises above the peak of the hill.

Mom shouts, "Go! The tunnel's right in front of you!"

Sung's gaze is riveted on his rearview mirror as he tries to see the threat, but Graham punches at the steering wheel and roars, "Sung, just go!"

Sung curses and stomps on the gas. We barrel toward the vertical rock face until we're close enough to see the massive, camouflage-painted metal doors set into its surface. "Will it open?" Sung shouts as we speed within a dozen yards of the cliff. But even as he says it, the doors swing inward, revealing a tunnel leading into the mountain. It's just wide enough to fit two SUVs side by side, but it's high enough to accommodate almost any kind of load.

"Congers has the scanner in his vehicle," my mom says loudly, peering out the back window, where we can see his SUV barreling toward us. "He needs to get into the tun—"

Her words are drowned out by another explosion. One of the Core vehicles behind us spins into the air like a toy, flames shooting from the windows. It comes down with a crash onto the road, blocking the progress of Congers's vehicle and the truck carrying the wreckage. With SUVs clustered on either side of the road, Congers and Race are boxed in and won't be able to get to the tunnel. They're caught out in the open, and the obelisk-shaped Sicarii ship is right on top of them. I shout for Sung to stop and let me out, but he shoots into the tunnel with single-minded purpose. He goes about a hundred yards and ignores at least five of my commands to halt before he applies the brakes. By that time, I'm made of adrenaline, every muscle jacked. The scanner. They're going to get the scanner. As soon as we've slowed, I throw the door open. Christina grabs my wrist, but I tear my arm away.

"I won't let them have it," I snap as the passenger door sends sparks off the stone wall of the tunnel. Sung notices that I'm getting out and finally lurches to a complete stop, but before he does, I'm gone, sprinting back toward the fiery glow that makes my stomach twist.

About a dozen vehicles have made it into the tunnel, and agents are pouring out of them, pulling grenade launchers and firing questions at one another as they make their way back toward the tunnel entrance. "Don't let that ship land!" I shout as I shove into their midst. If the Sicarii get the wreckage or the scanner, we could be doomed. My legs propel me past at least four SUVs, but the press of agents on either side slows me down, so I jump on top of one of the SUVs and go right down the row, leaping from roof to roof, desperate to get to my dad's invention, to do anything I can to stop these alien bastards from killing our chances of saving ourselves and our planet.

The explosions from outside shake rocky debris loose from the roof of the tunnel, pelting my shoulders and head with shards of stone. That Sicarii ship is taking out the SUVs one by one as the agents try to respond with fire of their own, everything from sidearms to grenade launchers. From behind me, someone calls my name, maybe my mom, but I keep going. There's a wrecked SUV in the middle of the road about twenty yards from the tunnel entrance, flames eating it alive. I swear, I can see a black silhouette inside, human and helpless. Or maybe H2. It doesn't seem to matter as the fire turns flesh to sooty carbon nothing. But just beyond it is my destination— through the smoke, I can see Congers's heat-warped silhouette as he leaps from his vehicle.

"Tate!" It's my mom, only a few cars behind me. I glance over my shoulder as I jump from the roof of the final SUV in the line. My mom pushes her dark hair out of her eyes and points upward. "The Black Box defenses will be triggered if the scout ship flies above the edge of the crater rim! The ship is too low and too close to the mountainside right now!"

"I got it, Mom. Get deeper inside the tunnel." Without waiting to see if she listens to me, I scramble to the metal doors that mark the entrance of the tunnel. Heat bathes my face as I peer up the steep hill. At least two hundred feet above me, the rock gives way to sky. If Mom's right, reinforcements are available—as long as I can get the Sicarii to fly a little higher.

The obelisk ship is just above the leafy branches, spinning this way and that to avoid the rocket-propelled grenades that are going off like fireworks, setting fire to the forest. Congers and Race are beside their vehicle, shielding their eyes from the explosions all around them as they try to direct a group of agents—including Devon, the weak-chinned guy who was dying to know where Black Box was—who are pinned down near a cluster of trees nearby. Devon makes like he wants to run toward Race and Congers, but they shout at him and the others to get to the tunnel.

I stay low and sprint toward the burning vehicle that stands between me and the scanner. We have to get the device into the tunnel, where the obelisk ship can't follow. If the Sicarii wanted to destroy it, this would all be over, but since they haven't fired on Congers's vehicle, I have to believe they somehow know it's in there—and that they want it.

That's going to work to our advantage. I sprint for Race's vehicle as the agents at the tunnel entrance fire a furious volley at the hovering ship. It spins gracefully, dodging the projectiles, but doesn't move lower. Its spiraling hatch slowly opens, and Race shouts and waves to his men, all urgency and noise. As I run toward him, I catch the desperation in his eyes. He cares for his agents. He doesn't want them to die.

But when the Sicarii ship lets loose, there's not a thing he can do. The hellish ball of bright yellow fire shoots from that hatch and roars over my head, hitting right at the tunnel entrance. Agonized screams fill the air as I'm thrown forward by the blast wave. I push myself off the soft, leaf-strewn dirt, my ears ringing, my heart pounding, and stumble around SUV wreckage to get to Congers and Race, whose brow furrows when he sees me. "Get away from here," he roars.

"They want the scanner!"

"And we're defending it!" Congers shouts, even as he hefts a grenade launcher onto his shoulder.

Not enough. It's only a matter of time before the Core can't hold that ship back. "Diversion," I say to Race, right in his ear, shielding my mouth just in case the Sicarii can somehow read lips. Hell, they found us here and they know where the scanner is, so I wouldn't put it past them. "When I go, get the device up your shirt and run for the tunnel."

His face crumples in confusion. "When you go . . . what?"

I ignore him and dive into the vehicle, frantically looking

around for what I need. Then my eyes light on the stereo. As a boom outside tells me Congers has fired his grenade, I remove the plastic cover and pry off the black rectangular ring that protects the edges of the stereo itself. I duck outside again and rip the Swiss army knife from Congers's belt. He doesn't seem to notice because he's so busy reloading his weapon. The obelisk ship is only about thirty feet overhead, firing deep, percussive blasts at the few SUVs that haven't been destroyed. Everything is burning. Bodies are scattered near tree trunks and beside flaming vehicles. Survivors like Devon have nowhere to run now, because smoke is billowing from the tunnel. I have no idea if anyone in there—including my mother, Christina, and Leo—is still alive, but I have to make this stop. I want that ship to *burn*. If it's killed the last few people I love, this is about more than survival—it's about revenge. I duck back into the SUV and try to steady my shaking hand as I run the knife around the edge of the stereo, feeling the metal catches give one by one. My blunt fingernails chip and give as I pry the block of metal and plastic from its slot.

I'm praying that the Sicarii don't know what the scanner actually looks like.

I tuck the stereo against my chest and slide outside again. My fingers clamp onto Race's shoulder. "I'm going to draw them away," I say, leaning close. "When I've got their attention, get the scanner to the tunnel."

"No," he says, reaching for my arm, but he's too slow. I'm

already ten feet from the road, hurdling burning debris that singes my legs and fills my nose with acrid fumes. I push all my fears away as I dodge and weave through the trees, their leafy canopies aflame, sparks and ash raining down. The mountain looms to my right, steep and menacing, and I peer through the smoky haze, looking for a route to the top. Blinking, I pause in a spot between two trees and turn toward the obelisk, which already seems to be tracking me. I make an obvious sort of movement with my arms, cradling the stereo protectively as the brutally elegant silhouette of the silver ship blocks out the sun. A thrill of grim pleasure shimmies through me when I realize it's slowly moving toward me.

Perfect.

But only if I'm fast enough. Only if I'm strong enough. I run through the trees, farther away from the tunnel entrance, to a spot where I can get a foothold. I shove the stereo into the back of my pants as I sprint—I need both hands if I want to make it to the top.

I'm only a few feet from the cliff face when someone crashes into me from behind. My forehead slams against stone. I'm ripped away from the wall of rock a second later, arms flailing. Hard fingers tear at the back of my shorts and shirt, and I pivot, smashing my foot into my attacker's knee. He roars and lets go of me, but when I turn to face him, he's already raised his gun.

It's Devon, grimacing as he shifts his weight to his uninjured leg. His gaze darts up to the ship overhead and then returns to me. "Surrender the device," he says calmly.

I try to swallow, but my mouth is so goddamn dry. I hold my hands out to the side and slowly reach for the stereo that's jammed under my waistband. "How long have you been inside that agent's body?"

Devon tilts his head and gives me a quizzical look. "I don't want to kill you. Give me the device."

I glance toward the tunnel, but it's too smoky to see the entrance. If I hand Devon the stereo, he'll know in a second that it's fake, and he and the ship will refocus on Race and Congers. But if I don't hand him the stereo, he's going to—

There's a sharp crack, and Devon jerks to the side, then falls, the side of his head shattered and bloody. I look over to see Race disappearing behind a giant oak, semi-auto in his hand. He's given me a second chance, and I won't waste it. I spin around and leap onto the vertical rock face, digging my fingers in. The toes of my sneakers wedge into cracks in the stones, and I'm moving. Up. Straight up. This whole plan is only going to work if I get to the top, and maybe not even then. But if all I end up doing is helping Race get the real scanner safely into the tunnel, then that's good enough.

Fingers hook over rock. Heave. Find a foothold. Surge upward. Jam my hands into a crack. Repeat. Repeat. I climb the cliff face with a frenetic energy fed by terror and determination. Searing heat licks at my spine, at the hairs on the back of my neck. The scout ship must be moving closer. It's so quiet—all I can hear is a low hum—but I know it's coming to get me—and what it thinks is the scanner.

They'd gotten to an H2 agent. Somehow, one of those aliens crawled inside him and took him over. No idea how—through his mouth, his skin, his too-large jug ears . . . I have to stop thinking about what it might be like to have a Sicarii invade my body. The merest inkling saps strength from muscles that need every ounce of blood and hope I can possibly give them. Fingers. Toes. Quadriceps. Biceps. Move. Climb. My pulse beats hot inside my head. My ears are awash with white noise. Time stops.

A rocket-propelled grenade slams into the cliff face about twenty feet above me, and I nearly lose my grip. "Hold your fire!" I yelp as rocks dash against my shoulders and arms, already knowing no one will hear me. Race must have rallied the surviving Core agents, and they're firing at the ship.

If they're not careful, they're going to knock me off the side of this cliff.

The low hum from the scout ship intensifies, and the loud explosion that follows tells me that it's taken a more permanent approach to the problem of ground fire. Sweat trickles down my back as I hear shouts and screams from below, making the metal stereo slip and scrape against my bare skin. Up. Up. I won't stop. I won't slow. My breath bursts from my lungs as I propel myself upward with frenetic speed. The top of the cliff is only about fifty feet above me now. My arms and legs destroy the distance; my lizard brain has taken over. At any moment, I could be blasted off the side of this rock, but the Sicarii ship floats behind me, graceful and quiet, maybe waiting for me to fall so it can catch me and take everything that's mine. Or maybe waiting for me to get to the top so it can land and scoop me up.

But if I heard my mom correctly, that's not going to happen. The defenses will be triggered if I can lure the ship above the edge of the plateau.

As I make yet another leap upward, my hand slips and my feet scrabble at the rock, trying to find purchase. For a few seconds, I'm still, clinging precariously with one good toehold and the fingers of one hand jammed deep into a crack. The lights from the ship brighten, turning the cliff face white and shimmering, and with a jolt of panic I'm moving again. Thirty feet. Lunge. Twenty feet. *Go.* Ten feet. *Almost there.* I heave myself onto the plateau at the top of the cliff, looking around with desperation and hope, gasping for air, praying for big guns or lasers or cannons or a squad of freaking special forces or whatever the fuck's going to keep this Sicarii ship from getting me.

What I see is . . . not much. The plateau is unnaturally flat and circular, at least one mile in diameter. There's a crater in the middle, protected by a rim that's at least a hundred yards thick . . . and in the center is a giant, empty bowl, from what I can see. No factory, no weapons. Nothing.

With dread flooding my insides, I whirl around to see the

Sicarii ship rise above the edge of the plateau. I wish I knew whether Race and Congers made it safely to the tunnel with the scanner and the wreckage. Whether this was worth it.

I pull the stereo from the back of my pants and wave it at the ship. "Want it?" I shout.

It moves closer. It gives off electrical pulses that I feel beneath my skin, like it's mapping all my weaknesses. I fold my arms over the stereo.

I'm about to start running along the plateau toward the crater, ready to hurl myself in if nothing else, when the ground trembles beneath my feet. The sound of rock sliding over rock makes my breath catch in my throat. It's a mechanical noise, very controlled. Gray shapes rise smoothly from the plateau all around me, the sun glinting off the metal panels. They give off a hum all their own as they spin into position.

Surface-to-air missile batteries. Five of them, positioned at intervals along the edge of the cliff. In the moment it takes me to breathe, they lock on to the Sicarii ship.

It's completely still for a moment, like the pilot inside is gauging the threat. Then, faster than anything I've ever seen, it streaks away over the trees.

Each of the missile batteries fires, rocketing toward the target that's hurtling over the forest, over the hill. *Faster,* I think, but after a second or two, I know it's no good. The Sicarii ship disappears behind a mountain miles away. The missiles slam into the base of that mountain a moment later, shaking the ground. And then suddenly, there's an eerie sort of quiet, and I don't know if we've won or lost.

I sink to my knees, all the panic and pain of the last several minutes hitting me at once and siphoning my strength away. The stereo clatters onto the rock next to me. My head hangs as I try to stand, to go see what's left of the Core, to find out if Christina, Leo, and my mom made it through.

Before I can, a whirring noise to my left has me crouching low, watching silently as a metal hatch slides open near the inner edge of the crater. A huge bear of a man emerges, followed by four other men, all armed.

All aiming weapons at me.

The enormous man strides toward me. Sunlight glints off blond strands in his thick red hair and beard. He tilts his head, his eyes narrowing as he peers at the stereo and then at me. "You look a lot like Fred Archer," he says in a rumbling voice.

"That's because I'm his son."

The man smiles, but it's not a jovial sort of thing. It's tinged with ferocity and war. I'm suddenly sure that he's the one who gave the order to fire on the Sicarii ship. "I'm Angus McClaren," he says. He gestures at his men, who immediately lower their weapons. "And you must be Tate. Welcome to Black Box."

TEN

THE DISTANT SOUND OF HELICOPTER ROTORS REACHES
me as I stare out the window of the infirmary within the Black
Box factory compound. It's been a few hours since the attack,
and several members of The Fifty have started arriving, trickling in from the international headquarters in Chicago, where
most of them had remained after the board meeting, given the
series of crises over the past week. I can see the helipad from
the gurney where I'm lying. Armed guards escort each patriarch and matriarch into this main building.

And then they're scanned. The device survived the Sicarii
assault, and Race surrendered it to Black Box as soon as he
emerged from the tunnel. Not that he had much choice—he was
surrounded by a horde of armed humans, all of whom knew
exactly what he was. Angus took possession of the device, and

after a quick aside with my mother and me, announced that all new arrivals, human or H2, would be scanned immediately, as well as all the factory workers, who apparently live on the compound. He switched on the device, and blue glinted across his skin and eyes as he showed the Black Box staff they had nothing to fear from it.

Unless they're Sicarii, of course.

The entire compound is on high alert, because thanks to one Sicarii—the creature who got inside Devon—the hostile aliens now know the location of this weapons factory. Perhaps that was their plan all along. They tried to grab the scanner before we entered the well-defended compound, but they gathered a shitload of information in the process. The single scout ship could come back with a squad of additional ships at any moment. The entire rim of this massive man-made volcano is bristling with missile batteries, and there are additional defense stations high on the sheer cliffs around the inner perimeter. But it's clear no one feels safe. People outside aren't walking from place to place—they're jogging, faces creased with tense frowns.

I'm sidelined for the moment, though. After our brief talk with Angus, my mom brought me straight to this infirmary—which is really more like a small hospital—pointing out injuries I hadn't even noticed before that moment. Rocky shrapnel had strafed the backs of my legs, my fingers were bleeding and torn, and there are first-degree burns on my shoulders and the back of my neck from the heat that came off that scout ship as it flew so close to me.

My nurse—a middle-aged woman with short brown hair, whose name tag tells me her last name is Cermak, a well-known family within The Fifty, according to Rufus Bishop—seems totally on edge. I don't blame her. In the last hour, nine Core agents have been wheeled in sporting injuries minor and grave. Nurse Cermak is scowling, eyeing the wounded H2 agents like they're going to rise up and zap her, like they're enemies instead of patients. All of them scanned red and not orange, but the difference doesn't seem to matter to her. The rest of the Black Box medical personnel seem to feel the same way . . . as do the black-uniformed guards who stand in the doorway with their weapons in the low ready position. We're in this enormous room, gurneys everywhere, blood on the floor, men with ashen faces and ghastly wounds, and mistrust hangs in the air like mustard gas.

I glance at Christina and Leo, who are sitting against the wall in plastic chairs as Nurse Cermak bandages the gash across the back of my left hand. It hurts like a bitch now that I'm actually paying attention. When I wince, Cermak says, "I have Vicodin. Might help you relax."

I raise my eyebrow. "Should I relax?"

The corner of her mouth curls with contempt as she glares at Graham Congers. He's looking like he dearly misses his

Glock as a male nurse stitches a laceration across his shoulder blade with rapid-fire jerks at the sutures. "Good point," she mutters. "I can't believe they let these H2 scum into our compound."

"They're not the enemy I'm worried about," I tell her.

Christina glares at Nurse Cermak, then gets up and takes my hand. She, Leo, and my mom were miraculously unhurt in the assault, and I'm endlessly thankful for that. "You're going to have to slow down at some point," she says softly. "You haven't slept since . . ."

"Since Congers was kind enough to sedate us after we freed your parents," Leo says. "But I didn't find that very restful."

Cermak's eyes narrow as she regards Christina. "Which family did you say you all were from?"

"Thomas," Leo mumbles, rubbing at his eyes.

"Archer," I say automatically.

Christina stares back at Cermak, unapologetic. "I didn't."

Cermak freezes, like her blood has just turned to ice. Her brown eyes dart to me, then back to Christina, then to Leo, who looks defiant as he gets up and stands next to Christina. "Does it really matter right now?" he asks. "We're all on the same side."

Cermak's mouth snaps shut, and she walks quickly away, stopping only to hiss in the ear of the supervising physician, a wiry African American man with a deep Southern accent and steel-gray hair—Dr. Ackerman, who Leo told me is also one of the board members of The Fifty. He looks over his shoulder at Christina before saying something quietly to Nurse Cermak, whose mouth becomes a white line as she heads for the supply closet.

"I feel so welcome here," Christina says as I hop down from the gurney, my bandages crinkling over my raw, torn skin. She nudges Leo with her shoulder. "Thanks," she whispers.

His cheeks turn pink. "No problem."

I pull Christina close. "Let's get out of here."

As we weave our way toward the door, I catch sight of Agent Sung, who's lying on a gurney and wearing an oxygen mask. His face is streaked with grime, and his buzzed black hair is damp with sweat. He and Graham were heading toward the tunnel exit to join the battle when the Sicarii ship fired into it, and Sung was one of several agents who suffered smoke inhalation. Looking gaunt and tired, he nods at me as I pass, and I find myself nodding back. Yeah, he's H2, and a Core agent at that, but we've been through something that erased the difference between us for a little while.

Plus, the Core took a heavy hit in the attack. Not including Devon, who was basically dead whenever the Sicarii got to him, ten agents were killed, and another nine were wounded seriously enough to need immediate treatment. Sooty and shell-shocked, the rest were corralled by the Black Box guards as they exited the tunnel and entered the giant crater that houses this compound. They were taken away at gunpoint, presumably until Race, Congers, and Angus McClaren agree on the specifics of their presence at Black Box—like whether they'll be allowed to carry their weapons and move freely around the compound.

Maybe all of that is why, on my way out the door, I stop at Graham Congers's gurney. Like Sung, he's now got an oxygen mask strapped over his face, and his shoulder is tightly bandaged. His eyes are bloodshot and swollen, but there's still no missing the anger there. Suddenly, I wonder if his dad bothered to make sure he was okay before rushing to take care of his other men. Something tells me he didn't. And something— namely personal experience—tells me that it hurts like hell. "Glad you made it through," I say to him.

His gray-green eyes meet mine, probably searching for sarcasm. "Thanks. And good job out there," he says in a muffled voice. He closes his eyes, and I take that as my cue to leave him the fuck alone.

Before she left me in the capable hands of Nurse Cermak, Mom told me to meet her and Angus in the CFO's office as soon as I was able. Leo, who's been here before on trips with Angus, leads me and Christina down a long hallway lined with paintings and then photographs of a bunch of people who aren't famous . . . except among The Fifty. As I read the nameplates, I realize these are probably the patriarchs and matriarchs of the families stretching back as far as anyone could document. Bishops, Fishers, McClarens, even an Archer or two that I wish I could stop to stare at for a while. Leo waves his skinny arm at a portrait of a man with a bushy beard and eyebrows. He's wearing a plaid sash across his broad chest. "That's Angus's great-grandfather. He led The Fifty for about twenty years, right after it formed."

"Why are all The Fifty coming here now?" I ask. "Seems dumb to flock to a place that could be attacked at any moment."

Leo squints up the hallway. "They know the H2 are here, and they've been raised to believe the Core are the enemy." He chuckles. "Some of them are probably pretty mad. The news of the Sicarii is brand-new and not yet credible. They might even think it's an H2 ruse to get inside Black Box. Their priority would be to protect their interests from those who they believe are the greater threat." He gives me a rueful look. "And I'm telling you now, they decide everything by committee."

We near the end of the hall, and I notice the birth and death dates beneath the portraits are becoming more contemporary. Then we pass a picture of a handsome blond man with a mustache and glasses. "Arthur Thomas," the nameplate reads. "1971–2007." Leo's dad. I look up the hallway with a sinking stomach.

Sure enough, Frederick Archer's nameplate is already affixed to the wall. The picture's not up yet, thank God. I wonder what my mom felt when she saw that. To me, it feels like I've been kicked in the gut. Christina doesn't say anything, but she moves close so her shoulder brushes mine.

"One day we'll be up there," Leo says quietly. "All the patriarchs and matriarchs are, after they've passed away."

I stare at my dad's nameplate. "Patriarch of what? A family of one?"

Leo reaches to push his glasses up his nose before remembering he doesn't have them. "Unless we have kids." His cheeks flush. "I mean . . ." He looks back at his dad's portrait. It might as well be an older version of the kid next to me, right down to the inquisitive bright green eyes. "Having a family someday would be nice."

This is the most awkward conversation I could possibly have while my girlfriend—who is an H2—is standing right next to me. I'm scared to even look at her. I clear my throat. "Do they make a big deal out of it? You know, you being the last of the Thomases and all?"

Leo gives me a one-shouldered shrug. "Not a lot. Not in front of me, at least. But several families have already tried to make arrangements with Angus for my . . . my—" He cuts an anxious glance at Christina.

She gives him a gentle, teasing smile. "Your hand in marriage?"

His face is beet red. "Um. Yeah."

"We should keep moving," I blurt out, grabbing Christina's hand and practically dragging her down the hall. I want to talk with Leo about this—he might be a few years younger, but he's been dealing with this crap a lot longer than I have and understands it better, too. I just can't talk about it in front of Christina. It's so weird. We never worried about the future before, but now that we might not even have one, it feels like I somehow have to think about it.

I'm the last Archer. A member of The Fifty, a group that's banded together to remain genetically "pure." Is that something I should care about? A pang of loss hits deep in my chest—I wish my dad were here to explain it. I wish we'd had the kind of relationship where I wasn't too busy fighting him to really learn from him. I squeeze my stinging eyes shut and force away these pointless thoughts. I need to focus on more important stuff now, like how to stop aliens from taking over the planet.

We enter a soaring atrium, walls of glass that give us a full view of where we are. In the cloudless afternoon sunlight, the grounds of Black Box look like this weird mix of parkland and industrial complex. There are wide expanses of lawn, copses of oak trees, and even a large lake on the eastern side of the crater. The entire compound is surrounded by a wall of rock at least two hundred feet high. They really did burrow into a mountain and make it their own. There are three tunnels in and out. Six perimeter defense stations have been positioned high on the rock wall, every half mile around the three-mile circumference of the crater. All smooth metal and big guns, those defenses have been anchored into the rock and jut outward, with two-person elevators ready to shuttle guards up from the ground to the bus-sized stations so they can defend the compound. And as I witnessed during the Sicarii attack, on the crater rim itself there are both manual and automated defenses, as well as sophisticated visual, geothermal, and acoustic shielding that prevent satellite spying, even though the compound lies under the wide-open sky. That technology is the reason it looked like an empty crater when I viewed it from the rim—it's a complete visual illusion. Basically, this whole compound is stealthed out.

Behind this main building, which juts up like a tower of glass with two gray wings on either side, is the actual factory. It's a hulking shadow right now, a literal black box. No windows. Steel doors and cargo bays. Massive and mysterious. I can't wait to get inside and look around.

"Have you ever been in there?" I ask Leo, nodding toward the factory.

"Oh yeah." He smiles. "It's badass. Uncle Angus won't let me go in there alone, though."

Christina looks over at him. "He's afraid you'll get hurt?"

He rubs at the back of his neck. "No, the last time I came here, I may have accidentally blown a hole in the south wall of the factory. They have some amazing artillery in there."

I wonder how much of it my dad designed. "Hopefully things that can take down a scout ship." I remember that obelisk leaving the Black Box missiles behind like they were moving in slow motion. We'll need to do better than that when they return. If Race and Congers are right about the scouts looking to control those with weapons and power in advance of the full invasion, then the Sicarii will target Black Box. It's one of the most heavily armed places on the planet, and if they're paving the way for a peaceful invasion, they'll need to take it out.

As we cross the atrium, urgent echoing voices draw our gazes. Along the front of the building's main entrance is a series of doors, and there's a security station there. The guards are out of their walled booth . . . and one of them is holding the scanner. This is where newcomers are being escorted, where everybody in the compound, including every worker who lives here, is expected to check in no later than three this afternoon—unless they want a warrant issued for their immediate arrest by Black Box guards.

A small squad of those guards is currently wheeling in several gurneys, each conveying a black body bag. With a rigid jaw, one burly young guard holds the scanner over each gurney as the others roll them by, headed for the freight elevators behind us. Red off the body bag, blue off the guard. These are the Core agents killed in the attack, probably being taken to a makeshift morgue. I count ten, and then three more roll in.

"I thought they said ten Core agents were killed," Christina says quietly.

Whatever's in the body bag scans orange.

"That's what they said," I reply. "One of them is that agent who tried to get the scanner from me. Race shot him."

Leo crosses his arms tightly over his chest. "The other two are George and—"

"Charles Willetts," Christina and I say at the same time. Our eyes are glued to the scene as the second and third body bags scan orange. The guards wheeling those three gurneys look like they can't wait to deliver their cargo and get as far from it as possible. They've probably been warned that there might be parasites within those bodies. My mom told me she's going to be in charge of the autopsies, so she's tasked with figuring out what exactly the Sicarii are.

After we watch all the gurneys disappear onto the elevators, we enter another hallway, this one marked with doors that indicate we've reached the executive offices. The first nameplate reads "Brayton Alexander, CEO." The office is dark, the door closed. The second reads "Angus McClaren, CFO." That door is open, and there are voices coming from inside. I enter to find my mom, Angus, Race, and Congers sitting stiffly on the couches and chairs in the large receiving area. There are a couple of smaller offices stemming from this room, as well as a back hallway that probably leads to a restroom or something.

Race, Congers, and Angus stand up as Christina, Leo, and I walk in. Angus glowers when he sees Leo, who walks quickly over to him. "Do you have any idea how much you upset your aunt?" Angus asks. "She burst into tears when I called to tell her we'd found you alive."

Leo scuffs at the carpet with the toe of his soccer cleat. "Sorry, Uncle Angus."

"She sent a suitcase full of clothes and a new set of glasses with one of the incoming patriarchs. It'll be sent to your suite when it arrives."

Leo nods, his gaze on the floor. "I didn't mean to scare you guys."

Angus's mouth trembles for a moment, and then he pulls Leo into a tight hug. The kid disappears within Angus's bear-like embrace. One of Angus's hands ruffles Leo's blond hair before he lets the boy go. It suddenly strikes me—Leo might be an orphan, but he has a lot of people who love him. Angus, George . . . my dad. I bite the inside of my cheek as he comes to stand next to me.

My mother looks me over, seems satisfied that I'm properly stitched up, and nods at the rest of the couch on which she's perched, inviting us to join. If anyone is tempted to ask why Christina is there, they manage to hold themselves back. We settle ourselves on the firm cushions, and that's when I notice a young woman sitting in the corner, behind Angus. She's got shoulder-length, white-blond hair, pale skin, round cheeks, and a delicate little chin. She's wearing a gray suit and heels. No name tag, but she looks vaguely familiar. She regards me soberly, her fingers poised over the tablet in her lap, where I suspect she's been typing notes. No one bothers to introduce her, so I turn my attention to the others. "What are we talking about?"

"We were discussing the housing of our agents while we're here," says Race in a tight, angry voice.

"Where exactly are they now?" I ask.

"Apart from the ones in the clinic or in body bags," says Congers, his face still streaked with soot, his clothes torn and dirty, "the uninjured members of our ranks are under guard in the main garage on these grounds. That wasn't what we agreed to when it was decided the Core would come here. We shouldn't be treated as prisoners."

This last part is directed to Angus, who gives him a sly smile. "Of course. It would be terrible if we treated one another with malice or suspicion." He glances at me and then at my mom. "I'm sure you treated members of our contingent with the utmost care while they were in your custody," he says to Congers.

"We're not in your custody!" snaps Race, but he shuts his mouth when Congers gives a slight shake of his head.

"We've come to you at substantial risk to ourselves," Congers says. "We've brought you technology that is, by all rights, ours."

"I beg to differ," says Angus. "We have been in possession of the technology for hundreds of years. I fail to see how you can call it your own."

Race's eyes light on me before moving back to Angus. "*You* have not been in possession of the technology."

"Fred Archer was one of ours." Angus settles heavily on a large chair, and somehow, the fact that he's sitting there makes it look more like a throne.

"Gentlemen, perhaps we could stay focused on the task at hand," my mother says wearily, like the testosterone in the room is giving her a headache. "I've had little sleep and less food in the past two days, and I have autopsies to perform."

Angus clears his throat. "Of course. Hopefully we won't be adding any more bodies to your queue. We expect to have all individuals on the compound scanned before the emergency meeting tonight." He rubs at a spot above his bushy red eyebrow, like he's trying to release the tension. "With The Fifty arriving, we've got more people to keep track of. Given the reported breach in the Core's ranks, they've already been scanned, though I think a period of observation might be in order."

When he sees Race open his mouth to protest, Angus holds up his hands. "Agent Lavin, I have hundreds of humans on this compound who believe to their bones that the H2 are the enemy. Most of them are armed. This is as much for your protection as it is a security precaution."

Race stiffens. He gives Angus a curt nod.

My mother turns to the Core agents. "Do you have any idea at all how the Sicarii could have gotten to one of your agents?"

Race clenches his fist and stares at the wall. "Devon Kerstein was stationed in Manhattan and participated in the raid at Tate's school. He remained in New York with his unit when I left to reacquire the scanner."

Congers looks down at the soot on his hands. "He helped in the search of the Archer apartment two days ago. He would have been aware that we'd departed for the facility in Jersey with the scanner. He probably called in both attacks. But I've now questioned the agents who were with him over the past two days. They said they noticed nothing unusual about him."

Mom's eyes narrow. "Is it possible the Sicarii can access the hosts' memories when they take hold?"

"Either that or they are very good at blending in and playing along," Congers says, rubbing the bridge of his nose. "Keep in mind that they have some experience with this type of subterfuge."

Mom tucks a lock of hair behind her ear. Her dark hair is in its usual ponytail, but several strands have escaped. "It's unnerving to know how easily they can infiltrate." I'm sure she's thinking of Charles Willetts. It was obvious she didn't trust him completely at the end, but because he was wearing the face of a friend, it took her a lot longer to pull back and be cautious. She raises her head and looks at Angus. "Do The Fifty understand the risks of coming here?"

Angus rolls his eyes. "They're more interested in making sure they have their say."

Mom glances at Race and Congers before returning her gaze to Angus. "You'll have to be very clear in your expectations for nonviolence."

"Something tells me you're worried about the Bishops." I sigh, setting my elbows on my knees, suddenly tired. "Rufus isn't going to be happy to see me, either. He only lost his son a few days ago, and I'm sure he blames me. He seems like the type who carries a grudge."

The blond woman in the corner shifts uncomfortably in her chair, like it's suddenly too hot in here. She taps something into her tablet.

Angus regards me for a few moments while he scratches at his thick beard. "I'm glad Rufus is coming, though. He could be helpful with upgrading the defenses. He understands the technology very well. He worked with Fred to set it up. We've already got those positions on the highest alert, seeing as the scout ships could return at any moment."

"We should be doing more than preparing for the next moment, though," says Race. "That scout ship outstripped your missiles easily. They're agile while your defense setup is largely stationary. We need more than that to protect your weapons factory—and this planet."

Angus presses his lips together, looking annoyed. "At the meeting tonight, we'll agree on next steps, including appropriating and reassigning factory operations to focus on the assault vehicle we were discussing. Fortunately, we do have a large order of heavily armored vehicles in assembly, so it's a matter of fitting them with the necessary tech." Angus crosses his arms, his thick fingers closing over his biceps. "They were meant to go to the US government, but if the situation is as dire as you describe, perhaps they'll need a more specialized machine like this one, and we'll be able to assure them we've road-tested them. We'll have to determine the function of each of those modifications, though. I have never in all my years seen a combat vehicle with a giant lens set into the roof."

Race and I look at each other. "The plans we found in my dad's lab?" I ask, and he nods. Those vehicles will be more nimble—and portable—than the perimeter defenses. I looked them over while the wreckage was being packed. My dad designed the vehicle with next-gen artillery and a complex weapons console with all sorts of specifications, but I need to find time to take a look at the plans to see exactly what all of it is for—including those lenses. "How much advance notice will we have if the Sicarii attack?"

Congers turns to Angus. "Did they come up on your radar?"

Angus shakes his head. "After Mitra called to report what she'd witnessed on the road, we heightened our alert level. Even with that, we had no idea it was coming until we captured the ship on our surveillance cameras. By that time, it was already on top of you. We've double-staffed the defense stations so that they can keep their eyes glued to the video screens, but that's as much as we can do."

"It's not much," says Congers.

"That scout ship certainly thought it was," Angus replies with a hint of offense. "We may not have taken it down, but we did send it off with its tail between its legs."

Race lets out a bitter laugh. "You underestimate them. Its retreat was purely strategic—it likely went to report the location and description of your compound to the others. We suspect there's a small squadron of them on this planet. If they attack en masse, the defenses might not hold."

Angus arches an eyebrow. "Which is why fortifying them is our top priority."

"Fortifications will be worth little if the full invasion happens," Congers says. "You're focusing on the wrong things. Planetary defense is just as important."

Angus glares at Congers as if the Sicarii are all his fault, but his expression softens as he turns to me. "Tate, we'll need you to figure out your dad's plans for using the H2 technology as some kind of satellite shield. My staff has looked at them but can't get past the security in the files. They've been downloaded and stored in the Black Box mainframe, which is half a mile underground—not likely to be penetrated by any artillery those Sicarii possess. Our team of developers is ready to assist you."

It suddenly feels like the weight of the world has been set on my shoulders. "Yeah," I say in a strained voice. "I'll take a look at all of it. Oh, and I'll need all available information about any satellites Black Box already has in the air." We're sunk if Ramses is the only one.

Angus's eyebrows go up, and he opens his mouth to say something, but—

"We have exactly twenty satellites currently aloft," says a voice from the hallway behind me. "And I think I should get to review Frederick Archer's plans as well. I might be able to help."

The blond woman jumps up, her sober expression spreading into a huge grin, her pale eyes bright. "Dad!" she says happily, jogging out the door and into the arms of the man in the hallway.

He wraps his arms around her and looks over her shoulder. His gaze meets mine. "Hello, Tate," he says. "I hope we can let the last week go. Water under the bridge."

I stare at him, his neatly combed blond hair, his round face, his stupid golf shirt. He may be well-groomed, but he looks tired, like he's been through hell.

As far as I'm concerned, that's what he deserves.

The last time I saw Brayton Alexander, he was trying to kill me.

ELEVEN

I SHOOT TO MY FEET. "WATER UNDER THE BRIDGE?" I point at Christina. "You shot at us. You could have killed us."

He nods, looking weary. "It was a desperate situation, and I made the wrong call in that moment. But as CEO of Black Box and the man who employed Frederick Archer, I know more about how we used his technology than anyone else, and I have every right to examine the plans, the scanner, and anything that was taken from his lab."

Angus clears his throat. "Well. You *would* have had that right. But as of Tuesday morning, the board voted to remove you from your position."

Brayton's eyes go round with shock. He looks at the blond woman next to him, who is obviously his daughter. "Is that true, Ellie?"

She winces. "I tried to call several times, but I didn't want to leave it as a voicemail or text. Where have you been, Dad?"

"In the custody of the Princeton police." His eyes narrow as he regards Angus. "I had just arrived in Chicago when I received the message that The Fifty were convening here." His jaw clenches. "After years of service, this is how I'm treated?" he says in a deadly quiet voice.

"You're lucky you're not still in jail," I snap as Christina's fingers twine with mine.

"I should have been given the chance to defend myself!" Brayton shouts at Angus, ignoring me completely. A vein in his temple is throbbing blue and thick, but the rest of his face looks hollowed out, his cheeks sagging inward from his rounded jaw. "Everything I did was on behalf of Black Box, and I should have had a chance to vote as the head of the Alexander family!"

Angus rises to his feet as Brayton comes closer. The two Core agents rise as well, touching their belts, where they would normally find their weapons. Both their holsters are empty.

But Brayton's isn't. And he looks unstable at the moment. "You were just waiting for your moment, weren't you? You've wanted the CEO chair for years."

"You brought this on yourself," says Angus, folding his massive arms over his chest. He's the only person in the room who doesn't seem the slightest bit nervous that Brayton's fingers are twitching near his waist. "And this wasn't about me—the decision of the board was almost unanimous, Brayton. We had a quorum, and we made the call. Your own vote wouldn't have saved you."

"You need me. I know more about Frederick Archer's work than anyone else," Brayton says, his voice echoing through the room, a hint of panic giving each syllable a sharp ring.

"No, you don't." That comes from several people at once. Me. My mom. And Race.

Brayton's lips clamp shut. I get the feeling his thoughts are little more than a string of shouted curses, judging from the vivid red color of his face. Ellie steps close to him, eyeing us all with defiance. But her expression softens as her fingers close over her father's sleeve. "Come on, Dad. You look so tired. I can walk you to your quarters."

He nods, then abruptly shakes his head, ripping his arm from her grip. "I don't need an escort," he growls. His eyes meet mine, then sweep over Race, Congers, and Angus. "I never thought I'd see the day when H2 were welcomed as guests and members of The Fifty were treated like pariahs. You think I'm the traitor? Look at yourself, Angus."

He turns on his heel and marches unsteadily from the room, leaving Ellie pink-cheeked and stricken in his wake. She blinks a few times, then takes a deep breath. Angus strides forward and puts his arm over her shoulder, and she doesn't resist. He pulls her close. "I'm sorry, Ellie. I know you're in a tough position."

"I can handle it," she says softly. "Excuse me." She walks from the room quickly, and I get the distinct impression she needs to cry and doesn't want anyone to see. Something like admiration stirs inside me. If my dad had been the pariah, wouldn't I have stuck by him?

"She's been my secretary for the past year," Angus explains.

Congers's nostrils flare, momentarily widening his narrow, hooked nose. "And you trust her?"

Angus looks at the chair where she was sitting, quietly taking notes on her tablet. "I do. Ellie's an ethical young woman, and she's given me no reason to doubt her."

"Was Brayton scanned?" I ask. "He was looking a little crazy-eyed." I see Christina nod out of the corner of my eye and wonder if she's remembering Willetts.

"He would have been scanned at the door. No exceptions," says Angus. "My orders were very clear."

We talk for a few more minutes, and then Angus gives us ID cards—Leo and I have ones that indicate we're patriarchs, and Christina gets one that signifies her as a guest who must be in the company of an escort at all times. My mom heads off to the morgue to start her autopsies, looking like it's the last place in the world she'd like to spend her time. Race and Congers are marched back to the garage with the rest of the Core agents, where they'll stay until The Fifty okay their presence here.

Angus announces that he needs to "herd some cats," and

goes off to cajole and coerce various members of The Fifty into actually granting the H2 permission to stay. I can understand why my mom respects him; he's adapted pretty quickly to the idea of the Sicarii and working with the Core, and he isn't wasting time moaning about it. In fact, he seems a little annoyed at having to deal with the politics, given the threat.

Leo, Christina, and I head for the computer labs. On the way, Leo and I discuss the perimeter defenses and guess at what they can do. I mentally catalog the name tag of each Black Box employee we pass: Bearden, Bradley, Cavalcante, Costa, Diop, Dos Santos, Engel, Hayashi, Jasinski, Juneja . . . one by one, I try to commit them to memory. There's a steady trickle of arrivals via helicopter and SUV, families having unexpected reunions as the patriarchs and matriarchs of The Fifty come looking for nieces and cousins and grandchildren, sons and brothers and sisters-in-law. We duck into a side hallway as we see Rufus Bishop stalk through the front entrance. He looks like a vengeful Santa with his bushy white beard and eyebrows, his big belly, and a glare that makes people sweat. The young guard looks a little nervous as he scans Rufus, who then stomps straight toward Angus's office.

I listen in on conversations in Japanese, Mandarin, German, and Portuguese as we walk by people in the halls. They're nervous. They're questioning whether the Sicarii threat and the earlier attack is an H2 ruse, a Trojan horse strategy to gain access to the walled fortress. Some of them wonder if Christina and I are H2 who should be locked up with the rest of the Core agents, but since we're with Leo, who they know, they're not sure. Leo, who understands almost as many languages as I do, introduces us to a few people, pausing awkwardly each time he gets to Christina.

"She's with me," I say. I end up saying it a lot. Each time, Christina's mouth gets a little tighter.

Finally, she sags against me. "I know that the apocalypse might be coming and there are a ton of things you need to do before then, but I'm tired of being treated like a second-class citizen. Is there a place where I can take a shower and lie down?"

I put my arm around her and give Leo a questioning look. My thoughts are buzzing with fatigue, and all I want to do is lie down next to Christina, but she's right—I have work to do. I persuade Leo to take her back to the fancy hotel-like dorm where members of The Fifty are staying, walk them halfway there so I can see where it is, and then plod to the computer lab, which is located in the main building. I walk back through the doors to find the scanner's light right in my eyes. As my chest takes on a blue glow, I ask, "Who's responsible for the scanner when it's not in use?"

"Why do you want to know?" asks a guard with curly light brown hair. He's seriously built, tall, and wearing a name tag that identifies him as a Fisher—one of George's relatives. He's also the one who scanned his dead family member earlier today. I wonder if he knew and how much these guards have been told.

"Because my dad's the one who invented the device, and I want to make sure it's secure." I pull out my ID card.

The guy's eyes widen a bit as he sees my name and picture. "I knew your dad," he says, almost reverently. "My name's Kellan. My uncle George and he were good friends." The way he bows his head and swallows tells me he knows his uncle is dead.

"I'm sorry," I say quietly, and he nods.

"Me too." He sighs, his broad shoulders curving forward like his chest hurts. "About your dad as well. I don't even know what's happening, man, but I know it's bad." He gazes at the scanner in his hand, this ordinary-looking, foot-long device with the three oddly shaped USB-type ports along its side, the thing we're depending upon to tell us who or what is in our midst. "Angus ordered us to store it in the vaults on the first basement level once we've got everyone scanned. That floor's got layers of security and surveillance."

"Good."

"You gonna be at the meeting tonight?" When I nod, he says, "My mom's the matriarch now that Uncle George is gone. I'll be there, too. I'm supposed to re-scan all the board members as they come in." He looks like he's dreading it.

"You don't think it's necessary?" This additional scanning is yet another thing I'm really glad to hear. The last thing we need is some Sicarii spy listening in on our high-level planning.

"Well, maybe it is, but . . ." His eyes meet mine. "I'm supposed to execute anyone who scans orange."

It's a huge responsibility for a guy who looks like he's barely graduated from college. "Can you do that?" I wonder if I could, especially if the Sicarii was wearing a familiar face.

He shrugs. "I have my orders."

I tell him I'll see him there and go to the computer lab, where I spend the next three hours going over my dad's various plans and blueprints. I'm not ready to share these with the team of developers quite yet. I want to think about it without other brains interfering.

Somehow, my dad figured out the technology—but he also discovered this third race, or at least guessed at it. Using the wreckage of the H2 ship, which is now stored in the same vault where the scanner will be kept, he built the scanner to identify each species. Yeah, the device might just be a tiny version of the giant satellite that's scanning the planet, but I'm not so sure it's only meant to scan. The satellites, after all, are rigged with lasers to zap incoming Sicarii, so maybe the scanner can do the same if I figure it out. I have no idea what those USB-type ports on the side are for. Are they supposed to connect it to something, or to communicate or store information? And why do the Sicarii want it so badly? Why did my dad call it the key to our survival? I'll have to request permission to take a closer look, but I can't now, because it's needed to ensure that Black Box is a secure place.

I turn my attention to the satellites, the top priority. If what Brayton said is true, all twenty of the ones listed in Dad's plans are already aloft, but only Ramses is activated. The rest of them are spinning through space, their most powerful capabilities dormant within their metal bodies. My dad was so secretive about the scanner, so I'm guessing no one else knew what he'd installed inside the satellites before they were launched. They're most likely meant to relay communications and to spy on the Core. But if the plans are accurate, those satellites are also armed with incredibly advanced lasers and the same scanning technology as the device Kellan's using out there in the atrium. And as Race said, if they're all working together, they'd effectively form a defense shield around the entire planet.

I just need to figure out how to activate them. My dad gave me the password—*Josephus*—to access the plans, but to activate the satellites themselves? It's a no-go. I try all the other ones I know he used, all the ones I ever used, and get nowhere. I'm realizing it's yet another riddle he left me to solve, but all I've got right now is what he scribbled in that notebook in Kentucky—*find it in 20204*. I try *20204* as the password and get shut out again, so I pull up a secure browser and look up 20204, moving past information about the zip code, the ID number for a Lego kit, its meaning in SQL computer code . . . I get all excited when I see that 20204 is a genetic identifier, until I read further and see that particular gene is part of the mouse genome.

I rub my tired eyes and think back: *20204* was written on the same page where he'd scribbled the word *Sicarii*. I resume my searching and type in *Sicarii 20204,* wishing the magic of Google would make this easy.

What I get is a lot more random shit, most of which is a trash-talking Russian with the username "Sicarii," spouting off in some RPG forum about nunchuk-wielding dwarves. The two search terms don't fit together; the 20204 piece doesn't seem to have any connection. Just in case, I spend an hour slowly translating, scouring the web page for the number, for any hint or connection, but it all feels like I've taken a wrong turn. My dad took stuff from history, not forums for hardcore D&D players.

So much for Google. My eyes now burning with fatigue, my wounds itching, my stomach growling, I close the browser. I have to figure this out—even if the Sicarii show up and destroy Black Box, which could happen at any moment, maybe everyone else on Earth would be okay if I could get the satellite shield working. Unless destroying Black Box would disrupt communication and control of the satellites. I don't see how it wouldn't.

Shit.

Having hit nothing but dead ends with the satellite shield activation, I turn my attention to the one thing that could buy us some time and security. When the Sicarii come back, we need to be able to defend ourselves. I do a little searching on the server and find my dad's plans for the combat vehicle, the eight-wheeled monster with the complex artillery system and giant lens set into the roof. I pore over the plans, trying to figure out what the hell the lens could be used for, brainstorming possibilities and coming up empty . . .

I jolt upright, shaking myself awake. My head aching, my thoughts mush, I glance at the time—and curse.

I have to go to this stupid board meeting, which starts in a few minutes. I can't miss it—I might be one of the few patriarchs who actually understands that the Core aren't the real threat, at least not right now, and we need their help if we want to survive a Sicarii attack.

I find Leo in the atrium, laughing with Kellan, who looks like he needs the distraction of a goofy kid to take his mind off what he's about to do—wield the power of life and death.

Leo, who's wearing clean clothes that actually fit him along with a new pair of glasses, waves cheerfully when he sees me, and I head over there. "Where's Christina?"

His smile falters as he meets me in the middle of the lobby. "I took her to my suite and let her use the shower. We got her some spare clothes from the infirmary. Just some scrubs she can wear until her clothes come back from the laundry. And I gave her one of my spare rooms." His cheeks are a little pink, like he's been caught stealing. It would be funny if I weren't worried about Christina.

"Did she say anything? Did she seem okay?"

"She just said she wanted to sleep."

"Does she know she has to stay in your suite until we come back for her, though?" I ask, eyeing Kellan. He's set the scanner on the counter and is, at the moment, making sure he has a round in the chamber of his Glock. Those things have super-light triggers. "The H2 haven't been granted any sort of status on the compound. It's not safe for her to be out." All it takes is one nervous guard, one twitch of the trigger finger, one bad moment to shatter everything.

Leo nods. "I'm not stupid. Besides, she already knew. She said she'd stay put."

It's as good as I'm going to get for now, but all of a sudden I'm anxious to get back to her. Instead, I have to gather all my fragmented thoughts and endure this board meeting, the first one I've ever attended . . . and I'm one of the board members now. I feel hollow. I miss my dad more than ever. He's the one who should be dealing with The Fifty, not me.

We walk down the administrative hallway, past Brayton's old office—his nameplate has been removed sometime in the past few hours—and past Angus's, until the hallway ends in a set of double doors that have been propped open. The conference room is huge, with a round table that seats exactly fifty, plus rings of chairs around it for all the heirs and senior members of each family. There's a secretary with a digital recorder, and microphones are positioned on the table in front of every seat. As we walk in, I see Race and Congers seated behind Brayton, whose eyes dart to me as soon as I enter.

In a semicircle around the two agents stand a row of armed Black Box guards. None of the other agents are in the room. The H2 look more like prisoners than guests, but they're being pretty stoic about it. Rufus is looking murderous on the opposite side of the table, and other patriarchs and matriarchs are taking their seats behind placards showing the family name. Yang from China. Abe from Japan. Soto from Chile. Engel from Germany. Ndebeli from South Africa. Fifty families from all over the world, ruled by old men, old women . . . and two boys with responsibilities too big for our wiry shoulders.

I head over to my mom as she stands behind the Shirazi placard. She looks tired and stands stiffly. She's removed the sling she was wearing to support her wounded shoulder, and is cradling that arm against her middle. Like me, she's probably been pushing herself past the point of exhaustion, trying to find the answers that could save us. The unhappy set of her mouth and the strain on her face suggest she's had about as much luck this afternoon as I have.

"I'm representing the Shirazis," she tells me as we reach her. "My father is the patriarch, but he's too ill to travel. You can sit here." She points to the Archer placard, which is next to hers.

Leo sits behind the Thomas placard, which has been placed

next to mine. We must look kind of pathetic, sitting here with no one behind us while most of the other families have at least one assistant or a whole herd of relatives behind them. The exception is Dr. Ackerman, who sits alone, staring at the H2 from his position next to Rufus Bishop. I wonder if the two of them see eye to eye.

A hush falls over the room as Angus strides in with Kellan at his side. Angus pauses when he reaches his own empty chair and faces Kellan, who switches on the scanner and waves it over Angus's chest. The blue light turns back to yellow when Kellan angles it at the floor once more, and Angus addresses all of us. "Before we discuss urgent matters, we need to make sure all of us are who we say we are," he says in a loud voice. "By now you've all been briefed, and I've spoken to many of you myself, so I know you'll cooperate as Mr. Fisher does his job."

He nods to Kellan and takes his seat. Kellan, whose hand shakes a little beneath the rapt attention of all members of The Fifty, scans himself, and then holds the device over our heads and slowly walks counterclockwise around the enormous table. His right hand is on his weapon. I watch the leaders as blue light cascades over their faces. Brayton eyes Kellan as he approaches, and my stomach draws tight, waiting for the light to hit him. But then the scanner turns the shadows beneath Brayton's eyes deep and dark, the wrinkles around his mouth become navy blue, and some of my tension subsides. He's definitely human. It doesn't mean I trust him any more than before, though. It just means he's not under the command of a parasitic alien.

Nor are the rest of The Fifty. Once Race and Congers scan red, Kellan leaves, and the debate begins.

God, it's annoying.

Everybody has to have their say, and everyone has a complaint. Half of them want the H2 escorted off the premises, and at least a third appear to want them publicly executed. Rufus glares at me while he talks about "H2 collaborators and sympathizers."

It's so fucking petty, and finally the arguing wears through any patience I had left. "Didn't *anyone* see the burned wreckage outside the west tunnel?" I shout. "Some of you flew over it just a few hours ago. Are you aware that ten men and women died there this afternoon? Do you know what killed them? A fucking alien spaceship like you can't even imagine! The Sicarii could come back at any moment, and we're rehashing the same H2 hate over and over. It's pointless and useless right now."

My mouth snaps shut when my mother's fingers close around my wrist, and she tugs me down. Sometime during my rant, I jumped up from my chair. The members of The Fifty are either slack-jawed with shock or glaring with the offense. Rufus's face is brick-red, and Brayton's is paper-white.

Angus, though, is unruffled. He leans forward and speaks directly into his mic, the whiskers on his chin brushing over its surface and providing staticky punctuation to his words. "I think what Mr. Archer is trying to say is that the enemy of our enemy is our friend." He glances over his shoulder at Congers and Race. "For the moment."

The conversation gets more reasonable after that. The board finally votes to grant the Core agents basic privileges within the compound, including allowing them to carry their weapons, as long as they're registered with the Black Box security staff. By the time that agreement is reached, my head feels like it's going to explode, and I'm wondering if Christina ever got anything to eat for dinner, because I know I didn't.

But we're not done. We move on to discussing how the scanner will be used and who controls it, and that leads to another hour-long argument. Rufus thinks only humans should control the scanner. Brayton suggests that it should be kept in the vault at all times. Angus and I argue that it should be used in any way that enhances our security and prevents Sicarii infiltration, including scanning workers before they start their shifts in the factory, as well as random checks of people on the compound.

"The Sicarii could spread like a virus, for all we know right now," says my mother, giving me a look out of the corner of her eye. "Until I've completed the autopsies and we're confident of how they take over a host organism, we should be vigilant. They could take hold with a single touch, a sneeze, an unobserved moment between two people. A Sicarii could be as big as a human or as small as a germ."

That's enough to jolt people into cooperating. Several of

them look like they want to hurl. Arms fold over stomachs and chests, hands discreetly cover mouths and noses like they're wishing for hospital masks, and no one wants to be too close to anyone else.

It's midnight when we adjourn, and I can't remember the last time I slept or ate. Leo's head is resting on his arms—he fell asleep about half an hour ago. The room spins as I rise from my chair, and my mom catches me when I sway and lowers me down again. While the rest of The Fifty funnel out of the room, Dr. Ackerman makes his way over to us.

"Young man, I think you're trying to do too much," he drawls as he takes my wrist and feels for my pulse.

"That's because there's too much to do," I mumble, leaning forward to rest my forehead on the table. My lips are tingling, and I shiver.

Mom touches my back. "Then maybe you should let other people do a little of it," she says gently. When I turn my head and look at her, she adds, "I walked by the computer lab on my way from the morgue. You were hunched over that computer—"

"Probably because I'd dozed off," I admit. "I didn't get a single thing accomplished. How are the autopsies going?"

Dr. Ackerman looks keenly interested as he peers at my mother. "I heard they'd brought the bodies that scanned orange here. Do you need some assistance as you examine them?"

My mother leans back in her chair and rubs her eyes. Her face crumples in pain, and she slowly lowers her hand. "In all honesty, I've only completed the external exam," she says quietly as she gingerly moves her wounded left arm. "I made that germ statement because I don't want anyone to underestimate the threat, but I don't have any idea yet. I'll resume the work tomorrow."

My heart clutches. She's been staring at the bodies of three men, two of whom she loved as friends. I wonder if she's dreading actually finding out what the Sicarii do to a person, and how much it hurts. I slide my hand across the table and take hers. She accepts it, giving me a grateful smile.

"We're dreadfully understaffed in the infirmary," says Dr. Ackerman, "but if you need it, Mitra, I can help you. I know it's important."

I watch my mom, wondering if she trusts this guy. He was quiet during the debate, but he voted with Angus and me every time. He doesn't seem to be a hard-liner like Rufus. "I might need some consultation on the actual dissection," she says to him after a few moments.

I sit quietly, too tired to move as they make arrangements to meet tomorrow morning. Dr. Ackerman advises me to drink plenty of fluids and to prioritize sleep. As he's telling me to drop by the infirmary tomorrow to have my blood pressure taken, the lights flicker. Dr. Ackerman looks around. "Well, that's not good. I've got two patients on ventilators."

Mom frowns. "You think there's an issue with the solar panels?"

Dr. Ackerman stands up. "I don't know. It happens some-times, but right now I'd say we need the lights to stay on." He strides out, his posture bent with fatigue. Everyone on this compound is both tired and jittery, a recipe for disaster.

After chatting with my mom for a few minutes about all the people I met this afternoon, who she knows well, who she trusts, who's aligned with Rufus and who's with Angus, I gather my strength and push myself up again, reaching over to wake Leo up.

A piercing alarm splinters the quiet, and the lights flicker again. Leo yelps and jumps to his feet, looking confused and bleary. My mother is wide-eyed as she gets up, too, and we all head for the door. Down the hallway, guards are shouting, and I break into a jog, adrenaline pouring through my veins. I reach the security desk near the main entrance several steps ahead of my mom and Leo. Kellan and the other guards are clustered together, talking urgently as they point to the surveil-lance screens behind the desk.

"What's going on?" I ask.

Kellan looks over his shoulder at me. "We've had a security breach," he says in a tight voice. "I think someone just tried to steal the scanner."

TWELVE

FOOTSTEPS GIVE US ABOUT THREE SECONDS' WARNING
before two figures come running in from the far side of the
atrium. Kellan's got his weapon up in an instant. "Freeze," he
barks.

"We heard the alarm, and we saw someone running past
the infirmary," says Graham Congers, his voice desperate and
angry, wincing as he raises his arms. His short brown hair is
standing on end, and his shirt is buttoned wrong. Sung is next
to him, looking winded but fierce, a soot-smeared undershirt
clinging to his wiry frame.

Graham takes a step forward, his gaze riveted on Kellan's.
"We're unarmed."

"Why does that not reassure me?" Kellan says. "You're
Core agents."

"And they've been in the hospital wing," I say. "They were injured in the attack."

"How do we know that's where they were just now?" says Kellan.

"Don't you have surveillance feeds?" asks Sung in a hoarse voice, his dark brown eyes full of frustration. "You'll see there was someone in that hallway, and it wasn't us."

Kellan gestures to one of his colleagues behind the guard desk. "Check video of the infirmary hallway for the last ten minutes."

My mom looks at the narrow-shouldered guard who's staring at the monitors at the desk. "You didn't see anything on the screens *before* the alarm?"

Kellan's jaw ridges like he's clenching his teeth. "We should have. We were watching the basement vault and the main corridors nonstop. Nothing seemed out of the ordinary—and then the alarm went off. One of our guards called up from the basement that the door leading to the vault had been breached. He's checking the vault itself right n—" Kellan's fingers move toward his ear, and he sags a little, the slightest smile of relief flickering on his lips before it disappears again. "Okay. They have the scanner. The door to the vault room was open, but the alarm must have sent the thief running."

"There's nothing on the video, Kellan," says the guard at the desk. "The infirmary corridor was clear the whole time."

Leo frowns and joins the guy. "Could you have been

hacked?" He reaches for the keyboard, and the guard lets him. Leo taps away for a few minutes, then rolls his eyes. "Seven minutes of video captures are gone. This thing's looped."

"Let me guess—it cuts off when the lights first flickered?" I ask, my heart sinking.

"Looks like," says the guard standing next to Leo.

Kellan shrugs. "That happens all the time. We're on solar, but sometimes there's a surge."

Leo doesn't take his eyes off the screen. The gray glow of it is reflected in the lenses of his glasses. "That only means that whoever tried to take the scanner knows the system and its idiosyncrasies, or figured it out pretty quickly."

"Where are all the board members?"

"I checked them out of the building myself," says Kellan. "They all went back to the residential quarters to get some rest. None of them were in the building." His gaze swings to the two Core agents. "So that leaves these guys."

Kellan's finger moves to his trigger, and Graham and Sung step back. "Hey, hey, we didn't—" Sung begins, then starts to cough. As he doubles over, Kellan follows the movement with his gun, like he's about to shoot Sung in the head. And I don't know why I do it, but I skip forward and stand between him and Kellan.

Our eyes meet, and Kellan's are brimming with questions and betrayal and fear. "Don't," I say, quietly enough so that only he can hear. "Ask them to bring the scanner up from the basement, and let's check everyone again. These guys nearly died trying to keep the Sicarii from getting the scanner. If they tried to steal it, we'll figure it out. But for now, be cool, okay?"

He stares at me, his nostrils flared, the tiniest tremble in his hands, which freaks me out, as do my mother's wide eyes, which I can see over Kellan's shoulder. I can tell she wants to say something, but she knows that one nervous twitch might cause Kellan to accidentally put a bullet in my chest. But after a few seconds, Kellan lowers his weapon. He jabs a finger at the Core agents and then to a group of guards by the door. "Go over there, and don't do anything to make us shoot you."

"Like existing?" Graham mutters.

"Thanks, man," Sung says quietly as he passes me.

Two more guards emerge from the elevators, and one's carrying the scanner. Both look spooked. Kellan accepts the scanner as they reach him. "Any sign of an intruder?"

One of the guards, who can't be older than midtwenties but has seriously receding hair, shakes his head. "I was there only a few seconds after the alarm went off, but there was no sign of anyone."

"I'm telling you, we saw someone running down the infirmary hallway," Graham says loudly, his voice pure frustration.

I turn to Kellan. "Is there an exit down that hallway? Could someone access it from the outside—or escape that way?"

Kellan uses his sleeve to wipe sweat from his brow. "Yeah.

There are exits in every hallway. And they all have surveillance cams, but I guess that won't help us."

"We should make sure everyone's accounted for at the dorm," says one of the guards.

"Don't forget the H2 in the garage," says another.

"Or maybe not. The H2 could be anywhere on the grounds, seeing as our wise leaders granted them status," snaps Kellan, glaring at Graham and Sung like they're responsible for all of it. "I'm calling Angus." He slides his phone from his belt and puts it to his ear as he walks away.

"We need to make sure Lavin and Congers know about this," Sung says to Graham.

Graham's staring at Kellan's back. Just as he opens his mouth to reply, Kellan pivots around and comes back to us.

"Let me guess," Graham says. "You're going straight to the garage to scan our agents."

"No," Kellan replies. I swear, he looks a shade paler than he did a moment ago. "We're going to the residential suites. Angus wants us to scan The Fifty first. The alarm was just for this building, and he said it can't be heard all the way down at the residential building, so everyone's still in their suites."

"Scanning the board members and the factory workers makes sense," Leo says, pushing his glasses up on his nose. "Whoever tried to steal the scanner knew exactly how to hack the system, and how to get away without being seen.

Considering the Core just got here and they've been held in the garage for nearly that whole time, they're a little less likely as suspects."

Kellan orders a small group of guards to go to the garage and make sure the Core are all accounted for, and then to keep them there until they can be scanned again. After letting the guard scan her, my mother announces that she's going to check the morgue to see if anything's been tampered with, and accepts a weapon from Kellan with gratitude. She looks haunted, as if the dead Sicarii could somehow be responsible for the attempted theft. Oddly enough, Leo volunteers to go with her. Part of me wonders if he wants to see George's body, to say good-bye, to convince himself that George was long gone even before his body was perforated . . . or maybe he just needs a mom right now, and mine is the closest he'll get. I don't know. But Mom agrees to take him and tells me she'll see me later. As for me, I'm eager to make sure Christina's all right before I get back to work on bringing the satellite system online, so I go with Kellan. He tries to order Graham and Sung to go to the garage under escort, but Graham smiles and shakes his head.

"You said we were granted official status. That means I'm not your prisoner. And I'm going with you, seeing as one of your people probably tried to steal the scanner."

Kellan's mouth is a tight, flat line as he switches on the scanner and waves it over all of us. When Graham arches an eyebrow, Kellan impatiently passes it over his own arm and scans blue. "Where were you guys before you entered the atrium?" Kellan asks me. "Everyone else went back to their quarters."

"At least, you hope so," says Sung.

"We were in the meeting room," I say. "Dr. Ackerman was with us when the lights first flickered. He can vouch for us."

"And can you vouch for him?" asks Graham.

We enter the crisp night air and walk toward the dorms of The Fifty, which is maybe a quarter mile away. The sky is clear, stars above us and lit defense stations glowing bright all along the rim of the crater. The guards inside are watching for the ships that could come at any time, ready to use all available firepower to protect us—but we may have an enemy within the compound, too. "I don't know Dr. Ackerman, but I can tell you that he was with us during the first flicker of the lights. He left after that."

Kellan's pace quickens, and a few of us stutter-step to keep up. My head is a little foggy. The jolts of fear and menace keep clearing the cobwebs, but I'm so tired that it doesn't take long for them to regenerate. I won't be able to go without sleep much longer. "Is the dorm building on the same circuit system as the main building?" I ask as Kellan breaks into a jog.

Next to me, Sung takes a wheezing breath, not yet fully recovered from the smoke inhalation. I'm wondering if he should have stayed in the infirmary. Graham is grim and silent as he takes smooth strides, but he's sweating in the cool mountain air, and by the tension in his arms, I can tell he's hurting. Why did they leave the infirmary? Did they really see someone running down the hall? Did they want to steal the scanner, or are they feeling as protective of it as I am?

When we reach the dorms, all is quiet. A few windows are lit, but most are dark.

"Is there a guard on duty?"

"At the front desk," Kellan says, yanking the door open and marching through a large entryway toward what resembles the lobby of a very swanky hotel. "But the first-floor hallway has another exit. Someone could come down the stairwell and exit that way without being seen by the guard."

Sung runs his hand over his buzzed black hair. "If they have the same seven-minute gap in surveillance feeds that you had in the main building, we might be screwed."

Graham curses. "We came here because it was supposed to be this technological fortress, but you guys can't even manage basic surveillance."

Kellan lifts his chin. "Can you? Those Sicarii got two of your people, and you led one of them right to our doorstep."

Graham's mouth twists, and I'm betting he's about to remind Kellan that they got George, too, but Sung nudges his arm, and he simmers down, thank God. "What's your plan? Are you going door-to-door?" asks Sung as we enter the lobby.

Kellan motions for the guard at the front desk to stay where she is. Then he looks around, and his posture sags a little. "I guess."

There's a brief flash of sympathy in Graham's eyes. He's used to being weighed and measured—and found wanting. "It's a place to start," he says to Kellan. "Let's get it done. We have the scanner now, and we can dissect this tomorrow, after we rule out the obvious. Maybe we'll get lucky."

From Kellan's expression, I can tell that he wouldn't perceive finding a traitor among The Fifty to be "lucky."

A hallway to my left has a metal plate on it that reads:

BISHOP

BELAY

BEARDEN

ARCHER

ALEXANDER

ACKERMAN

ABE

I guess my family suite is down there—as is Brayton's, Rufus's, and Dr. Ackerman's. Sung and Graham stare at the nameplate while Kellan questions the guard at the attendant's desk.

The elevator in the lobby dings. "Tate!" comes a shriek as the doors open.

My head swings around so fast that I'm dizzy. "Christina?" My heart hammering, I watch her emerge with two guards on either side of her. One of them has a gun aimed at her head.

I stride toward her, my hands up. "She's with—"

"Caught her near the stairwell a minute after you called, Kellan," says the guard with long brown hair pulled into a tight knot at the base of her neck. "She won't say who she is, and none of us recognize her."

Kellan switches on the scanner, and Christina winces as her skin flashes red. His broad shoulders tense as he realizes she's H2. "What the hell are you doing in this building?"

"She's my girlfriend," I snap, shoving past the guards, beyond caring whether they aim at me. "Step away from her."

Christina looks like she wants to reach for me but is afraid to move. "I was in Leo's suite and kept hearing people coming back from the meeting. I was coming down to see if you were in your room," she says to me in a broken voice.

"Is she some undercover Core agent?" the female guard asks.

I want to hit something. "Did you hear what I just said? She goes to my high school. She, like two-thirds of the population of this planet, is H2 and a *civilian*. Not every H2 is Core, and you know that."

"She's not one of ours," says Graham.

"We're wasting time," I say to Kellan. "I'm taking her to my suite, and you're checking each one, right?"

Kellan seems to note the edge in my voice. He's still regarding Christina with suspicion, but the guards are holstering their weapons. "Yeah."

He stalks toward the hallway, and I offer Christina my hand. Wearily, she takes it. We follow the others down the hall, reaching the Bishop suite first. I'm tempted to walk right by and let them handle it, but it's clear they've already hit a snag. Kellan is banging his fist against the door. "Mr. Bishop, just for a minute. We've had a security breach, and I need only a moment of your time."

"I can see the Core agents out there, boy," shouts Rufus from the other side. He must have his face pressed to the peephole. "If you think I'm coming out, you're insane." This is followed by a long string of threatening and colorful curses.

"Mr. Bishop, we need everyone's cooperation—"

"If you think those aliens are cooperating with you, you're even more stupid than the rest of your family!" Rufus shouts.

Kellan's cheeks darken. "Sir," he says, his voice turning gravelly. "I'm going to have to order—"

More curses. Kellan looks helpless. Purely out of impatience, I snatch the scanner from his hand and wave it over the door. Despite the barrier, it flashes blue. The thing can scan through walls and doors.

Sung's dark eyebrow arches as he notes the device's capability. "Good to know," he says.

I nod and hand the scanner back to Kellan as Rufus shouts, "You think the scanner protects you? Those H2 don't need to scan orange to do damage."

"Neither do you," Graham calls.

"It's all you're going to get tonight, dude," I say to Kellan. "Just do your scanning, and we'll sort the rest tomorrow."

He moves away from Rufus's door as Brayton Alexander emerges from his room at the end of the hall. "What's going on?" he asks, smoothing his rumpled blond hair across the top of his head.

"Someone tried to steal the scanner, Mr. Alexander," says Kellan.

Brayton's eyes go wide, and then he scowls. He closes his eyes as Kellan scans him blue. His cheeks still look sunken with fatigue, and I swear there are new streaks of gray in his pale hair, though that may be the light. "Obviously the thieves didn't succeed," he says in a tight voice. "And equally obvious, it needs to be guarded more closely."

"Agreed." I tuck Christina a little tighter to my side. "I'm betting they'll try again," I say. "Speaking of, Brayton, you must know the security and surveillance systems of this compound pretty well, right?"

I look to Graham and Sung, who said they saw someone running down the infirmary hall. Graham shrugs and looks at the floor as he mutters, "It was dark, and the guy was moving fast."

Brayton leans back against the wall, his face pinched with anger. "I do know the system well." He leans forward and glares at Kellan, the circles under his eyes making him look like a ghoul. "But I don't appreciate being under suspicion, especially since we both know the surveillance cameras would have detected any intruder."

Kellan stands his ground. "That's what we're talking about, Mr. Alexander. They were hacked."

Brayton blinks at him. "What?" He pushes himself off the wall. "I can take a look if you'd like."

"We're just trying to scan everyone in the building right now," says Kellan. "Then I'm reporting to Angus."

Brayton slumps a little. "Tomorrow, then," he says quietly, and Kellan nods.

I'm about to remind them that we might not have a to-morrow because the scout ships could come for the scanner at any time, but Christina leans on me like she agrees with them, and my own fatigue is making me feel so heavy that I'm about to sink to the floor. And suddenly, I realize I'm not holding Christina up—it's the other way around.

"Gentlemen," she says, "if you're done with me and Tate, I'm taking him to his room. He hasn't slept in nearly two days, and I'm sure you can manage without him, seeing as it's your job."

Graham snorts with laughter, and he, Sung, and Brayton step out of the way. "You want me to let you know if someone scans orange?" Kellan asks.

"I'm sure the gunshots will give me a clue," I mumble. Because I'm done. Someone on this compound tried to steal the scanner, and the surveillance that protects it is inadequate, and all of that will have to be figured out. And if I'm really lucky, someone else will handle it so I don't have to. I have enough to do.

Christina is digging in my pocket. She pulls out my ID card and slides it into the card reader at the door of the Archer suite, then guides me inside. "I have to go back to the computer lab and work on bringing those satellites online," I say.

Christina puts her arm around my waist and leads me toward the bed. "Doing that won't stop the scout ships from coming here."

"But it could keep the invasion force from taking over the planet." I try—and fail—to stifle a yawn. "I have to figure out the password to activate the satellites. One password." Something I've done dozens of times in the past, and it's never been this hard. Possibilities flash in my brain and then evaporate. I'm too exhausted to hold on to a single one.

"Tate, if you try to keep going, you're going to pass out," Christina says, placing her warm palms on my cheeks. "You've been awake for almost forty-eight hours. You've been through so much." She draws me down and gives me a featherlight kiss. "You're not at your best."

"I'm sorry I left you alone for so long," I say as she gives me a gentle shove onto the bed. This is a huge suite, with several bedrooms, an office, and a kitchenette. I force myself not to think of the fact that my dad was the last person to spend the night here. "I had to try to figure it out. I should go back right now and keep trying. It's not just the satellite shield. It's the combat vehicles, too. I have to—"

"You will, Tate," she says softly, pressing a glass of water into my hands. "After you rest."

"What if I fail?" I whisper, closing my eyes as I sip the water, then concentrating hard to set it on the bedside table without dropping it.

"You won't." The bed dips as she settles her body next to mine. She gently lays her head on my chest. "Go to sleep. *Please*. Just for a few hours. We're all right at the moment, and we'll figure out the rest when you wake up."

I want to argue, but I'm so exhausted that I can't even open my mouth. *I'll only sleep for an hour, then I'll wake up and figure this out*. It's the last thought in my head before my brain shuts down and takes the world away.

THIRTEEN

I WAKE SLOWLY TO MORNING SUNLIGHT FILTERING through the curtains. "Shit!" I bolt upright and scrabble for the phone by the bed, frantically checking the time. It's nearly nine. There's a note on the pillow next to me. *Went to breakfast with Leo, but wanted to let you sleep.*

A jolt of frustration makes me crumple the paper, but then I notice something written on the other side:

Please don't be mad ~ C

My fingers trace the initial she used to sign off, realizing, as I look again at the date display on the phone, that it's Sunday morning, and our prom was last night. That was where we were supposed to be, laughing and dancing and being stupid with our friends. And instead of getting a hotel room and hoping for the best, I was here. Christina was with me, but it wasn't exactly the romantic scenario I'd envisioned.

This last week has stolen all my hopes for a normal, care-free end to my junior year. What it hasn't stolen is how I feel about Christina. That's only stronger every time I look at her, which makes it both awesome and terrible that she's here.

I get up and shower quickly. As I dress in some of the clothes my father left in the drawers, I remember all the sim-mering tension of the night before, the hair-trigger suspicion of the Black Box guards, the way they collared her just for be-ing a stranger, the way they looked at her when they discovered she was H2. As I walk to the main building, where the cafeteria is located, I call my mom. She doesn't pick up, so I leave a mes-sage. "Just checking in. I hope everything's all right." I wonder if she ever left the morgue last night.

The guards at the main entrance don't scan me, and I'm not sure what that means.

I make it to the cafeteria in time to catch Leo and Chris-tina finishing their food. Christina gives me a nervous look, but when I smile, she relaxes. They're at a table with Angus, Race, and Congers, and for a moment I pause, struck by the weirdness of that sight. Christina still has stitches in her head because one of Race's agents shot her last Tuesday. And now she's listening politely to something he's saying while she sips her coffee.

I grab some cereal and milk and join them, noticing that the scanner is sitting in the middle of the circular table like a centerpiece. "Why aren't we scanning people as they enter the building?"

Race wipes his mouth with his napkin. "Everyone on the compound was located and re-scanned by six this morning. Now it's a matter of priorities. There's a lot we don't yet know about the device, and we're wondering if our time wouldn't be best spent trying to figure out whether it has additional capabilities." He runs his fingers down the side of the scanner, across those little ports. He's noticed them, too.

Congers, his hair neatly combed with a perfectly straight part, looks around at the people in the cafeteria. Several factory workers, wearing gray coveralls, hunch over their scrambled eggs while they stare coldly at a group of Core agents quietly eating their own breakfast at a table across the room. The agents' tense postures tell me they're glad their weapons have been returned. "I'm not sure any amount of scanning will reassure either side."

Angus pulls his napkin from his lap and drops it over his half-eaten plate of food. "It'll take more than a day to resolve centuries of mistrust. It has nothing to do with the scanner or the Sicarii."

"But maybe it should," I say. "I'm not saying one has to be a Sicarii to try to steal the scanner; I'm just saying we shouldn't rule it out completely. There's a lot we don't know about how they operate."

Angus shrugs. "All we know is that everyone is accounted for and no one scanned orange."

"Are we going to figure out what happened to the surveillance system?" Leo asks, using the bottom of his shirt to clean his glasses.

"It's on a long list of things we have to do." Angus rolls his head on his neck. "I have a team on it. Rufus is leading it up."

I nearly drop my spoon. "What?"

Angus scrubs a hand over his face and scratches at his beard. "He's an expert in the kind of power grid we have here, Tate."

"My point exactly," I snap. "He wouldn't even come out of his room last night. How do you know he's not hiding something?"

"I'll be providing oversight," says Congers.

Leo's eyes get wide. "Oh, man. Rufus won't like that."

"We need the mutual accountability," says Angus, putting his enormous hand on Leo's skinny shoulder. "If each team is a mix of humans and H2, we have a built-in watchdog system Neither side is going to cover for the other." He gestures from the Core agents to the factory workers. "It means we'll have less of this mistrust."

"Or more of it," says Christina softly, staring into her cup of coffee.

I touch her leg under the table, and she takes my hand. "Are there Core agents helping in the defense stations?" I ask. "It might be good to have fresh eyes on the horizon."

Congers nods. "There are also agents working in the factory, to build the mobile attack units your father designed."

Angus runs his thick knuckles along the underside of his chin. "There's been a lot of debate about the plans. It calls for a hole to be cut into the roof of each vehicle, to allow for the placement of that giant lens. Some folks on the design team think it's a flaw."

"They haven't been able to determine the intended purpose for those lenses?" I guess I shouldn't be surprised. My dad designed for himself. He didn't bother writing explanations so everyone else could keep up.

Angus shakes his head. "Some of the design team want to eliminate that part of the modifications. I can't say I disagree. It seems like a risk to have a giant glass lens in the roof of the vehicle—especially if you're fighting something that's flying overhead."

Race frowns. "Do you realize what Frederick Archer accomplished before he was killed?" As soon as that word comes out of his mouth, he cuts me an uneasy glance and clears his throat. "He was working with alien technology more advanced than anything on Earth. And he not only figured out how to make it functional—he extrapolated an entire defense system that might be the key to protecting this planet from total annihilation." He leans forward, and his voice rises. "And he basically accomplished all of it with a blindfold on. No plans, no explanations, and almost no context. Yet still, he did it. The scanner. The satellite shield. And these mobile attack units.

The building blocks are all in place—all we have to do is figure out how to put them together and use them." Race sits back, his nostrils flaring.

Angus blinks at him. "I guess you're of the opinion that the lenses should stay," he says with a bemused chuckle.

Race looks at me. "I'm saying that if Fred Archer had designed a weapon using peacock feathers and rubber bands, I'd build it and trust that it would do the job."

Something in my chest loosens, even as my throat gets tight. "Yeah," I say hoarsely. "Dad never designed things without a purpose." But it's one more thing to figure out, and we may not have time. It's been nearly twenty-four hours since that Sicarii scout ship discovered the location of Black Box. Why haven't they attacked yet? What are they waiting for? "I'll take a look at it later if the weapon design team can't figure it out, but I have to get back to work on bringing the satellite system online this morning."

Congers stares at the scanner, his expression grim. "Assuming we can activate that satellite shield, will it still be functional if—"

"If those Sicarii come in here and blow us up?" I interject.

Angus regards me steadily. "The servers are very protected, deep underground. Bombs probably wouldn't do it. But if these Sicarii get boots on the ground and gain control of the compound, they could probably take it down."

We sit in silence for a moment, and then Angus scoots his chair back abruptly. "We'd better get moving," he rumbles as he stands up.

Race turns to me. "In the spirit of mutual trust, Tate, I was thinking you and I could work on the satellite defense system together, maybe figure out the technology, which pieces of the wreckage your father used to create the system and the scanner."

I look into his eyes, the whites still shot through with crimson. It's not possible to trust him, not completely, but after what he said about my dad, it's a bit easier to think about working with him.

Also, there's no way I'd let him look at the satellite plans by himself. "Sounds good."

Leo pokes my arm. "Can I come?"

Race looks to Angus, who nods. "Don't underestimate this boy," Angus says proudly.

"He knew my dad well," I say. My voice sounds hollow. I think he knew my dad better than I did.

As I dig into my breakfast, eating as quickly as possible, Angus asks Christina if she'd like to help out on the factory floor. They need all the assistance they can get. Christina looks relieved at the idea of having something to do and eagerly agrees. Angus waves to a ridiculously tall, lanky guy with black hair and olive skin, and when the dude comes over, Angus introduces him as Manuel Santiago, oldest son of the Santiago patriarch and a member of the weapons design team. He appears to be in his midtwenties and, like so many others, looks short on sleep and highly caffeinated this morning. He shakes Christina's hand and tells her he could use some help inputting raw data to create a simulation to test the weapons systems for the combat vehicles. I'm not sure whether it'll be boring or cool, but Manuel seems easygoing and friendly. He doesn't ask her what her last name is. He seems interested only in having an extra set of fingers to enter data, considering the urgency of getting the vehicles battle-ready. Christina kisses my forehead and leaves with him, telling me she'll see me at lunch.

I'm shoveling the last bit of cereal into my mouth when Brayton walks into the cafeteria. He slept in, and it's done him loads of good. His face has lost the sunken look it had last night. He strides over to our table, doing that meticulous hair-smoothing thing as he reaches us. "Good morning," he says to Angus.

"Morning," says Angus. Both Race and Congers sit back a little, watching. "You look like you got some rest."

Brayton smooths his hair again. "I heard you needed some help figuring out how to bolster the security around the scanner," he says, nodding at the device. "I told the guards last night that I'd assist."

"We did need help," says Angus. "We put Rufus Bishop and Mr. Congers here on it."

"But I know more about it than either of those two,"

Brayton says, his brow furrowed. "I was the CEO, for God's sake. I know all the systems within this compound. It's very shortsighted of you not to use my expertise."

Angus gives Brayton a friendly smile that does not completely mask the cold look in his eyes. "I had every intention of using your expertise. We were hoping you'd assist in managing the logistical team."

"The logistical team . . ." Brayton begins.

Angus nods. "Sanitation, janitorial services, laundry, and cafeteria services."

Brayton stares at Angus. "You don't trust me," he says slowly, tilting his head. "Have you *ever* trusted me? Was I an idiot to think you did?"

His tone is so controlled, but I've seen Brayton get mad—on Monday in Princeton when I wouldn't give him the scanner, and again yesterday when he found out he'd lost his job. My stomach tightens as I wait for the explosion.

Angus puts his hands up. "Brayton, this isn't the time to rehash the past—"

"Then I won't," Brayton snaps as he takes an abrupt step back, looking from Angus to the scanner before meeting each of our eyes. "I will work to regain your trust," he says, gentling his tone. Then he pivots on his heel and marches out, his hand shooting out to grab a granola bar from a rack as he makes his way to the exit.

"He took that better than we anticipated," Race comments.

Angus lifts his shoulder slightly, a noncommittal sort of movement. "We've had our differences over the years, mostly over his accounting, but also over how brilliant men like Rufus Bishop and Fred Archer were driven away from our ranks because Brayton prioritized profits over anything else. He went after the scanner on his own last week. I had no idea he was trying to buy it from Fred, and no idea how far he'd go to get it. And what he did to Tate is unconscionable." He folds his arms over his chest. "He'll be watched."

"He's not the only one who should be monitored," I say, frustration creeping in. I don't disagree with anything Angus is saying, but Brayton was in his room last night, and he looked too tired to be sprinting down corridors in the main building. Rufus was also in his room, and I can't imagine him sprinting anywhere ever. But maybe neither of them needed to. "This attempted theft was aided, at least, by someone who knows the technology. But maybe whoever masterminded it had help." I get up from my chair, struck by an idea. "Where's the scanner going to be?"

"For now, when we're not examining it, it will be in a storage room adjoining my office. I'm taking it there now," says Angus. "All the security staff are needed today to work in the defense stations at the perimeter, since we're concerned about another attack after yesterday. When I'm not in there to watch over it myself, guards will be posted outside the door, at least until Rufus and Bill render the electronic systems foolproof."

Computers aren't that hard to fool, I want to remind him. But instead, I say, "I'll meet you at your office." I tell Race I'll be in the computer lab in less than half an hour, then make for the door. Leo follows me out.

"What are you up to?" he asks as I head for the infirmary.

"Low-tech alternatives," I say, and he grins.

I stroll into the clinic to hear Dr. Ackerman's voice emanating from behind a curtain. In his soft, Southern drawl, he instructs a Core agent to inhale and let it out. The open hospital room still contains a few of the injured, a guy with burns and two others still wearing oxygen masks. For a half second, I consider trying to talk to Dr. Ackerman about where he went after he left the meeting room last night, but if he's guilty of trying to steal the scanner, I can hardly expect him to be straight with me.

Besides, I'm going to catch the thief if he has the balls to try again. I ask a nurse if I can access some of their basic supplies. I show her my ID card that marks me as a patriarch. She leads me to a closet with bandages, soap, various ointments and nutritional supplements . . . and what I want—vitamins. I grab a bottle of B12 tablets and make my exit, Leo at my heels.

On our way to the elevator, we pass all the portraits of dead patriarchs and matriarchs again. Leo looks away as we pass his dad. I wonder how well he remembers his parents. "Hey, can I ask you a question?"

"Yeah, sure," Leo replies.

"What family was your mom from?"

"Fisher," he says. "Uncle George was her cousin."

I look up the hallway toward my dad's nameplate. "Did your parents ever tell you how they met?"

"It was an arranged thing. Like most marriages within The Fifty."

"Does that bother you?" I ask. "Knowing that these families are picking out some girl for you to marry?" The vitamins rattle in my hand, taut with nervous energy.

Leo shrugs. "Honestly, I don't spend a lot of time thinking about it." He gives me a sidelong glance. "Are you asking because of your thing with Christina?"

God, she's not even here, and still this feels awkward. "Yes and no. I mean, it's not like we're at the point where we'd even talk about a permanent commitment." I pause for a moment, about to mention her college plans, and then realize all of that might be totally irrelevant given our present circumstances. We'll be lucky to make it through today. "I guess I'm just trying to figure out how important it is. You know. To keep the families totally human, genetically speaking."

Leo stops in front of my dad's nameplate. "Weird being part of an endangered species, isn't it?"

I nod. "Is it our responsibility to keep it going?" Honestly, as I think about the differences between H2 and humans, which come down to our origins and some discrepancies in molecular structure so tiny that they can only be detected by extraterrestrial tech, it's hard for me to understand why it matters, except in principle. I stare at the blank space where my father's portrait will hang. "I wish I could have talked to him about it." I close my eyes. "Did he ever talk about it with you?"

Leo is quiet for a few seconds. Then he sighs. "Kind of? At the March board meeting, one of the Bearden matriarch's daughters—her name is Kim—decided to marry a guy who wasn't a member of The Fifty. There was no way of knowing if he was H2 or human." He chuckles. "Well, I guess there was, but your dad wasn't telling anyone about it. And there were big questions about whether Kim could remain a member of The Fifty if she didn't marry within the group. Some people, like Rufus, were really outraged that the Bearden family was even still speaking to her. I guess he expected the Beardens to completely cut her off." He pushes his glasses up on his nose. "Your dad was really quiet in that meeting. I don't know how he voted. But afterward, he said it was a decision every family would have to face, and he hoped they would remember what was important."

My heart beats a little faster. Christina and I had just gotten together in March, and my dad must have known she was probably H2, just based on the odds. "Did he say what was important?"

Leo's brow furrows. "I asked. And he just said that every family had to decide that among themselves."

I grit my teeth. Dad put off all those conversations, and now they'll never happen. And meanwhile, as he was keeping me in the dark, he was talking to Leo, who's almost three years younger than I am.

I want to put my fist through the wall, right where Dad's picture will be.

I want to sit down on the floor and try to breathe, because it's almost impossible right now.

I can't do either. I need to stop a thief, hack some satellites, and save the fucking world. "Next stop, morgue," I say briskly, swallowing the lump in my throat. "My mom's probably already down there, if she ever left at all."

We get on the elevator. Leo shuffles his feet as we descend. "She's having a hard time with the autopsies," he says.

"Why did you go with her last night?"

"I wanted to know if Uncle George suffered," he mumbles, confirming my suspicions. "She said it was quick."

I don't parse the death of George's body with the death of George himself, because we don't really know how it happened, what the Sicarii did to him. Maybe my mom has some answers by now. The elevator opens onto a basement level brightly lit and completely sterile-looking, white tile and white walls. Cold as hell. I shiver as my sneakers squeak along the hallway, following Leo to a swinging set of doors. It opens into a room with drains in the floor, a row of sinks along the back wall, and a long table containing a shitload of medical equipment, centrifuges, a mass spectrometer, and a set of microscopes. This place isn't just a morgue—it's a forensic lab. Awesome. "Mom?"

"Tate?" she calls from a room to my left. "In here. Hang on." A tap switches on, and a moment later, she comes out, wiping her hands on a towel. She's wearing a rubber apron that makes her look like a butcher. "I'm in the middle of the dissection," she says somberly. "Dr. Ackerman was too busy with patients to help this morning. How are you?"

"Rested. Fine," I tell her. "You?"

Her mouth twists at the corner. "I may have found something, but I'm not sure yet."

"What is it?" Leo asks.

She gives him a sympathetic, motherly sort of look, one that seems odd on her serious face. "Are you sure you want to hear this, Leo?"

He folds his arms over his chest. "I'm not a child."

She puts her hands up. "Okay. I've discovered some anomalies in George's skin."

"Anomalies," Leo says quietly.

"In addition to the sweat glands, there are secretory glands that I've never seen before."

"Like, they grew there? Something alien?" I ask, trying to wrap my head around what she's saying.

"Perhaps."

"What do they secrete?" Leo asks in a tight voice.

"Unknown, as of yet," Mom says gently. "I'm using caution as I examine them, but at this time, I can tell you that the structures are definitely unnatural. I'll have more answers later today."

"You're being careful, right?" I ask. "We still don't know how the Sicarii go from body to body."

She gives me a smile. "I wear full protective gear when I'm working. I'm taking every precaution."

"Good." I look her over, her dark hair pulled back in a ponytail, her brown eyes rimmed with red. And I think of my dad, how he left so much unfinished, including his relationship with me. "I don't want anything to happen to you." It comes out rushed. Soft. I'm the one who sounds like a child.

My mom's eyes get shiny. "Like I said, I'm being careful." She clears her throat. "And I need to get back to work."

"We'll leave you to it, then," I say. "I just came down here to see how you were doing and to grab some things. Do you have a black light?"

She points to a cabinet over the set of sinks. "There's a wand light in there. Why do you need it?"

I walk over to a shelf that contains all sorts of chemicals and take down a bottle of ethanol. "To catch a thief."

Leo grabs the black light from the cabinet, and I snag a metal bowl, stirrer, and specimen brush. My mom doesn't bother asking me what I'm up to, but she gives me an amused, fond . . . *sad* . . . look that tells me I'm reminding her of my dad. She says she'll call me if she discovers anything and retreats back to her autopsy, and Leo and I walk back to the elevator.

"I approve," Leo says as he looks over our supplies. "Your dad would have thought this was hilarious."

"He's the one who forced me to learn this kind of thing." I don't say that he never cracked a smile while he did it, either. I can barely fathom what "hilarious" looked like on my dad, and it kind of kills me that Leo knows.

I swallow back the bitterness on my tongue. "Leo? Was my dad . . . I don't know. He talked to you about a lot of stuff. But what was he like when he was with you?"

"What was he like . . ." he says thoughtfully, then pushes at the bridge of his glasses. "He was sad, Tate. He was nice, but he always seemed kind of sad. And honestly, sometimes he seemed sadder after spending time with me."

"I'm sure you didn't make him sad, Leo," I say, my stomach aching. *But I probably did.*

"No, I know I didn't. I think . . ." His eyes meet mine. "I think he kind of wished I was you."

Guilt lances through me as I say, "I don't know if you're right. He and I fought. A lot."

"He never talked about that. He did talk about you, though. All good stuff." He glances at the ethanol and vitamins I'm carrying. "All true stuff."

I bow my head. And all I can think is *why*. Why, if he could talk to Leo about me and say those nice things . . . why couldn't he just say those things to me? Why was he so shut down? So machine-like, except for those final minutes when I held his hand and watched him die? Why does it have to be like this? And why does it have to hurt this much?

We find Angus in his office suite with Kellan. They're standing next to a closed door, which is locked using yet another electronic code vulnerable to hacking. I assume it's the storage room Angus told me about. He frowns as he looks over my armload of supplies. "Do I even want to know?" he asks.

"It's just a backup," I tell him as I sit on the floor and dump the bottle of B12 pills into the metal bowl, then crush them with the heavy ethanol bottle. Next, I pour the ethanol over the pill debris and stir until it's dissolved. "Maybe don't mention this to anyone else?" I say to the two of them.

Angus nods in this bemused kind of way as I use the specimen brush to paint the dissolved B12 solution over the electronic keypad, the door handle, and the threshold in front of the door. I stand up and switch on the black light, and Kellan's eyes go wide.

"Vitamin B12 is fluorescent under black light," I explain, gesturing at the bright yellow glow beneath the light. "You can hack the code, but it still takes a pair of hands to open the door and swipe that scanner. Assuming we can keep this between ourselves, the thief won't know he has this stuff all over his fingers and shoes. It can be easily wiped off and reapplied." I pour the remaining solution back into the ethanol bottle and hand it to Kellan.

Angus gives Kellan a hard look. "We'll definitely keep this between us."

With that done, Leo and I clean up and head to the computer lab. Race isn't here yet, but that's fine with me. I sit down in front of a monitor and bring up the plans, using *Josephus* to access them. Leo settles next to me. "So we have to figure out the password to wake up those satellites?"

"Yeah," I say, bringing up the satellite files. "I've been chasing my own tail trying to think of what it could be."

"Were the Black Box developers helpful?"

I bite the inside of my cheek. "I haven't talked to them. I didn't think they knew Dad well enough to know what he might have been thinking."

Leo scratches at a spot on his shoulder. "Sounds like you're putting a lot of pressure on yourself. Nobody said you had to figure this out alone."

"I'm his *son*," I blurt out, louder than I intend. Suddenly, my eyes are burning. I turn my head and stare at the wall, willing away my envy, my stupid desire to prove I'm worthy.

"You don't have to rub it in," Leo says quietly. "Trust me, there wasn't a moment I spent with him that I wasn't aware of it." He scrubs his sleeve across his face, a quick, angry movement. "I was so jealous of you, I could barely stand it."

I blink and turn back to him. We glare at each other for a few moments. "Sorry," I finally say.

"Me too," he mumbles.

I draw in a breath and let it out slowly. "I think he'd be glad if we did this together."

Leo lets out a raspy laugh. "Yeah. I think he would. So let's do it."

I gesture at the satellite plans on the screen. "If these do what we think they'll do, anything hostile that tries to come through—and specifically, anything that scans Sicarii—gets zapped."

He gazes at the schematics. "Do you think your dad knew what the Sicarii were? He did scribble that word on his paper, along with the two-zero and the two-zero-four."

"No way of knowing. But since the H2 scanner technology detects three species, he probably deduced the third was bad news. It's possible he didn't activate the satellite system because he really wasn't sure yet, and he thought he'd be alive to make the decision when the time came. Or maybe he was just about to do it and simply didn't get the chance." I rub my throat as I click the button that says "enter activation code" and bring up the password box. I should be used to talking about my dad in past tense by now, but I'm not. "Right before he died, he told me that 'when the time comes, it's Josephus.' That's all he got to tell me. Turns out it was the password to access the files. But to actually activate the whole satellite network?" I point at the cursor, blinking in expectation of a magic code that will unlock a way to protect our planet against invasion.

"Your dad never did anything without a reason," Leo says, echoing what I already know. "Why do you think he chose 'Josephus' as the password to access the files?"

"No idea. But—"

"Just let me try something." He scoots to the next terminal and wakes the screen. "Does this thing have a browser on it? Oh, here it is." He clicks it open and Googles *Josephus*. The first several results are for one guy. A second later, he's at Wikipedia. "Josephus was a Jewish historian from the first century."

I read the page over his shoulder, realizing I shouldn't have discarded Josephus as an avenue for further investigation simply because it had already given me access to the plans. "He was part of an army defeated in battle by a guy named Vespasian who later became a Roman emperor." I return to my own computer and try *Vespasian* as a password, but it's a no-go, just like every other freaking option I've tried.

"The battle was at a place called Jotapata," Leo adds, still reading. "Try that?"

I do. Nope. Once again, the terrible odds, the ticking clock, the failure, my own stupidity, all of it starts to weigh heavy again. "Any other options there?"

He squints at the screen. "Well, he was a historian . . . He wrote two books: one called *The Jewish War*, and one called *Antiquities of the Jews*. I don't suppose you've read them?"

I let out a dry chuckle. "No, not yet. Have you?"

He rolls his eyes. "It's probably on my reading list." He clicks on the hyperlink and scans. "Oh, this is interesting. The Antiquities book contains passages about Jesus. Like, outside the Bible, Josephus's book is considered possible evidence of his historical existence."

It's interesting, but I'm not sure it's useful. Still . . . "I don't suppose those books are available online?"

"You mean, like on Amazon or something?" He's already typing. "Huh. It's right here."

Forget Amazon—there's a website with the whole damn thing. "How long is it?" If the answer's there, maybe I can get a team together and scour the pages to find it.

He groans. "Did I say it was one book? According to this, it's twenty. Twenty. Books. This guy really needed an editor."

My heart kicks. "Twenty?"

He nods, already starting to read the first. I shove his shoulder. "Leo. Think about what you said to me a second ago. My dad had scribbled two-oh-two-oh-four on that notebook page. I thought it was one number. But that's not how you said it a second ago."

He looks over at me. "That's because there was a little space between the first zero and the second two."

He must have a nearly photographic memory. "Exactly," I say, waiting for him to make the connection and then getting too impatient and blurting, "Go to book twenty?"

"Oh!" he says loudly. As he scrolls down, I notice the little notations before the sentences, kind of like Bible chapters and verses, and my heart starts to pound. "Is there a verse or line two hundred four?" I whisper, my mouth dry.

"Yeah, there is." His voice trembles as he reads it. "Tate, look."

. . . *as soon as Albinus was come to the city of Jerusalem, he used all his endeavors and care that the country might be kept in peace, and this by destroying many of the Sicarii* . . .

I turn back to my own terminal. Carefully, letter by letter, I enter the name *Albinus.*

And the reaction is instant. The password screen disappears, and words begin to scroll down the screen.

RAMSES: Active
AMENHOTEP: Activating
THUTMOSE: Activating
HATSHEPSUT: Activating
ARTAXERXES: Activating
DARIUS: Activating
HAKOR: Activating

And on and on, all twenty of them. I'm standing up before I know what I'm doing, and I lunge for the hallway just as Race walks in. He blinks as he sees me pull up short. "What's wrong?" he barks.

"I've activated the satellite network!"

His mouth drops open. "You did?"

"Yeah. It was Leo's idea," I pant, elbowing the kid as his cheeks darken. "How to find the password, I mean. The system's ramping up right now."

Race stares at me for a moment more, then a smile breaks across his face. "It's possible you kids just saved the world."

I laugh out of sheer relief. We did it. *We did it.*

Race opens his mouth to say something else, but he's drowned out by the shriek of an alarm. My heart is in my throat as we emerge into the hallway. Panicked shouts and thumping footsteps from the atrium fill in the gaps between the screams of the alarms. We barrel into the atrium and turn in the direction of the commotion, gazing through the stories-high wall of glass at the back of the main building, behind which is the Black Box factory.

Thick smoke billows into the air. The factory is on fire.

FOURTEEN

"CHRISTINA," I CROAK AS I SHOVE OFF AND SPRINT FOR
the rear exit of the cavernous atrium with Leo right behind
me. There are no windows in the factory building, so there's
no efficient way to vent whatever poisonous fumes are carried
in that black smoke, which chases the factory workers as they
tumble from the exits. Their faces are black and red, and their
eyes are wide with horror.

We bust through the exit of the atrium and into the wide
courtyard between the two buildings, covering our mouths and
noses with our sleeves. My eyes sting as I hit the smoky air,
and I squint, searching every face and figure for the one I most
need to see. Distantly, I hear people shouting for the hoses,
for the two emergency trucks located somewhere on this compound, for Dr. Ackerman . . . for mercy, for their mothers, for
the pain to stop. Some are dragging limp, burned bodies from

the building while others are frantically gesturing, trying to let us know exactly how bad it is inside.

Which is where Christina is. We weren't ready for this. I can tell by the panicked strain in all the voices I hear. Rufus and Brayton both come barreling out of the atrium and end up next to me and Leo, huffing and gaping at the disaster unfolding in front of us.

Rufus glares at the sky as he jogs forward. "Was it those alien bastards? Why didn't the perimeter defenses go off?"

"It couldn't have been," says Leo, pushing at my back. "The fire looks like it started inside the factory, not as a result of a shot from the outside." He points at the roof. It appears to be intact.

"Oh, God," Brayton says between heavy, harsh breaths, looking at the carnage around us. "This shouldn't have happened."

"Maybe it wouldn't have if you'd listened to me when I told you to overhaul the vent system ten years ago," Rufus shouts, lumbering for the building. "There are still people in there!"

I follow him, but we're swimming against the current as worker after worker staggers from the building. One of them is on fire. She falls forward and is immediately smothered by others who leap to help her with no regard for their own safety.

All I can think is *that could have been Christina.*

If she's not already dead, that is. My chest is tight and my limbs are buzzing as I let Rufus part the crowd, his massive frame allowing me to stumble along in his wake. Leo's behind me, and right before we reach the door, I spin around. "You need to stay out here."

He shoves against me, his eyes on the black smoke billowing from the door. "Get out of the way."

I grab his bony shoulders. "Leo. Look at me! I have to go in there and get Christina, and I can't focus if I'm worrying about you," I shout.

"I can help." He bucks, trying to throw me off. "She's in there!"

"I *know.* Please. Stay out here, and help in any way you can." Seeing Angus appear behind us, his shirtsleeves rolled up and his hair wild, I shove Leo into his arms. The big man wraps himself around Leo and drags him back, and I whirl around to find Rufus gone. Brayton disappears into the factory a moment later, and I'm on his heels. As soon as I make it through the door and into the blazing-hot interior, he shoves a gas mask toward my face. He's pulled it from some emergency stash near the entrance.

"Get that on, if you have to be in here," he says, and then he runs off, probably looking for Ellie or one of his family members, plowing down a relatively clear aisle toward the back.

I wrestle the gas mask over my face and take a moment to look around the unfamiliar building. I'm thinking there has to be a sprinkler system, but it's almost impossible to see the ceiling of this four-story factory because the smoke is so thick.

It roils like poisonous thunderclouds with nowhere to go, but staring at it makes one thing clear—if there *is* a sprinkler system, it's not working.

The workspace is dense with mechanical bays, each of which contains a combat vehicle in various stages of assembly. There must be at least twenty rows of ten vehicles, lined up nose to tail with aisles along the walls and between each row. The apparent epicenter of this disaster is near the middle of the factory floor, which must be pushing a million square feet—a cluster of combat vehicles is on fire. Workers are fleeing from the burning vehicles as the flames creep up supply lines toward the ceiling and along the row in either direction, effectively cutting off the escape route of anyone who's on the other side of the conflagration.

I grab one guy as he runs past, practically clotheslining him. "Is there live ammunition or fuel in these vehicles?" I shout, my voice distorted by the filter on the mask.

He shakes his head. "Just the dummy shells in the combat vehicles that Manuel was testing at the back." He gestures wildly toward a space on the other side of the flaming vehicles. "But the rest of these are empty."

The combat vehicles that Manuel was testing. And Christina was with him. "Have you seen him or the girl he was working with?"

"No," he says, coughing. "Not since before the shelving started to collapse on us." He wrenches his arm from my grasp and lunges for the door. I try to catch him to ask exactly where, but an explosion on the far side of the flaming vehicles has me whipping around again, sprinting through waves of heat and vapor. There could be people—including Christina and Manuel—trapped on the other side of that inferno. My shirt is soaked with sweat as I climb atop one vehicle and begin leaping along hoods and roofs, careful to avoid the hole that's been cut in each of them to accommodate the lenses in my dad's design.

I crane my neck, trying to peer between dancing spirals of flame, trying to identify anything human and breathing in the chaos on the other side of the fire. Just beyond the flames, instead of mechanical bays, there are massive three-story-high shelving units, which hold metal panels, boxes of parts and tubing, and equipment. One of them has buckled and collapsed onto its neighbor, which is leaning precariously. It looks like all of them are going to go down like building-sized dominoes. Meanwhile, the smoke is now so thick that it's drifting down from the ceiling toward the floor—where survivors would be, if there are any.

I'm within three rows of the fire and looking for my opening when I catch movement on the other side. A long, lanky silhouette staggering between aisles of shelving. "Manuel!" I shout.

The silhouette pauses. That has to be him. I make it close enough to the fire that it feels like the hairs on my arms and legs are getting singed. All that stands between me and the rear of the factory is one long, burning row of combat vehicles. I'm so close, but I can't go any farther. But hanging around me are tools, suspended from scaffolding two stories above me, their thick power cables like vines in a mechanical jungle. I leap onto one and begin to heave myself upward, praying it holds. My palms are slick with sweat, causing me to slip every time I grab the cable and pull, but I make steady progress.

Without my gas mask, I'd be falling to earth, suffocated and still, but it filters the air and keeps me breathing as I begin to swing on the cable, reaching for another that's hanging about twenty feet over the flames. I want to stop and look for Manuel again, to make sure I'm heading in the right direction, but right now I have to focus on not tumbling into the fire below me. I pick up momentum, pumping my legs and swinging closer. My vision narrows to the orange cable in front of me; all I hear is a roar of white noise. Just as I arc forward, I let go and throw myself at that orange cable, my fingers closing over it . . . and sliding.

I clutch at the sweat-slick cable as every muscle in my body tenses, like the rest of me knows what my mind hasn't accepted yet—the inferno below me is awaiting my arrival, ready to reduce me to ash. My fingers are white-knuckled over the cable, stopping my downward progression. With my legs kicking less than five yards above the flames, I cling desperately to it, afraid to move lest I start to slide again. It feels like my legs are starting to cook in the raging heat that rolls off the fire below me. I heave myself up with one arm and slowly climb, twisting the cable around my hand to keep from slipping down, until most of my body is tangled with the long orange cord.

Then I begin to swing again. Two rows of combat vehicles—two sets of cables—away, Manuel is waving his arms in quick, uncoordinated motions as he leans heavily on the massive scaffolding of the shelving. He doesn't seem to notice it leaning dangerously over him, and he startles when a box falls from three stories above and slams to the ground nearby, hurling bolts and screws against his back as he hunches over more debris at his feet. He's barely visible through the fog, but I can tell from the dark blob of his face that he's got his shirt pulled up, desperately trying to block the fumes. His movements are sluggish and weak as he tugs at the pile of rags on the ground between his legs, trying to pick it up.

My heart clutches as the pile shudders and shifts, revealing dark blond hair and pale skin. Christina is lying at Manuel's feet. There's a swath of smudged cloth tied around her face. Her name is the pulse in my head as I kick and swing, and when I grab for the next cable, I'm ready for the sweaty slide and tangle the cable around me before I can lose momentum and altitude. I force my eyes away from Christina's body and concentrate on making it to her, moving like a clumsy Tarzan as I lunge for the next cable, which hangs close to the huge, leaning shelving that Manuel is huddled under. I hope it's strong enough to hold my weight without collapsing.

I swing just far enough to grab onto the shelving two stories above the floor. It creaks and wobbles, but it's enormous—like one of those three-story-high shelves at Home Depot—so it tolerates my weight. It takes me only a few seconds to climb low enough to drop to the ground, landing next to Manuel.

"The back entrance is blocked," he wheezes into my ear. His black hair is plastered to his face, and his eyes are red and swollen. "I was trying to get her out the front, but the smoke—" He doubles over, coughing.

But he's said enough. If the back exit is inaccessible, we're trapped, because although there's a slim possibility that Manuel could climb the shelving and swing himself to safety, as I kneel and pull Christina into my arms, I know there's not a chance in hell that she could follow.

I have to find another way. Huddled over her, I stroke her hair away from her face. I can't see any obvious injuries, but the smoke has done its work. She's barely conscious. Sooty tears streak out of the corners of her eyes. I start to rip the mask off my face to put it on her, but Manuel grabs my hand.

"Keep it on," he says hoarsely, still bent over and bracing his hands on his thighs. "You're our only chance to get out."

And if I don't move quickly, if I don't think smart and fast, we're all going down. Still holding Christina against my chest,

I look around. Beyond the shelving are more combat vehicles, but none of them are fueled—which is lucky, since they'd be exploding if they were. And none of them have live ammunition, but . . .

"Are any of these vehicles armed?" I say loudly, just as an explosion shakes the factory floor and causes boxes of equipment to land heavily around us. If we don't move, the shelves are going to collapse and bury us here.

"Only with dummy rounds," says Manuel between coughs. "You can fire the cannons on the roof from a console in the back or the hood-mounted cannon from the driver's seat."

"That's our way out." I tug his arm. "Which one can I use?"

He peers at me, looking confused, and I realize his brain is probably a tainted stew of delirium-inducing chemicals that he's inhaled from the smoke. He's not exactly at his best.

"Manuel, which one is armed?" I shout.

He blinks and squints at the combat vehicles around us, then shoves off the scaffolding and staggers down the aisle, which is now completely closed in by the leaning shelving above it. It's a miracle we're not crushed as I scoop Christina into my arms and carry her, following Manuel along the aisle littered with debris.

We emerge on the other side to see more collapsed shelving against the back wall, but one small area is reasonably open, a set of combat vehicles sitting peacefully while the smoke swirls in lazy tendrils above them. "There." Manuel points to the three vehicles in a row near the wall to our left. "We were testing the cannons on the roofs of the vehicles. Christina's really good at . . ." The rest of his sentence is in Spanish. He closes his eyes and takes his head in his hands.

I heave Christina over my shoulder, curling one hand around her thigh as her arms hang down my back. With my other hand, I grab at Manuel's sleeve to lurch him into motion. We make our way over to the first vehicle, a looming SUV with the gaping hole in the top. All these eight-wheeled fighting vehicles have two cannons on either side of the hole in the roof, but they're not the usual stationary turret you'd see on an armored personnel carrier. These are each on rails that enable them to slide and rotate three hundred sixty degrees, allowing the gunners to operate both cannons at once. It must take mad skills, and I'm hoping I've got them. I gently lay Christina on the ground, and Manuel sinks to his knees next to her, coughing and heaving. I climb onto the combat vehicle and drop through the hole in the roof, landing awkwardly in a chair surrounded by a circular console.

In the tiny metal-encased world of the combat vehicle, I peer through the hazy air at the targeting system, which is giving off a dim green glow that tells me it's connected to a stable power source, probably a battery. I've never seen anything like this, the three-hundred-sixty-degree video display, the odd things that look like blood pressure cuffs on either side of the seat, the two metal sticks jutting up from the floor like double helicopter controls. Wishing I'd studied my father's blueprints a little more closely, I flip the safety off one of the control sticks and flinch as the thing kicks in my hand. Above me, one of the roof cannons slides along its rails, whizzing past the circular hole above my head, a dark shadow in the fog.

Now that I know how to move the cannons, I lean close to the video monitor.

What I need is wall space. To my immediate right, the area is blocked by those massive shelves. Right in front of me, one of them has toppled over and is blocking the rear doors. But to my left, there's some space. I grip both control sticks and feel the jolt of movement above me as the roof cannons slide back and forth along their rails. The vehicle wobbles in its metal carriage that suspends it above the ground so that people can work on its underbelly.

I'm aiming when an explosion rips through the air, shaking me with the percussion and the wave of heat. I shoot to my feet and nearly clip my head on the metal edge of the hole in the roof, thinking of going out and bringing Christina and Manuel in here, but then I realize—I need to focus, and I need to save them.

I sit back down. My thumb hovers over the red button at the side of the control stick, and as the cannon swings into position, I push it all the way down. With a heavy *thunk* and a muffled boom, a projectile flies out of the cannon and slams into the wall to my left. On the monitors, I wait for the cloud of dust to clear.

As it does, no daylight greets me. I fire again, both cannons this time. The heavy dummy artillery collides with the wall in almost exactly the same place. But it doesn't penetrate. As the smoke grows thicker around us, I grab two more dummy missiles from the stack inside the vehicle's cabin and load them into the cannons, then fire again. And then I do it again. And again. On the fourth try, a section of the wall collapses outward with a loud crunch, and smoke is sucked out of the hole. The flames will follow, so I load up again and fire twice more, trying to make the opening larger. It's about six feet off the ground, jagged and gaping, when I let go of the control stick. The lingering vibrations tingle through my bones as I climb out of the combat vehicle and jump to the ground.

Both Manuel and Christina are unconscious. I don't check their vitals. I don't want to know. I yank Christina up by the arm and stagger toward the smoky hole through which I can see daylight. I make it to the wall as the three-story-high shelving near the fire starts to collapse. If I don't make it back to Manuel, he's going to be crushed. Already I can see the shifting of the metal monster behind him as it buckles and tangles with the shelving next to it. Boxes and paneling crash to the ground, raining destruction onto the fire and the space around it. Flames and cinders shoot into the air. My grip on Christina is so tight that I'm leaving red marks on her pale, clammy skin. Panting, I lift her, planning to let her slide out of the opening and onto the ground—

Leo's head appears in the opening. He's wearing a gas mask. Kellan appears next to him, his arms outstretched. "I knew it was you!" Leo shouts as I hand Christina to Kellan, who must be standing on something outside. He wraps his arms around her slender body and pulls her into the open air.

"I have to get Manuel!" I yell, and turn back to the carnage without waiting for a response. But before I make it more than a few steps, Leo is next to me, matching my strides as I weave my way toward Manuel—and the collapsing shelving. We reach him as the unit nearest us begins to come our way. I don't need to tell Leo what we have to do. I grab Manuel's right arm and Leo hooks his arm under Manuel's left, and we drag him as fast as we can, his long legs sliding across the floor as we scoot toward the hole in the wall, where Kellan is climbing through to help.

A rush of air and a roaring sound make me look over my shoulder to see the combat vehicle I was sitting in buried and crushed beneath the heavy metal shelving. Leo and I lug Manuel to his feet, and Kellan helps us pass him to some Black Box employees outside. With one last look at the flames and all the destroyed combat vehicles, I give myself up to the arms reaching for me, the voices shouting my name. The gas mask is torn from my face, and I suck in a burning lungful of toxic air before an oxygen mask is clamped over my nose and mouth.

People swarm all around me, putting victims on gurneys in

the courtyard and helping others into the atrium of the main building. Two massive fire trucks are only a few yards from the factory, one aiming its foam cannon into the hole we escaped from. I let two guards drag me away, my thoughts buzzing, my mind drenched in dread. I have no idea how many people have been killed. I have no idea if Christina is one of them. But I do know one thing: Our chances of winning a ground battle against those Sicarii scout ships have just gone up in flames.

FIFTEEN

THE ATRIUM OF BLACK BOX IS A SEA OF PAIN AND
misery. I lean against one of the big columns at the edge of the
room, forcing myself to down a granola bar as I stare. People
lie shoulder to shoulder on the floor, some on gurneys, some
in the arms of a relative. Manuel Santiago is two gurneys away,
his hands fluttering at his sides as he sucks down purified oxygen and tries to clear his head. Dr. Ackerman zips from person
to person, taking vitals, barking orders, having his staff whisk
the burn victims up to the infirmary and commanding them to
bring more oxygen tanks down in order to meet the needs of
those who will remain here while we take stock.

We don't know exactly what caused the fire. I've heard
whispers of everything from a bomb to a hydrogen leak ignited
by a spark. It wouldn't even be clear it was a deliberate act—except that the sprinkler system was disabled sometime last night

or early this morning, as was the automatic system that was supposed to raise the massive cargo bay doors. We need to find out, but we've got other priorities at the moment. Even before the fire was out, Congers and Race had dashed off to warn the guards in the perimeter defense posts to look out for signs of sabotage. If the stations are disabled, we're dead.

My mother is here. She came rushing up from the lab in the basement and gave me a fierce hug as I walked into the atrium. Now she's helping Dr. Ackerman care for patients. She's shed the sling for her left arm, but her mouth is tense with discomfort every time she moves the limb. Her eyes keep darting over to me with concern and frustration. I'm wondering if she's discovered something in the autopsies, but I've only got half a mind for it. Christina lies on a stretcher next to me with a mask strapped to her face. Her cheeks are streaked with grime, beneath which her skin is pink like she's been sunburned. Dr. Ackerman said her vitals were strong, and her eyelids are twitching like she's waking from a long sleep, but I still feel sick and shaky. My mind keeps replaying the moment I realized I was looking at her unconscious body. That image lingers in my brain, along with the seconds I spent in the same situation after a Core agent's bullet tore along the side of her head. Too many close calls. She's been lucky. But somehow I know: Our luck is running out, and I'm terrified that, sooner or later, one of us might not get up and walk away from the carnage. I'm not sure I'd ever recover, knowing that my actions had resulted in her death. I'm already carrying the burden of my father's death on my shoulders. I'm not strong enough to manage the weight of another life snuffed out because I got us all into this.

I'm leaning down to kiss her hand as a dark shape rolls into my periphery. Rufus Bishop is a few feet away, also tethered to an oxygen tank and sitting in a wheelchair. His belly sits like a beach ball on his lap, and he rests his hands over it while he watches what's happening with narrowed eyes.

His steely gaze lands on me. For a moment, we stare at each other. I wait for him to go off on me, to accuse me of murdering his son, to threaten me. But instead, as the seconds pass, his face creases with hard, desolate grief. And I remember looking down at Aaron, Rufus's oldest son, and watching him take his last breaths. I remember how scared he looked.

"I'm sorry about Aaron," I finally say. Because I am. I wish he hadn't chased me. I wish he'd been more aware that other members of his family had brought their deadly defense system back online. He shouldn't have been so damn determined to get back the scanner.

Rufus's nostrils flare. His face turns red beneath his Santa beard. He pulls the oxygen mask away from his face with a trembling hand. I brace for his rage.

"Did he suffer?" he finally says, his voice rough.

I blink at him. "N-no. Not for long." I honestly don't know. When I sprinted away, he was still alive. But if Rufus is asking me this, it means Aaron was dead by the time he was found. "He went pretty quickly."

He nods and bows his head. "He was trying to get the device for *me*," he says in a strangled voice. "He'd heard me say we needed it. Stupid boy was loyal to a fault." He stares at his knees as he lets out a sad, raspy chuckle, and my chest hurts. I expected him to tear in to me, to blame me, but somehow, his raw sadness is worse.

His head jerks up as someone shouts from the back of the atrium, and Ellie Alexander bursts through in a puff of smoke, leading four factory workers using a tarp as a kind of sling, within which is a body. She screams for Dr. Ackerman as they lay their burden down on the stone tiles. Her light blond hair is plastered in wisps against her forehead and cheeks. "Medic," she shrieks.

On the tarp, Brayton Alexander lies as still as a corpse. His pale blond hair is gray with soot, and his cheeks are sunken. My mom comes rushing over and kneels next to him, feeling for a pulse but drawing her hand back in surprise. "How close was he to the fire?" she asks Ellie. "His body temperature is very high."

Ellie joins my mom on the floor. "He never got that close to the flames. He just . . . I don't know. Fainted?" A tear slips from her eye and carves a pink path through the grime on her face. "Was it the smoke? Or a heart attack?"

My mother pulls a pulse oximeter from the pocket of her

lab coat and slips it onto one of Brayton's limp fingers. He winces and tries to pull away, but she holds his hand firmly, then shakes her head. "His pulse and oxygen saturation are in the normal range." She lays his hand back on the tarp. "But his temperature is 103.5. The fever may be why he collapsed. We'll have to consult Dr. Ackerman, but since Brayton appears stable, it may be a few minutes." Dr. Ackerman is presiding over the transport of a badly burned factory worker at the moment.

Ellie strokes her dad's arm and glares at Rufus, then at me. "Constantly having his loyalty questioned has taken a huge toll on his health."

Rufus gives Brayton a pitiless sneer, all his grief submerged beneath his decades-long hatred for the former CEO of Black Box. "If he hadn't gone off the reservation in an attempt to acquire the scanner, no one would question him," he says in a low, gravelly voice.

Ellie clenches her teeth. "I've heard stories about how you tried the same thing, Mr. Bishop."

Rufus's chubby fingers curl over the armrests of his wheelchair. "I was trying to protect the human race from annihilation. He was trying to make a profit."

"At least he's not a paranoid maniac."

"I'd rather be a paranoid maniac than a traitor!" Rufus says in a hoarse shout.

"Leave her alone," whispers Brayton, opening his eyes. His cheeks look like he's been smacked over and over again.

Crimson. He lifts his head, but it falls back just as quickly. "This is my fault. Not hers."

His voice is raspy and soft, but Rufus hears him. He grunts. "For once, I know you're telling the truth."

Brayton doesn't respond. He lies there as Ellie strokes his sweaty hair, and I guess this isn't the right moment to start questioning him about why he's saying he's to blame. Rufus apparently disagrees. He leans forward, his shoes squeaking on the footrests of his wheelchair. "Did you hear what he said, Ellie? It's his fault. Ask him why." He wheels himself a little closer. "What are you up to, Brayton? Did you and your H2 buddies sabotage the factory? Are you and the Core working together? Are you planning to sell them our technology like you have in the past?"

Brayton swallows painfully. "What are you talking about? You said it yourself—I didn't upgrade the vent system. The smoke—"

"How dare you accuse my dad of sabotage!" Ellie blurts out, tears shining in her eyes. "Do you have one shred of evidence, or is this your paranoid psychosis leaking out?"

Mom turns to Rufus and snaps, "This is a ridiculous time to carelessly toss around accusations, Rufus—and a dangerous one. If you are truly concerned about the welfare of the inhabitants of this compound, try not to sow needless suspicion and discord."

He arches a furry eyebrow at her, but backs off. Brayton's

chest shudders. He's red-cheeked and drawn-looking, his breaths coming fast. Despite my mistrust, I have a hard time understanding why Brayton would do something so utterly destructive as destroying the factory, especially since he said he wanted to earn back people's trust. What would he gain from that kind of sabotage, apart from petty revenge for being removed as CEO? He seems more motivated by profit than vengeance. And I don't buy for a minute that the Core would work with him to do something like that, not after I've witnessed their desperation to stop the Sicarii.

In fact, what would *anyone* gain from the factory fire . . . except the Sicarii?

The frustration of that thought makes me tense. We've scanned everyone repeatedly, and no one flashes that violent orange that indicates the presence of a Sicarii. So why can't I shake the idea that we've got one somewhere on the compound?

Christina's fingers brush my hand, and I look down to see her blue eyes gazing into mine. Her lips curl upward beneath the oxygen mask, and I lean over her. "How are you?"

She nods but points to her throat and grimaces. I smooth her hair off her forehead and kiss her brow. "You don't have to talk. I know it hurts. I'm just so, so happy you're alive." My voice gets more unsteady with every word.

God, I want to tell her I love her. The words are right there on my tongue.

I nearly lost her again today, and we may not have much time left, and I don't want to leave things unsaid. My heart pounds within my chest. "Christina," I say, touching her forehead with mine. "I—"

The lights go out, and two loud popping noises make both of us flinch. Despite the billowing black smoke outside, there's still plenty of daylight to illuminate the atrium through its glass walls. Heads swivel in the direction of the hallway where the noise came from. Angus, on his knees next to a red-haired young man who is probably a family member, looks over at me, and I can read his thoughts easily.

The scanner.

I let go of Christina's hand and sprint toward the hallway, joined on the way by Angus, Kellan, and two other armed guards. We enter Angus's office and are confronted by an echo of the carnage in the atrium—horrific, but on a smaller scale. Two guards lie sprawled in front of us, blood haloed around them and sprayed on the wall next to their bodies. There's no one else in the office or the long hallway outside.

Angus lets out a strangled roar when he sees the bodies. "Get Ackerman down here now!" he shouts, and one of the guards with us peels off to get the doctor.

One of the guys on the ground is a Core agent. It looks like he was shot in the back of the head. But the other guy—a Black Box guard—is on his back, his lips gray and his eyes staring at the ceiling, his fingers clutching weakly at the hole in his chest. My mind does a lightning-fast reconstruction as I try to puzzle out whether it could be possible that these two shot each other. But nothing clicks into place. While I move past them to the storage room where the scanner is being kept, Angus sinks to the ground next to the guard, speaking in soft, comforting tones.

The door is hanging open, and the room is empty. I clench my teeth around the string of curses threatening to emerge. Race and Congers arrive, a little out of breath. "The scanner's gone," I say. "Whoever took it planned the perfect distraction."

Race's eyes glitter with fury as he gazes down at the dead Core agent. "McClaren, is your guard saying anything?" he asks Angus.

Angus shakes his head. "He's in shock," he says in a shaky voice, scooting back as Dr. Ackerman joins us. The doctor's brown skin is sheened with sweat, and his eyes are full of horror and sorrow, but his movements are calm as he assesses the guard's vitals and applies pressure to the wound.

It won't help, though. I can tell that the guard is doomed. My eyes squeeze shut against the certainty of it. I rub my hand over my face and focus on Race and Congers.

"Someone in this compound has the scanner," Congers says. "We need to alert all guards at the tunnels to the outside. No one goes in or out until it's found."

"I'll take care of it," Angus replies, getting up slowly as Kellan—who is trying to look tough but seems on the verge of breaking down—helps Dr. Ackerman move the Black Box guard onto a gurney. Angus disappears into his office, and soon after, we hear the low rumble of his voice as he communicates with the perimeter guards.

I nod at Kellan, whose broad shoulders are slumped. "The guards need to take the black light and do a systematic search. Use it like you did the scanner. Anyone with the B12 solution on their shoes or hands should be brought in for questioning."

Congers and Race look surprised, but Angus comes out of his office and says, "It looks like your old-fashioned safeguard is the only one we have, because the surveillance cams have once again proved useless." His mouth is working like there's a bitter taste on his tongue.

Kellan glances at Angus. "No one's going to like being under suspicion again, not when everyone fought the fire together, not when so many are hurt."

Angus nods. "Don't tell them they're under suspicion, then. Try to be subtle. Scan everyone, even the injured, and then move on quickly. I'll get the guards down in the residential building to round up anyone in their suites and make sure they don't go anywhere, and the guards on the grounds will bring in anyone who's not here already. But start the search."

Kellan sighs and runs his hand through his curly brown hair, leaving it sticking up on top. "Yes, sir."

My chest is tight as I look around the empty storage room one more time, and then head back to the atrium. Congers stays behind with Angus, but Race falls into step with me. "Do you have a list of suspects?" he asks as we emerge into the open space, where dozens of grimy, sweaty, injured individuals are still lying in rows, grateful to be breathing. Through the high glass walls, I see that the fire is well under control now, only faint wisps of gray smoke spiraling from inside the building. The hole I blasted in the wall is gaping now, because one of the fire trucks rammed right through the weakened barrier to get inside.

Leo is now hunched over Christina, and even from here, I can see their smiles. He's brightened this horrible day for her, and I'm grateful. She's not alone, and at the moment, she's not scared.

My eyes settle on Brayton, who's on his feet, his arm slung over Ellie's shoulders. Without thinking too much about it, I head over there, noting that Kellan is slowly walking along the rows of patients, the black light on, staring at their hands and shoes, looking for the incriminating fluorescence. Most people seem too thrashed to even notice him, which must come as a huge relief to poor Kellan. Brayton and Ellie eye him with suspicion, though.

I quicken my pace. Rufus is still sitting in his wheelchair, and Christina and Leo look up as I approach. Rufus sneers at Race. "Happy now? We're defenseless. Easy pickings."

Race regards him somberly, no doubt recalling all the

shouted accusations from Rufus during the board meeting last night. "I have over a hundred agents here, some of whom are gravely wounded. One of whom has just been shot in the back of the head. Angus has ordered the perimeter guards to forbid anyone to go in or out. We are caught here, just as you are, but the difference is that we are on unfamiliar ground and vastly outnumbered. Tell me the logic behind accusing the Core of creating this tragedy."

Rufus's face becomes a mottled maroon shade. "Tell me why we never had a fire in our factory until you H2 came onto our compound!"

"Maybe the H2 aren't the only ones here," I say.

"Everyone's been scanned," Brayton replies wearily, looking like he could collapse again at any moment. "Rufus does have a point. And now we all need to prioritize rebuilding and getting everything back online. All I've been hearing since I arrived on this compound is that we're under threat of imminent attack."

"We've already taken care of the bigger threat," says Leo, his pride glowing through the sooty smears on his skin. "We got the satellite defense shield working."

Race squeezes his eyes shut at Leo's careless disclosure.

"That's incredible," says Brayton. He looks at me. "I heard rumors you were having trouble accessing the satellites. It's a relief to hear they were wrong."

"But it won't help us much, considering there are already

scout ships *here*," growls Rufus. "Just like scanning everyone didn't help us. But go ahead and scan us all again if it makes you feel less helpless, boy. Oh, wait. I see Kellan's already at it." He glares at the young Black Box guard, who is trying and failing to look casual as he walks toward us, holding the wand light over every person he passes, whether they're upright or lying unconscious on the floor. I'm relieved to see that the wand light resembles the scanner from a distance. But then Kellan passes it over a Core agent, and the faint blue light stays blue. Rufus sits back. "That's not the scanner. What the hell is he doing?"

Leo's eyes go wide when he realizes it's the black light, and before I can stop him, he blurts, "Someone tried to steal the scanner again, didn't they? Did they get it?"

Race's jaw clenches, and he looks away. We're playing a game of secrecy, and Leo's giving out information left and right.

Rufus throws up his hands. "Now the scanner's been stolen? I didn't think I could be more ashamed of being part of The Fifty, but apparently it's still possible." His hands close over the wheels of his wheelchair. "I'm leaving."

Race steps in front of him. "The compound has been sealed until we find the scanner."

"I'm a patriarch of The Fifty!" Rufus shouts. "And no H2 will ever be my master!"

Kellan meets my eyes briefly as he raises the black light and approaches Ellie and Brayton, who looks weak but defiant as he turns his gaze to me. "This wand light test was your idea, wasn't it? What do you think you're going to find, Tate?"

"I'm sorry, Mr. Alexander," Kellan mumbles. "It's just a precaution. It won't take more than a second."

"We were right here when the lights went off," Brayton says quietly, his eyes locked on mine. "All of us were."

Kellan shrugs and moves closer. I stop breathing as the light slides over Brayton's fingers, twined with Ellie's. Nothing. Kellan shines it at their shoes. Nothing. Brayton and Ellie's other hands. Nothing.

I relax a little. Then Kellan moves to Rufus.

And as soon as the light hits the Bishop patriarch's chubby fingers, the fluorescence is nearly blinding. Kellan's eyes go wide. "Guards!" he shouts.

Four of them rush over before Rufus has a chance to move his wheelchair anywhere. "Take him to the designated holding area," Kellan says in a shaky voice as Rufus begins to rise from his chair. Kellan wrenches his weapon from its holster and points it at Rufus's head. "Don't push this now, Mr. Bishop. I don't have that scanner to see if you're really who you claim to be, so I'm going to have to judge by your level of cooperation."

"I was *right here*," growls Rufus. "This is outrageous."

"But you might be working with someone who wasn't," says Race. "And we know you tried to get into the room with the scanner." He nods at Rufus's hands.

Rufus's mouth snaps shut, and he sinks back into his chair.

His eyes glassy with rage, he allows the squad of guards to wheel him from the atrium. He holds his head high and looks neither left nor right. Everyone else watches in shock.

Movement to my left brings my attention back to our little group. Brayton is sagging against Ellie, who is struggling to hold him up. He weakly raises his head and looks at Race. "I need to talk to Angus," he says, his words garbled. "He doesn't . . ." His head lolls, and he groans.

"I need to get you back to your room," Ellie says firmly.

"Infirmary," he mumbles.

"There won't be any space in the infirmary. They're dealing with enough. But I can get Dr. Ackerman to—"

"I'm fine," Brayton mutters. "I can go by myself. You stay here and . . ."

She rolls her eyes. "Shut up, Dad." And with that, she guides him slowly toward the front exit, headed for the dorms.

"Maybe Christina should get back to the dorms, too," Leo says quietly.

She props herself up on an elbow. "No way," she rasps, looking at Manuel, who nods at her.

"What are you talking about?" I take a step closer to her, recognizing that look of determination on her face. "Remember an hour or so ago when you *almost died*?"

She pushes herself up to sitting. "Remember why we're here in the first place?" she says, rubbing her chest, which makes my fists clench.

Manuel walks over, each step looking like an effort. "We were onto something when the fire broke out," he says in a hoarse voice. "We need to see if any of the combat vehicles survived. We don't have the luxury of days, do we? We were told the Sicarii could attack at any time, and now that we've been decimated . . ." His look is hard—he's heard the tales of the scout ships, and he's seen the injuries and destruction they caused.

I put my hands up, sweat beading at my temples from the heat of my frustration. I need to get away from here. I need to punch something. All of this feels like my fault, but I can't fix it or control it. Everything is *so* far out of control, in fact, that I'm not even sure where to start. The factory is destroyed. The scanner is gone—and maybe Rufus Bishop is behind it. So many people are dead or hurt.

Where would all of us be if I'd never taken that scanner from my dad's lab?

It feels like a great chasm has opened in front of me, threatening to swallow me whole.

"Tate."

My attention snaps back to Race. "What?"

"We have things to do." He inclines his head toward the elevator, guiding me away from Leo, Christina, and Manuel, who are already talking among themselves about how they're going to reenter the factory.

"We need to post guards around any terminal that can

access the satellites," I say quietly. "Leo just announced to the entire atrium that the shield is live. If there's really a saboteur—"

"It's done," says Race. "I did it before the fire was even under control."

"Good." Of course, if those scout ships attack, even that might not help. If the Sicarii can gain control of this compound, they could take the shield down themselves, opening the door once again for a massive invasion. "Rufus was right about one thing—we're sitting ducks."

"Then we should get to work." He moves toward the elevator.

"On what?" I snap, staying where I am. I'm so tired. I've done everything I knew to do. And we're still facing defeat.

He hooks his fingers around my elbow and leads me toward the elevator. "On figuring out why the Sicarii want the scanner."

"Seeing as it's been stolen—how do you propose we do that? Do you really think Rufus will talk?"

"Let Angus deal with him for the moment. He's well-equipped to handle that, and he'll call if he makes headway with Rufus. What he can't do is figure out our technology." He presses the DOWN button, and we wait for the elevator door to open. "Your father built the scanner and the satellite system—and he did it by using the wreckage of the spaceship."

The one thing I haven't explored yet. A reluctant, grim smile creeps onto my face. Maybe that's where we'll find the answers that will save us. Maybe that's where I'll discover the key to all my dad's plans. Maybe that's where I'll find him again. "Okay. Let's go take a look."

SIXTEEN

AS WE ENTER THE ENORMOUS VAULT-LIKE STORAGE
room where the wreckage is stored, I talk to Race about what
I suspect. "This stuff was stowed on the defense ship that escaped the H2 planet, but I think the Sicarii must have gotten
some demonstration of what the scanner tech could do when
Congers's ancestor went to that final meeting. Congers himself
said as much a few days ago. It can be made into a weapon."

"True, but maybe it wasn't that powerful, or else his ancestor would have walked away," says Race as we flick on the
lights.

"We don't know that. It could have been so powerful that
he couldn't control it, or that it took him out, too."

Race peers down at the twisted hunks of wreckage. "You
think they're after the scanner here because they know exactly
what it can do."

"And maybe because they want to use it against us."

I kneel next to the biggest piece and brush some of the dust from its surface.

"Then I hope Rufus Bishop and whoever's working with him hid the scanner well," he says in a grim voice.

I turn to him. "Do you really think he's responsible for the theft?"

"Aren't you the one who laid the fluorescent powder trap?" he says, his red eyes glinting with something like amusement.

"Yeah, but Rufus was in the atrium the entire time."

"That doesn't mean he didn't scope it out prior to the factory fire."

"I know, but . . ."—I can't believe I'm saying this—"I think Rufus is a bigoted, paranoid asshole. But I also think he's extremely intelligent and has his own code of honor."

Race's mouth tightens like he's about to laugh. "Well said. So you think a Sicarii took it? Or do you think he *is* a Sicarii?"

I press my knuckles into the tile floor. "No idea. How are they here, if we've scanned everyone repeatedly and no one is orange?"

"Perhaps Dr. Shirazi will have some answers after she completes the autopsies."

I nod and return to my inspection of the wreckage. Most of it looks like ordinary-yet-severely-damaged, high-tech gadgetry, in that there are screens and chips and wires. "Maybe we should pull some of these chips out and see if we have any way to interface with them."

Race's eyebrow arches. "It's quite advanced."

I mirror his expression. "And yet somehow, my dad built an entire satellite shield from it. And look." I point to one open control panel. There are fingerprints along its edge, and inside . . . "It looks like something's been removed." There are ports within the compartment, little odd-shaped holes that are strangely familiar.

"The scanner has ports that looked just like those," I blurt out as the connection is forged inside my mind.

Race leans in, squinting. "You're sure?"

"Fairly. I thought the ports on the side of the scanner were USB, but they weren't shaped quite right. There were three of them, though." I jab my finger at each of the three holes where something used to connect.

"So your father removed the chips," Race says slowly, clearly turning over possibilities in his mind. "And the scanner has ports identical to these—"

"I said it looked like they were, but—"

He holds up his hands, granting me my uncertainty. "It had ports similar to those. So if we knew what they were—or if we could find the missing pieces that fit into them—we could figure out what the scanner's full capabilities are."

"Which would be awesome if we actually had possession of the scanner," I say with a humorless laugh. I move to a crumpled piece of debris as tall as my hip and touch one of the chips inside a gaping crack in the panel. As soon as I do, the hunk of metal scrapes along the floor and falls back before I can catch it. The thing splinters, spilling and scattering a dozen different components and chips that had been nestled within.

I go to pick up a few of them, but Race grabs my wrist. "Don't." He nods at one of the chips, which is oozing something viscous and brown onto the tile. "We have no idea what that is."

"My mom can help us figure it out," I say, feeling my muscles tense with energy and curiosity. A clue. A lead. Something to pin my shredded hopes on. We grab a broom and dustpan and carefully scrape the chips and the ooze onto the pan, then carry it to the morgue.

"Mom?" I call, immediately recognizing the whine of a bone saw coming from behind the closed doors of her autopsy room. When he hears it, Race winces and tells me he'll wait outside.

A moment later, the whine stops abruptly, and my mother leans out of the chamber. She's wearing goggles and gloves. A face mask is tucked beneath her chin. "Tate," she says wearily. "I've just gotten started. Dr. Ackerman was going to assist, but once again he's got his hands full."

I glance around, noting the hum of a mass spectrometer against the wall. "Are you sampling those anomalies? Any signs of a parasite or anything like that?"

"I have a handful of odd cellular and chromosomal findings, but that's it. I've done the thoracic and abdominal dissections.

No findings that indicate parasitic activity." Her lips press together for a moment. "In fact, all three of them seem perfectly healthy apart from the bullet wounds," she says in an unsteady voice, reminding me that two of the men she's been cutting open had been her friends for years.

"What are the odd findings? You mean the weird secretory glands in their skin? Did the other two bodies have them, too?" I ask, trying to bring her to a more objective place, where she can think of them as a collection of lab results instead of dead comrades, at least for the time being.

She switches into scientist mode quickly. "All three bodies had the additional secretory glands. I haven't had time to further examine their function, though. But I've confirmed the DNA profiles as Charles and George, so even if the Sicarii somehow took them over, it didn't change their basic genetic makeup. However, their chromosomes are somewhat strange. The telomeres are unusually long, and their levels of telomerase are off the charts."

"Telomeres . . . like, the ends of their chromosomes?"

"Correct. The parts that protect the DNA sequences from degrading or mutating."

"Aren't they associated with aging or something?" It was all over the news last year, the idea that telomerase, this enzyme that causes those telomere endcaps to lengthen, might slow the aging process.

"That's the theory. As chromosomes replicate, they degrade,

resulting in a loss of genetic information and integrity. Telomeres keep that from happening as quickly, but they shorten over time, and when they get too short, the cell stops dividing and dies. Lack of telomerase and short telomeres are common in people with various premature aging disorders."

"And both George and Willetts have a lot of telomerase."

Her dark eyes are steady on mine. "The deceased Core agent does as well. Far beyond the normal range. Basically . . . immortal."

My mouth drops open. "Like, they'd stopped aging?"

She nods slowly. "I've just started the intracranial examination. Perhaps I'll find some answers there."

She's cutting their skulls open to look at their brains, hence the sound of the bone saw. "I just wanted to drop these components off," I say. "They're from the ship wreckage. I'm wondering if you can take a look at these?" I hold up the dustpan full of oozing chips.

She frowns and blows a wisp of hair upward, away from her face. "When I'm finished."

"I think these might help us figure out what the scanner was supposed to be used for," I tell her. "And what Dad meant when he said it was the key to our survival."

She eyes the chips as I set the dustpan on the stainless steel lab table in the center of the room. "He might not have meant the specific device. He may have been referring to the overall tech—"

"No," I say firmly, my throat getting tight. "I was there. I know what he said, Mom."

She stares at me for a few seconds, and then the lines in her expression soften. "Okay. When I find a stopping point, I'll take a look."

I thank her and join Race in the hallway. He's leaning against the wall with his eyes closed, and I wonder if he's slept at all since arriving on the compound just over twenty-four hours ago. As much as I want to hate him, like Rufus, I feel a begrudging respect for him and the pressures he's been under. He's not the cold, merciless machine I thought he was when he was chasing us to get the scanner, and I understand his desperation now. He also cares about his agents, and he seems to regret what happened with my dad. I wonder what Dad would think if he knew we were working together now, if he'd be furious or if he'd understand that I have no choice.

It's one more thing I'll never know about Frederick Archer. Race opens his eyes when he hears me coming and pushes himself off the wall. "How are the autopsies going?"

I fill him in about the secretory glands my mom discovered in the men's skin, as well as the strange telomere and telomerase findings.

"But no signs of the parasite?" he asks.

"None."

His jaw clenches. "So we still have no idea how they move from host to host."

"Mom's working on it. She said she'd take a break to look at those chips, though. Even if we can't figure out the Sicarii, maybe we can find a way to beat them."

He crosses his arms over his chest once we reach the elevator banks. "We could do that a lot faster if we actually had the scanner."

"Maybe we should go check how Angus is doing with Rufus," I suggest.

It feels a little weird as we stride down the administrative hall together, me and Race Lavin, teaming up to fight a common enemy. I mean, on Thursday morning—just *three* days ago—I was choking him out on the floor of a Walmart. But he's a calm, steady presence at my side, and right now, that makes me feel less alone in all of this.

We find Angus in the CFO office, mostly by tracking the hoarse barks of Rufus's outrage.

"Did he confess?" Race asks as we enter. Rufus is nowhere in sight, but I can hear his grumbling coming from an office down the hall.

Angus glances at us and shakes his head, which is when I notice Congers across the room, tight-lipped and grim as he talks into a com device. My stomach drops. "Is he talking to the defense stations? Have they spotted scout ships?"

"No, thank God. No sign of them," says Angus.

"Yet," says Race.

Angus gives Congers a concerned look. "We're bringing in

another suspect. Rufus said he only approached and touched the keypad on the secure room after seeing someone else there."

Race looks back and forth between Angus and Congers. The tension in this room is stifling. "Who?"

"My son," Congers snaps before returning to his conversation. He's telling his agents to stand down, and he's obviously getting some pushback.

"If he really saw someone in the hallway who shouldn't have been there, why didn't he report it immediately?" I ask.

"Because of the fire in the factory!" Rufus roars from the other room, his gruff voice accompanied by the rattling of what I can only assume are handcuffs. Rufus must be close to having a stroke.

"Weren't you working with Rufus on the security system?" I ask Congers as he ends his phone call.

He nods. "Just before the fire broke out, Rufus was supposed to be checking the surge protection in the circuit breakers along this hallway."

"Making it either the perfect opportunity or an unfortunate coincidence?" Race says.

Angus scratches at his beard. He's got grime smeared across his shirt, and his sleeves are rolled up, revealing his massive, freckled forearms. "I'd been in here all morning since you put that stuff on the door. But maybe five minutes before the fire, I'd left to go to lunch, and when I reached the atrium, I sent two guards from the main entrance back to my office to guard the scanner. It couldn't have been unguarded for more than a minute or two."

Kellan walks in with two other guards, surrounding a cuffed Graham Congers, who is stone-faced and pale. "Sir, I did what you asked. The guards searched Mr. Bishop's quarters, and they're in the process of searching the Core agents' quarters as well. We haven't found anything yet."

That's the reason Congers was telling them to stand down. No doubt the Core is pissed at having suspicion cast on them again. The whole thing is exhausting and frustrating. Someone has the scanner, and I'm desperate to have it back in my hands. It's a vulnerable feeling, not knowing who the enemy is. For all we know, Rufus is being controlled by something that's infiltrated his body and mind.

Kellan jerks his head toward Graham and touches the black light wand at his belt. "His hands were covered in the vitamin solution. Bottom of his shoes, too."

"Because I was here and touched the keypad," Graham snaps. "I told you that already."

"Why?" Congers demands. "Why were you even in this office?" He looks utterly disgusted with his son, and my gut clenches.

Graham turns to his father, their gray-green eyes locking in a silent battle. "I wanted to catch whoever was trying to steal the device," he says. "And I saw someone go in after Mr.

McClaren walked out." He looks away, swallowing hard under the anger in his father's expression.

"Did you recognize him?" Angus asks, his gaze slanting toward the office where Rufus is being held.

Graham looks at me and then at Angus. "Yeah. He's one of you guys. Pale-blond hair."

"Brayton?" I ask.

Graham shrugs. "I don't know his name. He's a middle-aged guy. He was starting to punch in a code when I peeked in here, but he stopped when he saw me and took off." He points to a back hallway across the suite. "The guy was sprinting. I was suspicious."

"Where does that hallway lead?" Congers asks.

"To some other offices, an emergency exit to the building, and another hallway leading to the main corridor," says Graham. "After I checked to make sure the storage room door was still locked, I went back there. That's where I was when I heard the explosion. But the blond guy was long gone."

Angus's brow furrows. "Brayton is very ill. The last thing he can do right now is sprint."

"He looked pretty damn healthy at breakfast this morning," Congers says in a hard voice. "And you did deny him access to anything but janitorial duty, I believe. Plenty of reason for him to be upset."

"He was definitely out of breath before he went into the factory," I add. "But . . . his hands and shoes were clean when

Kellan scanned them after the fire. No fluorescence. And if the timing is as you describe, he would have run straight from the hallway into the atrium, because the alarms went off a minute or so later."

"Not to mention that I saw him come out of the elevators when the alarm went off," calls Rufus. "I hate the bastard, but I can tell you he didn't come out of this hallway."

I rub at an aching spot on my temple. "We can't forget that both Brayton and Rufus were in the atrium when the actual theft occurred. Even if either of them was trying to take it before, neither could have shot the guards and stolen the device."

"Which means we may be dealing with a conspiracy," says Congers.

"I had nothing to do with this," Graham says quietly. "You know I'd never do anything like this." He starts to take a step toward Congers, but the Black Box guards grab his arms. Graham grimaces. "*Dad*. You know I wouldn't!"

Congers's gaze snaps to his son. "You didn't follow orders." He looks away quickly, so he doesn't see Graham's shoulders hunch forward, like he's been punched in the stomach. "Do what you need to do," Congers says to Kellan.

Kellan and his guards lead a shell-shocked Graham to a separate office to question him further while Angus returns his attention to the surveillance footage, which is full of gaps. His meaty fists are white-knuckled with bottled-up anger.

I take a step back, the same frustration and fatigue rolling over me. "I need to go find Christina," I say. "I'll check back with you guys later."

Congers barely acknowledges me because his cell phone is ringing, but Race makes as if he's going to follow me out. "They were going to try to salvage the combat vehicles, weren't they?" he asks me. "I was hoping we could take another look at the plans and the actual vehicles, in case your father used some of the same wreckage components."

But as we reach the door, Congers calls out, lifting his chin away from the phone at his ear. "Lavin. Get back here."

Race waves me on. I head down the hall and into the atrium, which is quiet now that all the patients have been moved. The acrid stench of burning still hangs heavy in the air, though, and the smoke outside lends a grayish cast to the dwindling daylight as I emerge into the open courtyard between the main building and the factory. A large squad of uninjured workers is busy clearing out debris from the factory floor. Then I hear a cheer from the parking lot, so at odds with the grim scene in front of me. I look out to the lot beyond the burned-out factory, and there's a crowd clustered around what is unmistakably a row of combat vehicles. Six of them. I jog over to see more workers tinkering with them, wiping their shiny exteriors, welding panels, oiling the rails of the autocannons. Arrayed in front of the vehicles, a few feet beyond their hoods, are weapons consoles much like the one I used to blast a hole in the factory wall this afternoon. They haven't been placed inside the vehicles yet and are hooked up to huge generators rumbling off to our right.

"Tate!" Christina's hoarse voice is like pure relief to me, and I turn to see her walking toward me. Her eyes are red and swollen, and she's rubbing at her throat, but still she looks happy. "Wait until you see this. Manuel is a genius."

Standing head and shoulders taller than the cluster of folks near the consoles, Manuel blushes at her praise. "We were able to salvage these six from the factory floor, and we gassed them up and got them out here so we could complete assembly as quickly as possible. I've set up an interactive simulation using the available information about the Sicarii scout ships. It's based on witness reports from Mr. Congers, Dr. Shirazi, and some of the other agents, but it was the best I could do. So as my volunteers do the simulation, I'm going to gather data on the system capabilities so I can calibrate these babies before we install them."

He gestures at Christina and Leo—and Daniel Sung, who is among a small group of Core agents who has joined the effort to salvage the combat vehicles. "Leo said you got some kind of satellite shield up to protect the planet," Manuel says to me, lowering his voice. "I want to do my part to protect that shield. Which means protecting Black Box."

"Thanks," I say. "I had no idea you guys would get this far so soon."

"We're not done yet," Sung says as he flexes his fingers.

His dark brown eyes shine with eagerness as he gazes at the weapons console in front of him. Right now he looks less like a disciplined young agent and more like a caffeine-fueled gamer about to try out the newest *Call of Duty*. "You want us to hop in and just start shooting, Manuel?"

Manuel chuckles. "You can try. It's harder than it looks."

Leo, Sung, and Christina get into three of the four gunner pits, settling in on the swiveling seats. Leo's spinning like a top, but Christina sees me eyeing the fourth console. "Hey, Manuel, can Tate give it a try?"

He shrugs. "I don't see why not."

Leo snorts. "He already knows how to use them, as evidenced by the massive hole in the factory wall."

"What am I supposed to do with those?" I point to the two padded circles that look like automated blood-pressure cuffs positioned in front of the cannon control sticks. "Didn't exactly have time to figure it out during the fire."

"They have these sensors in them that detect muscle contractions. Not exactly sure why." Manuel's black hair falls over his brow as he bows his head. "We're following your dad's plans exactly. I'm still trying to figure out what those lenses do. He didn't leave a lot of explanations."

That's true in so many ways, and once again, my chest aches. "I know. I'm sorry—"

"No, don't be. Your dad was a genius. I want to do justice to his designs, because, man, they are brilliant." Manuel pats the hood of one of the vehicles. "I was thinking we should call them Archers. You think he would have liked that?"

The ache turns to a sharp pang. *Would* he have liked that? I return Manuel's smile. "Yeah," I say, my voice catching. "I think he would have thought that was cool."

"Archers it is," says Manuel, grinning. "Let's see what they can do."

With the Archers looming behind us, crawling with workers racing against the clock to get this tiny assault force battle-ready, I climb into the gunner pit. We all settle our arms in the cuffs and fiddle with the stick controls, which swivel along a circular track, too, that's set closer to the view screens. Once we're all in, Manuel fires up the consoles. On my viewing screen a shockingly familiar shape appears, one of the hovering obelisk ships of the Sicarii.

"If you see that round hole in the bottom half open up," says Manuel, "watch out. We're hoping the armor can withstand a hit, but Dr. Shirazi said it turned her armored minivan into a crushed soda can with one shot."

"Let's see if we can't take them out, then," mutters Sung, his chair swiveling, his eyes riveted to the shimmering obelisk on the screen. He jams his thumb on a button. On our screens, we see a blast of light fly at the Sicarii ship, but it spins out of the way.

We all start shooting, but as it turns out, Manuel is extremely good at creating simulations. The alien ships move just like the ones I've seen, fluid and lethal. Our consoles bounce and jitter as the program moves us across all types of terrain. We can't control the exact direction or speed of the vehicle, because we're gunners—not drivers. It takes two to operate an Archer. And it's a good thing this is a simulation, because if this were real life, we'd be toast. Our shots fly wide, short, wild, high, *off*. Our consoles are rigged to shut down once we've taken three hits from a Sicarii ship, and I've taken two before I know what's happening. My arms are sweating inside the cuffs, and I'm fighting to get my seat to swivel.

"These things have eye tracking!" Sung calls out. "It brightens the part of the screen you're focusing on."

Manuel scribbles something into a tablet, smiling. "Cool."

I growl with frustration as I try to turn my seat. I'm a fairly accurate shot, but only when I can aim my guns. This console works as a three-hundred-sixty-degree display, and I can't get my freaking chair to spin. One of the Sicarii ships on my screen keeps flying to my starboard and firing from there. "You're going to have to oil these seats, Manuel," I call out. "It's fighting me."

"You're fighting *it*," says Christina as hers turns smoothly. I glance over to see her eyes focused on the screen as she speaks, like she does this kind of thing every day. "I think the cuffs are connected to the seat swivel. Stop trying to control it yourself and let it do some of the work."

Boom. She hits a Sicarii ship right in its artillery hatch, and it explodes on my screen. Behind me, a handful of workers let out a cheer.

A few minutes later, I'm out of the simulation after taking the requisite number of hits. Leo, Sung, and Christina battle it out while other factory workers and Core agents gather around to watch. Sung's movements are a little jerky, and I think he's doing the same thing I was, trying to force the chair to swivel instead of letting the cuffs detect his movements before he consciously thinks about it. But he's a great shot, and he's the one who figures out that the eye tracker is how to achieve weapon lock on a target.

It doesn't save him, though. Soon he's out, too, and it's down to Christina and Leo. Both of them are grinning, swiveling and firing both of their guns at once while they taunt each other like brother and sister. Leo's faster, but Christina's more accurate. No matter where those ships move, she tracks them, and she gets more deadly the longer she works at it. The spectators start to make bets on whether Christina or Leo will stay in the simulation longer. It's a badly needed few minutes of lightness and even fun in what has been a day full of tragedy, and I think everybody needed a break from the tension. And as I watch Christina and Leo take on those silent, smooth scout ships, I find myself wondering if even six Archers might be enough to make a difference.

"This looks like fun," says a soft voice just behind me.

I turn to see Ellie Alexander, her white-blond hair tucked

behind her ears, watching the simulations. She's taken a shower and cleaned off all the soot, but it wasn't enough to wash away the heavy weight that seems to be pressing on her. Rufus gave her a pretty hard time earlier, but the worst thing she's done is to be loyal to her dad, and I can't blame her for that, even if I don't like him at all. "Hey," I say. "How's Brayton? Still feverish?"

She gives me a pained look. "He's just worn out. These past few days have been awful for him." She looks around, noting the hulk of the factory behind us, and hugs herself, rubbing her arms. "But I guess that's true for everyone here."

I nod. "Just so you know, a Core agent is telling people he saw your dad in the administrative hallway just before the scanner was stolen. He said Brayton ran when he realized he was being watched."

She scoffs. "Does my dad really look like he could run anywhere? He's completely drained." Her fingers are bloodless as they clutch her biceps. She's so protective of him. "Don't tell me—they're going to search his quarters." She rolls her eyes. "They won't find anything except painkillers. He's being blamed for everything, when all he wanted to do was regain everybody's trust."

"That's going to take longer than a day, after what he did." I say it gently, but I have to be honest with her.

She presses her lips together and stares at the blacktop. "Everything takes longer than it should," she whispers.

I take a step back. As much as she needs it, I'm not the right person to stand here and sympathize with her over how her dad's been mistreated. He brought it on himself, and no matter how hard he might be trying to make things right, I still don't trust him. I believe Graham about seeing Brayton in Angus's office before the fire. I just have no idea what Brayton was up to—and I hope Angus is planning to bring him in for questioning.

"Look, Ellie, I need to help with getting these vehicles up and running. I hope Brayton feels better," I say. When she gives me a nod, I retreat inside the back of one of the Archers as Ellie steps forward to watch Christina and Leo shooting down simulated spaceships.

The interior of the vehicle smells of oil and iron. There's a large open space where the weapons console will fit. Scraping above me draws my eyes upward in time to see two women lowering a giant lens over the hole cut in the roof between the rails of the autocannon. It fits into the opening with a muffled *thunk,* and their faces and bodies above the glass lens are instantly distorted, suddenly appearing miles away instead of only a few feet. I slide my finger along the curved underside. "What are these for, Dad?" I whisper.

"Tate!" My mother's voice is so sharp and urgent that I jump up and nearly crash my skull into the thick glass lens.

"Yeah?" I climb out of the Archer to see her jogging toward me.

Her dark hair flies around her face as she reaches me. "Race said you were here. I found something. I'm going to tell the others, but I wanted you to be part of it."

For a moment, we stare at each other, and I realize that she's deliberately including me. Not because I have any real authority, but because she wanted to show that she respects me. "Thanks, Mom."

A shadow of a smile crosses her face. "You earned it, Tate," she says softly, then heads for the atrium, and I follow her all the way to the administrative wing. By the time she reaches Angus's office, her cheeks are pink and she's out of breath.

"The DNA doesn't match," she announces.

Angus, Race, and Congers, who had all been clustered around Congers's cell phone, which I assume is on speakerphone, turn to her.

"Elaborate," says Congers, holding the phone in front of him. "We have Dr. Okpara on the line from our Washington lab."

Mom glances at the phone and hesitates only a moment before continuing. "DNA from tissue samples matches what we had on file for George Fisher, Charles Willetts, and Devon Kerstein. But samples from their brains don't match at all."

I blink at her. "Like . . . their bodies were actually them, but their brains belonged to someone else?"

She gives me an odd look, and I can tell her scientist's mind is struggling to find an alternative explanation. Congers looks down at his phone. "Did you hear that?" he says to it. "Now repeat what you just said to me, Dr. Okpara."

A tinny male voice on the other end begins to speak. "I have just completed an autopsy on a partially decomposed body found one day ago in the basement of the building at the University of Virginia, where Dr. Willetts resided. DNA samples—*all* DNA samples, mind you—confirm that the body lying on my exam table is, in fact, Charles Willetts."

Congers raises his gaze from the phone to look at my mother. His voice is dead calm as he says, "So who do you think you have on *your* exam table, Dr. Shirazi?"

SEVENTEEN

"UNTIL ABOUT FIFTEEN MINUTES AGO, I WOULD HAVE told you it was definitely Charles," my mother says slowly. "But at the moment, I'm unsure."

"So we have one body that appears to be Charles's in Washington, and another here that is . . . mostly Charles," says Race.

"There are two of them," I mutter, my brain churning to make sense of it. "I wish we could scan the body in DC."

"We already know the one in our possession scanned orange," says Mom. Her brow furrows, and she leans forward to speak into Congers's phone. "Any unusual findings in your autopsy, Doctor?"

"Only that it was unrecognizable as Charles Willetts by simple visual exam," says Dr. Okpara. "It was bound and hidden in a large antique trunk that was discovered when agents searched the basement. At first it seemed like an unrelated crime, because no one in the building had been reported missing and no one could provide a visual ID, but the body was brought to my lab anyway."

"Could they not tell who it was because it was decomposed?" asks Angus, looking faintly sick.

"No, Dr. Willetts hadn't been dead longer than twenty-four hours, though there were indications that he had been in the trunk for a good deal longer than that."

Angus pales. None of us want to contemplate what "indications" those might be.

"Oh, God," my mom whispers. "Tate, if he was in the basement for days—"

"Then who were we staying with in Virginia?"

She puts the back of her hand to her mouth, then speaks to the phone again. "If he hadn't been dead for long, why was he unrecognizable?"

"Charles Willetts was sixty-three years old at the time of his death," says Dr. Okpara. "The body in the trunk appeared to be decades older than that. It's hard to estimate, but I had thought I was doing an autopsy on a centenarian."

Angus's eyes widen. "He looked over a hundred years old? Why would that happen?"

Mom and I stare at each other. "Did you do any chromosomal analysis?" she asks in a weak voice. "Telomere length and telomerase levels specifically?"

Race, Angus, and Congers all peer at her with keenly

curious expressions while Dr. Okpara huffs into the phone. "Not yet," he says. "I was just—"

"Do it," snaps Congers. "Do it now and call me as soon as you have results." He ends the connection, and his hand falls to his side. "Now explain why that's important, Dr. Shirazi."

Mom explains the telomerase findings in the bodies she's autopsied as I ponder the fact that two versions of Charles's body have been found, and one of them was tied up and stuffed in a trunk in the basement of the building where we were staying with Charles a few days ago.

"There are two of them," I mutter, rubbing my temple. "One with lots of telomerase—who you said had stopped aging . . . and one who looked over a hundred years old. Mom"— she pauses in her explanation and looks over at me—"what if the Sicarii aren't parasites that invade a body? What if they leech something *from* the body?"

Race's eyebrows shoot upward. "How would they do that?"

"I don't know." Though I'm betting those extra secretory glands Mom discovered have something to do with it. "I'm making a guess based on what we know, and one of the things we know is we have two copies of Charles, one of which has different DNA in his brain, and one of which is prematurely aged . . ." My heart pounds. "Brayton," I say in a choked whisper, backing toward the door. "It's Brayton."

Everyone looks at me like they haven't quite connected the pieces. "He was unaccounted for a few days before he arrived here at Black Box," I say. "He said he'd been in police custody and then traveling to Chicago, but we really don't know, and his own daughter couldn't reach him. And he's been sick. Thrashed. Looking—"

"Like he's aged ten years in the last ten days," says Angus. "But he scanned blue every time."

"What if he smuggled something else in, though?" I ask quietly. "Something that looked exactly like him . . . only healthier?"

"Like when we saw him at breakfast," confirms Angus.

"This makes my son's report of him sprinting away from this hallway while Rufus saw him get out of the elevators a lot more credible," says Congers.

"It also explains why Brayton's hands were free of the B12 residue even after Graham saw him touching the keypad," says Race. "It wasn't actually him."

My mother shifts from foot to foot, like she wants to get back to her lab. "We may have a Sicarii on the compound after all."

Race and I move for the door at the same time. From behind us, I hear Congers and Angus barking into their respective phones, mobilizing agents and guards to patrol the compound in search of Brayton Alexander. We sprint down the hall and out of the main building, taking in the distant sounds of cheering still coming from the side lot where the Archers are sitting. "If Brayton is working with the Sicarii, he could have given it all kinds of information," I say as we run toward the residential building. "He could have given it everything it needed to sabotage the factory floor and compromise the surveillance systems. And maybe that's why the scout ships haven't attacked yet—they had someone on the inside working to get the scanner."

"Why would he help them at all, though?" says Race between breaths. "Spite seems like a poor reason to facilitate a hostile alien invasion."

A man staggers out of the residential building through a side entrance. The sinking sun illuminates his dull blond hair and sallow face. Race and I run toward him and stop a few feet away. Race draws his gun and disengages the safety, but he keeps his finger off the trigger. "Mr. Alexander, we have some questions for you. Assuming you are, in fact, yourself."

Brayton, the circles under his eyes a hideous purple, the lines around his mouth deep creases, rubs his wrists as he works to hold himself upright. "I'm ready to answer any questions you have, but first—Ellie. I need to find Ellie." He sinks to his knees. There are angry red welts on his wrists—like he was tied up. *Just like Charles Willetts.*

Race holds the gun to Brayton's temple, and Brayton doesn't even flinch. "Did you allow a Sicarii to take on your appearance?"

"Did I allow it?" He lets out a hoarse chuckle. "He found me in Princeton."

"*Who* found you?"

"He said he was a Core agent who wanted to negotiate a truce with The Fifty, and he had identification. We went to a safe house to discuss what we could do for each other." He closes his eyes and sways in place like he's about to go down. "That's all I remember from that night. And when I woke up, he . . . looked just like me. He told me he was part of an alien race, very advanced, and that they want to make contact with Earth. But he said he had to have the scanner."

"*How* did he take on your appearance?" I ask.

Brayton shudders. "He puts his hands on me." His face contorts with disgust, and he sinks to the pavement. "This . . . stuff oozes out of his skin."

Now the strange secretory glands my mom discovered in the Sicarii bodies totally make sense. "How long does it take?"

"No idea about the first time," he says, lowering his head until his cheek is against concrete. "But he's done it every day since. It takes several minutes." He winces. "And each time, I feel worse," he whispers.

Each time, it leeched more telomerase from Brayton's body, stealing years from his life.

Race stares coldly down at the crumpled man on the sidewalk. "Did you smuggle it onto this compound?"

Brayton nods. "You have to understand. All it wanted was the scanner. It promised me that I would be their emissary when they began official communication with our planet." He lets out a wretched, agonized sob. "None of this was supposed to happen. He said their intentions were peaceful, and he only wanted the technology. He said it would help the three species understand one another, but that it could be very dangerous if it wasn't secured before they revealed themselves to the other inhabitants of this planet, especially the Core, who would treat them as enemies unless the first contact was handled carefully. He said he was trying to *prevent* loss of life!"

"And you believed him?" Race asks.

I tilt my head. "At the time Brayton brought the Sicarii onto the compound, he had none of the information we had, like what happened on the H2 planet. How they took over."

Brayton raises his head, but it looks like it takes a lot of effort. "I heard everything when I got here, but the Sicarii said it was H2 lies." His watery blue eyes peer at Race with suspicion. "He said you destroyed his home planet before coming here."

Race glares at him. "Your misplaced trust in an alien who— by your own report—stole your appearance and hurt you in the process has resulted in heavy casualties."

Brayton grimaces at the gun still leveled at his head. "I wanted to tell Angus everything. I asked to speak with him earlier, and I would have—"

"Too late." Race looks more than willing to shoot him. "Does the Sicarii have the scanner now?"

"He does."

"Did you tell it the satellite shield was live?" Race barks, and Brayton nods. I've never seen Race show this kind of emotion, but suddenly I'm wondering if he's going to execute Brayton right here. Maybe it's a good thing that I can already hear the running footsteps of a cadre of guards headed in our direction. "Where is the Sicarii now?" he shouts.

Brayton shakes his head.

Race's finger closes over the trigger. "Where is the Sicarii?" he roars.

"Kill me," says Brayton, rolling onto his back. "But then find Ellie."

"She's fine," I say. "She's with a bunch of factory workers testing the few Archers that . . ." I trail off as Brayton points to the residential building.

"He took her away," he whispers. "She thought he was me. You have to find her."

My stomach drops. "Race. We may be looking for the wrong person."

"Did it take her appearance?" he shouts, leaning down and pressing the barrel of his weapon against Brayton's forehead.

Brayton closes his eyes, sprawled on the pavement, looking like a drained, exhausted old man. "He took her away," he says again. "He said I was useless. And he was right. I couldn't protect her."

But less than an hour ago, I was talking to Ellie . . .

"Shit," I snap. "The Sicarii is with the Archers!" I take off, my feet pounding the pavement as I fly toward the side lot, dread beating a pulse in my head as pieces of a horrible, devastating puzzle click into place. The Sicarii stole the scanner. It knows our satellite shield is live and controlled within this compound. If it gets out or signals its friends that it has what it came here for, there's nothing stopping them from coming in and destroying us.

Race is a few paces behind me. He calls out to the guards to secure Brayton and search the residential building for the real Ellie as I veer to the left and bolt for the side lot. Workers are busy with the interiors of the Archers, and in just the past hour, they've loaded the consoles into the heavy vehicles and are installing the systems. Several others are rolling carts carrying the live ammunition toward the Archers, and some of the workers are loading the cannons. The sun is setting, and the glitter of the massive lenses beneath the overhead stadium lights is nearly blinding, but so are the smiles on every face as they prepare these powerful machines to defend the compound.

No one realizes the enemy is right next to them.

Christina, Leo, Manuel, and Ellie are standing together at the rear of one of the Archers, watching as a worker secures the console to the floor. Christina sees me first, and her face lights up, but when she takes a good look at me, her smile dies. Ellie frowns as she sees Christina's reaction, and her head whips in my direction. I don't have to say a word. Her mouth goes tight, and she takes a step backward, looking around, assessing options. Leo's brow furrows, and he looks back and forth between me and Ellie.

Ellie darts behind one of the Archers.

"Stop her!" Race shouts from behind me, but the crowd of workers is too stunned to move quickly. They look around as if wondering who Race wants them to stop.

An engine roars. The last Archer on the line rolls forward. Leo sprints for it just as it snaps the cables tethering its undercarriage. "No, Leo!" Christina and I shout at the same time.

Leo's fingers skim the side panel of the massive armored vehicle as it lurches forward, trying to get a grip on it, but he stumbles when it zooms away. I change direction quickly, sprinting for the Archer that had been next to it, diving into the back and feeling the console rattle when I push past it to get to the driver's seat. The gunner's pit isn't bolted down yet. It may not even be connected. As I look above me and notice that this one doesn't even have a lens in place, I realize I may have picked the wrong ride. This one's not battle-ready. No time to go for another, though—I can already hear a distant explosion. Cursing, I throw myself into the driver's chair, twisting the square key in the ignition as I do. The engine roars.

At least there's gas in the tank. I shove it into gear and shudder with the deep vibrations as the Archer rolls forward. Through the tiny windshield, I can see that the Ellie-Sicarii has made it halfway across the compound.

And it's firing its hood cannon at the nearest perimeter defense station. I thunder after Ellie while I scan the controls in front of me, looking for a way to fire my own hood cannon.

"Damn it!" a voice shouts from a few feet behind me, star-tling the living shit out of me.

"What the hell, Leo?" I yell, jumping a curb and skimming around the lake that covers the eastern quarter of the compound.

He must have dived into the back right as I took off, and now he's squatting in the entrance to the cramped driver's compartment. "I wanted to be your gunner, but the weapons console isn't hooked up back there!"

One of my wheels rolls over the side of a boulder as I try to avoid hitting a tree. "Is there a harness back there? Buckle yourself in!"

He doesn't respond, and I focus again on reaching Ellie. All I can see is the rear of her vehicle—and then the bright burst of fire that zings from her hood cannon toward the perimeter station set into the inner edge of the mile-wide crater's rim. The station explodes in flames, debris and bodies flung out-ward and colliding with the ground a few hundred feet below. I can barely hear Leo's shouts of rage and horror over my own.

Ellie makes a sharp turn just in time to avoid colliding with the crater wall and roars toward the next station, only a half a mile away. I veer to the left and head after her. Movement on that side draws my attention, and I see another Archer in pursuit of her as well.

The autocannons on its roof are as still and silent as ours, which means that either they're not hooked up or there's no gun-ner in the back. I grab the small control stick on my console and try to aim my hood cannon at Ellie, but while I'm dodging trees and boulders and signs, it's nearly impossible to get a weapon lock on her vehicle. My target is small and moving quickly—but hers—the defense stations—are huge and stationary.

"She's going to reach that station in less than a minute," Leo snaps. He wedges his torso next to my chair and reaches for the control stick beside my steering wheel. The hood cannon jumps to life again. His deft maneuvering spins the cannon around, its thick barrel aimed straight at the rear of Ellie's vehicle. He jams his thumb down on the black button at the tip of the stick.

Nothing happens . . . except that Leo starts cursing fluently. "It's not loaded!"

"She was watching long enough to know which ones were armed," I mutter, trying to close the distance.

"Why aren't the stations shooting at her?"

"They probably have no idea what's happening! She's supposed to be a friendly."

Leo rips his hands off the hood cannon controls and withdraws into the low doorway between the rear of the vehicle and the driver's compartment. "I should have been paying more attention," he says, his voice thick with anger and frustration. "She's the Sicarii?"

"Yes. I'll explain lat— No!"

Ellie fires again, the shot flying wide and slamming into the rocky wall of the crater right next to the second perimeter defense station. The station's massive guns are swinging around, but they're slow. I can only imagine the chaos within that station, where the guards are probably shouting and scrambling. They were prepared to meet an enemy coming from above, from outside the crater, and now one of our own best weapons is firing on them.

And she does. Again. Direct hit. From behind me, I hear only clanking and a strangled cry. I grit my teeth and push the gas pedal to the floor, seeing my chance. Ellie careens to a stop and reverses to head for the next station. Already, the other Archer is racing ahead of her to protect that defense station, but the mixed signals and destruction must have terrified the station's occupants, because their giant guns are gliding around and aiming at the friendly Archer, which careens out of the way as they fire at it. I push away the fear that Christina might be inside that Archer and focus on drawing even with Ellie, trying to get my vehicle in a position where I can run her into the crater wall to her right. We skim along the edge, her Archer just a few yards off my front bumper. I push my own vehicle a little farther, slowly gaining as her hood cannon once again aims at a defense station. There are only six, and she's destroyed two. She's coming at this one from the side instead of straight on, and the people in the station are obviously thinking the other—friendly—Archer is its enemy, because they're focusing on it and not her. My stomach drops as Ellie fires, hitting a spot just below where the station juts out from the crater wall. A hail of rock and dust billows outward. I'm now only a yard from her bumper. If I can just—

Something flies across the distance between our two Archers and lands on the roof of Ellie's vehicle, right next to the massive lens.

It's Leo. He must have crawled up through the hole in my roof. "Goddamn it, Leo!" I shout as I watch him cling to the autocannon rails and inch toward the front of Ellie's vehicle.

My heart is in my throat. I have no fucking idea what to do. I can't ram her. I couldn't fire, even if we were armed. Leo is out in the open, his wiry body clinging to the back of a metal monster in an arena of rock. I'm helpless.

But the defense station isn't, and its heavy cannons are now rotating toward us. "Please see him," I whisper as I race along behind Ellie's Archer. "Please don't shoot."

I'm not just talking to the defense station. Because Leo has made it all the way to the front of the Archer and hurls himself onto the hood as Ellie sends another blast toward the defense station. It takes out the large cannon and part of the floor of the station, and I try not to look too closely when I realize one of the guards is dangling from the shattered paneling and wires.

I focus on Leo, who is crouched on the hood of Ellie's Archer. Blood streams from his ears—the last blast shattered his eardrums. His arms are wrapped around the barrel of the cannon. He's the reason Ellie's last shot wasn't a direct hit.

He's kicking at her tiny windshield, but there's no way he'll penetrate the bulletproof glass. He is distracting her, though. She swerves to the side, clipping my front panel and fishtailing. Leo holds tightly to the cannon, his little muscles standing out in sharp relief as he wrenches at it. One of his hands is working at something at the cannon's base, but I only catch glimpses as Ellie weaves back and forth across open ground. The other Archer has circled around, but the driver obviously sees Leo, too, because the vehicle is hanging back instead of racing toward Ellie. It's put itself between Ellie and the next defense station on the west side of the compound.

Ellie makes a sudden, sharp U-turn, churning up turf like bunched fabric beneath the Archer's massive wheels, and flies back toward the damaged defense station.

Leo's body bucks as Ellie's hood cannon swings forward, taking him with it. I can see his frantic movements, his desperate attempts to keep the heavy metal barrel from aiming at the men hanging from beneath the shredded metal and sparking cables.

I see the moment he makes his decision. His body goes still. He stops struggling with the cannon.

And he plasters himself across the narrow strip of windshield, including the camera ports for her display screens, completely blocking her view.

Ellie veers back and forth, trying to throw him off. My mind becomes an abstract whirl of physics calculations. Speed. Acceleration. Force.

Oh God.

"Oh God," I whisper aloud.

She picks up speed with frightening abruptness. She's only a few hundred yards from the crater wall. "Leo!" I shout. "Jump off! Get off that thing!"

He doesn't.

Ellie makes a sudden left just before it reaches the edge of the crater, so violent that when its front right side slams into the rock wall, the Archer rolls. I watch, helpless, as Leo's skinny body disappears beneath the vehicle.

And as the Archer rolls away, he's left behind. Lying in the grass, not moving.

I slam on the brakes, my chest filling with dread, and throw open the small driver's door. My feet hit the emerald-green grass, and for this random second beneath the lights of the damaged defense station, I think how beautiful the color is, how full of life and promise. And then I force my head up as I run around the side of my vehicle and sprint for the crumpled figure at the base of the rock wall.

Leo's on his side. His fingers twitch in the grass. His blond hair is streaked with blood. The fabric of his shirt has been melted to the skin of his arms and stomach by the heat of the cannon. But he's alive. I drop to my knees and skid as soon as I get close. "Leo," I say.

His glasses are gone, and his green eyes are bright with terror and pain. His mouth moves, but all that comes out is a broken whimper. I blink and focus, taking in the rest of him.

It's broken, too.

His legs are twisted in an odd way, and my thoughts scream as my gaze moves up his body . . . *spine shattered, organs twisted and hemorrhaging, ribs splintered, lungs perforated.* Afraid to move him for fear of doing more damage, I lie on my side so he can see me. I gently smooth his hair from his brow, noting with a sinking feeling the blood dripping from his nose and mouth.

"Someone call Dr. Ackerman!" I shout over my shoulder before returning my attention to him. "You crazy idiot," I say, trying to steady my voice.

"Did we stop her?" he asks in a halting, wet whisper.

I have no idea. "*You* stopped her. She wrecked." I nod, too, because the blood leaking from his ears reminds me that he can't hear me.

The corners of his mouth curl up as he watches my face, but when he parts his lips, the gurgling noise he makes is almost unbearable. "Tate?"

"Yeah." I take his hand, the one that's twitching on the grass. I squeeze it. I'm not sure if he feels it. My eyes are burning, like the air is filled with caustic fumes. "I'm here. I'll stay with you."

"Scared," he mouths, still watching my expression.

So I smile, but God, it hurts. "You're the bravest kid I've ever met."

The choked, agonized cough he lets out might be laughter,

but then his face twists with pain. "Tell me," he rasps, his chest shuddering. "Tell me it's going to be okay."

But then his eyes become unfocused, sliding away from me.

"It's going to be okay," I say, but I can barely get the words out, because his hand twitches once more before going limp in my sweaty grasp. I feel for his pulse.

And I can't find it.

His eyes are half open. Blood is still dripping from his mouth, but his chest isn't moving anymore. "Leo, *please*," I whisper. "Don't do this."

He's already gone. The certainty descends on me like an avalanche, burying me with a million separate impacts. I've only known him for a few days, but somehow, it feels like I'm losing another member of my family. A brother. I rub at my eyes, my fingers coming away wet with tears.

A humming, rumbling noise behind me snaps me back to the moment, and I turn quickly, in time to see my own death roll to a stop less than thirty feet away. It's a dented disaster.

But the hood cannon is functional, and I'm crouched in the grass next to my dead friend, staring right down its barrel.

EIGHTEEN

I CLOSE MY EYES.

The roar of an engine makes me open them again—in time to see another Archer T-bone Ellie, right on the driver's side. Both of the vehicles are armored, so they withstand the impact fairly well, but hers is shoved across the grass. No sooner have both vehicles skidded to a stop than Race jumps out of the third Archer, and Christina gets out of the back. Weapon drawn, Race wrenches Ellie's door open. He shoves her to the ground and presses his gun to the back of her head.

Christina falls to her knees and throws her arms around me. She's breathing so hard. Shaking. My head hangs. I know Leo is lying dead behind me. I know I have to face this. But I can't make myself look at him again. And I can't make myself look at Christina, either.

"I should never have let you come here," I say in a dull voice. "It's going to get you killed. Just like it got Leo killed." My voice breaks over his name.

She only holds me tighter. "Leo did what he did to save others. He didn't just get himself killed." Her body shudders with a sob. "It meant something."

"Meaning or not, he's still dead," I snap. "And no amount of meaning would make me feel okay if you got hurt, too." I try to push away a vision of Christina's body crushed like Leo's. "I wish you'd never come here. I wish you could leave."

She shakes her head. "Even if that were possible right now, I don't want to hear it."

"What do you want to hear, then?" My voice is shaking. *Because I can't think of anything else to say.*

"Tell me I'm all right," she chokes out.

"You're all right," I whisper.

"Now tell me you're all right."

"I'm all right," I lie.

"And tell me we'll do this together."

"We'll do this together, Christina." Despite those words, I still feel alone, carrying this collection of knowledge that feels like it should save us, failing at every turn, unable to protect the people I love.

The sob lurches out of me. "At least I don't have to worry about Leo anymore," I say hoarsely as tears streak my face, as

I lose control completely. I'm glad he's not here to see this. More than anything, I want to make his death count, but I don't know how.

I am vaguely aware of Christina's mouth against my ear, of her fingers in my hair, of her arms around me. I want to tell her I'm sorry, that I'm powerless, that I've failed, but I can't even gather the syllables.

Then she takes my face in her hands. She kisses my eyes, squeezed shut to keep the world out. Her lips graze my cheeks, my temples, my mouth. She holds me steady. "If Leo was still here," she says quietly, "he'd tell you not to give up. And he'd remind you that you're not alone."

"Bullshit." I let out a raspy laugh. "If Leo were here, he'd call me a coward." He was amazing, that skinny orphan kid, so easy to underestimate, braver than he had a right to be. My dad must have loved him. I was starting to love him, too. It feels like the whole world needs to stop and acknowledge that he's gone. But as I raise my head, I realize it won't.

Like it's happening in slow motion, Race waves a bunch of guards over. They wrestle a struggling Ellie . . . who I guess isn't really Ellie . . . into a waiting SUV. His severe face all angles, his eyes violent red, Race turns to me. Those eyes slide to Leo's body and then flick back to my face. His mouth tightens as I shake my head. *He's gone.* Race nods toward the SUV, inviting me to join.

I stay where I am. How can I walk away from Leo?

"I'll stay with Leo, Tate," Christina says quietly. "I won't let him be alone. You need to go."

She gives me the gentlest of pushes toward Race, away from Leo, away from everything that's happened. I climb into the backseat of the SUV. Ellie is cuffed and trussed in the middle, with a guard on either side of her and thick plastic bags encasing her hands. She turns in her seat and looks back at me. Her eyes shine with cold curiosity.

I stare back. It occurs to me that I could reach her from here, strangle the life out of her, crush her windpipe and stop her heart, and my hands are rising from my lap when Race taps my shoulder. I pull my gaze from Ellie's. "They've radioed back to the main building," he says. "They'll send another car to pick up the boy." He nods in the direction of everything I'm leaving behind. "And I'm sorry," he adds quietly.

By staying with Leo, Christina's done me a favor. I've left all my heart at the crater wall, so now I'll just be a collection of logical, emotionless thoughts, which is exactly what I need. I don't care about the people in this vehicle. They're moving parts in a machine, nothing soft, no nerves. Or, at least, that's what I'll tell myself. I breathe in and out. "Okay. And thanks."

As we drive back to the front entrance of the main building, Race radios Angus. He says that I'm safe and breaks the news that Leo is dead. There is complete silence on the other end of the line as Race ends the call.

When we arrive, Race and I disembark and walk into the

atrium ahead of the guards and the Ellie-Sicarii. Congers emerges from the administrative wing with Angus, whose normally ruddy complexion is gray. Next to him are Graham and Rufus, who have apparently been relieved of the suspicion and the handcuffs.

Angus has the scanner, and he holds it up as we approach. "It was in Ellie's quarters, as was Ellie," says Angus. He scrapes his knuckles along his bearded jaw. "Looks like it strangled her after it . . . did whatever it does. Her body had aged dramatically. But Brayton is still alive, though gravely ill—Dr. Ackerman is with him."

"He won't live much longer," the Ellie-Sicarii comments in a quiet, calm voice.

Congers's eyes blaze as he stares at the alien, the creature who has stolen so much from us. "Neither will you."

It doesn't even flinch.

"Where's my mom?" I ask Angus. I'd expected her to be part of this.

Angus steps aside as the Sicarii is led down the hall. "She's still in the morgue. I've called to tell her you're all right. She said she needed to look at some spaceship components you dropped off?"

The Sicarii lets out a low laugh, and Race and Congers stiffen like it's a personal insult. Graham takes in the look on his father's face and jogs ahead to assist the guards. We follow them down the hall and into Angus's office, where they shove the Ellie-Sicarii into a chair and cuff its wrists to the armrests. Rufus lowers himself to a chair in the corner and simply watches.

Graham helps fasten its ankles to the legs of the chair and moves back to make room for his father, who stands in front of the Sicarii. "Sorry we couldn't let you leave just yet."

The Sicarii arches an eyebrow. "Your posturing is amusing. By all means, continue."

Congers's nostrils flare, and Race steps forward. "Have you been communicating with your colleagues outside this compound?" he asks. "How much do they know about our defenses?"

"And your lack of intelligence is encouraging," the Sicarii says.

"Why do you want the scanner?" I blurt out.

"Now that is a more interesting question." It tilts its head, looking eerily like Brayton did this morning at breakfast—except it wasn't Brayton; it was the creature in front of me. "I was present at the gathering when that weapon was first deployed. It was . . . impressive in both its intensity and specificity. I was the only one who escaped. I injured the one who wielded it, but he destroyed himself and the device before I could acquire either."

Angus looks at Congers and Race. "You told us that happened hundreds of years ago."

The Sicarii turns its smile on him. "It did." It gives us all a speculative sort of look. "You are so lost. All of you."

"No," I say. "I don't think we are. You somehow drain the telomerase from your victims—"

"We refer to them as donors," it says.

"Donors? They let you shorten their lives willingly?"

It shrugs.

I can't tell if the Sicarii's nonchalance is bravado, or if it's so old that it really doesn't care. I think it might be the latter, because it's clear that threats don't impress it much. So I decide to take a different tack. "Tell us how it works."

It seems intrigued by my curiosity. "We were driven to this out of necessity. Five hundred years ago, we were a thriving species. Much more advanced than the creatures on this planet. But our advancement came with consequences, and our world grew sick. The weather, the soil, the water. There was a worldwide famine that threatened our extinction, but we had the technology to artificially stimulate the environment into producing food once again." Its pale blue eyes meet mine, and there is something ancient and cold behind them. "But the consequence of this irradiation was more complex than my ancestors initially realized. Infertility rates rose exponentially, and we began to age twice as quickly. We discovered that our bodies' ability to create telomerase had been decimated. I was born among the last generation of our species, but we were all genetically damaged, destined to age quickly and die young and childless. We were a species rapidly going extinct. We tried so many things, synthesizing telomerase, injecting it, rubbing it on our skin, drinking it . . ." It sighs. "None of it worked. Until, one day, our planet was visited by an alien species from a nearby galaxy."

Congers and Race go very still. "H2," Race says quietly.

"You didn't call yourselves that at the time," it replies with a condescending smile. "But yes, they were on an exploratory mission, and they found us. We were happy to welcome them. A few weeks of experimentation was all it required for us to realize the potential of a donor species."

"Experimentation," Congers says in a flat voice.

Its brow furrows. "Our entire race was dying out," it says to him. "By that time, our population was only a fraction of what it had been. What we did, we did out of necessity."

"What you *did* was torture explorers who were there to make friendly contact!" Congers snaps.

The Sicarii ignores him, returning its attention to me. "I was part of the initial test group to take telomerase from the H2 donors. A few genetic and physical modifications were all that was required."

It's probably talking about those anomalous secretory glands, like the ones Mom found in the skin of George's and Willetts's corpses. "You somehow pull telomerase from the other body through the skin, right?"

"The process requires time and extensive physical contact, but yes. It would have been our preference to artificially siphon the required enzyme; it's really a simple sort of chemical. But the way it works in a humanoid body is much more complicated, and our bodies could no longer create or use telomerase at all. Hence the need for a complete DNA transfer." Which also makes them look like the person they're leeching the telomerase from. "Unpleasant, but it allows us to prolong our own lives, though not to procreate." For the first time, a shadow of sadness passes across the Ellie-Sicarii's face.

"It allows you to lengthen your life—for how long?" Race asks.

It shrugs again. "I witnessed the miracle of this discovery myself, and I'm still here."

"Are you saying you could live forever?" Angus asks, incredulous. "How long does the effect last?"

"As long as we have donors, our life spans are unlimited," it says. "But our need for new telomerase donors has accelerated over the centuries. At first, the effects lasted for several months. Not long enough to reproduce, but long enough to thrive for a while at least. Now the telomerase from a single donor only keeps us whole for a few weeks at most. Which brings us to Earth."

"What happened to our planet?" Graham asks suddenly, like he couldn't hold back another second.

It stares at him, and though he's a tall guy and the Sicarii is wearing the body of a petite young woman, it looks like it believes it could snap him in half. "Despite careful and systematic breeding, your species did not reproduce quickly enough to be a sustainable source of telomerase."

In other words, over the last few hundred years, the Sicarii have been slowly using up the H2 population, breeding them in captivity generation by generation, and now they're pretty much extinct. Graham's jaw goes rigid with hatred. Congers's hand drifts to the weapon at his belt. He draws it slowly, like he's not fully aware he's doing it.

Graham and Congers are direct descendants of the man who tried and failed to save their planet all those years ago. Their family has carried their history through generations, just like mine did, and to them, this fight with the Sicarii is deeply personal.

Race puts his hand on his colleague's wrist to stop him from doing anything rash. "Your ability to take on your victims' appearances allowed you to subdue the H2 population with few casualties," he says to the Sicarii. "And that's what you planned to do here."

The Sicarii nods. "Armies are full of young, healthy donors. We have absolutely no desire to destroy them. It's so easy for you to brand us as evil. As monsters. But we are only trying to preserve our race. We kill out of need, not malice. Strategically, not indiscriminately." Its eyes light on the scanner.

"How did the H2 not notice that there were two versions of someone walking around?" I ask. "It took us a while to figure it out because it was only Brayton, but a complete government takeover has to involve dozens, if not hundreds of Sicarii doppelgängers."

The cuffs clank as the Sicarii moves its legs. "Unless we have good reason, the donor does not survive the initial exchange. We sap the creature of all its telomerase and then euthanize it."

"You mean you murder the person," Race says, his voice deadly calm.

Angus's huge fists are clenched. "Like you murdered Ellie."

"Call it what you will, if it makes you feel righteous," the Sicarii says. "But if the donor can serve some purpose, we can drain its body of telomerase more gradually, which enables it to remain alive until it is no longer useful to us. Brayton Alexander led me to believe he had more access and credibility than he actually did. Still, he was helpful."

"You mean he was a traitor," Congers snarls, his finger twitching toward the trigger of his weapon. "But if there was complete genetic transfer, why do you still think like a parasitic alien instead of like your victim?"

The Sicarii only seems amused by his fury. "We have been genetically and biochemically modified so that our minds are preserved even as our bodies undergo the dramatic changes that come with the DNA transfer."

"But you needed Brayton as cover, and to provide information," I add. "You left him alive. Charles Willetts, too." I almost ask about George, but I don't want to think about it.

The Sicarii nods, blond hair falling across its forehead. "Like we did on the H2 planet, scouts were sent ahead to identify and neutralize potential threats. Our squad has been on

Earth and investigating for several weeks, and were already aware of the Core and The Fifty. We had begun to infiltrate and gather the information required to quietly dispose of you, but when we saw the report of the scanning device on television, we knew we needed to move quickly to acquire it."

"Why?" It's all I can do not to shout that word. I stride across the room and snatch the scanner from Angus, and he's too surprised to stop me. I flip it on and wave it in front of the Sicarii's face. It squints against the orange light until I switch it off and point to the ports on its side. "What are these for?"

It seems baffled. "How did you create the defense system, if you are so ignorant?"

Because my dad held all the knowledge in his head. "We know it differentiates the three species," I say, trying to keep my voice steady and low. My fingers are running along the ports. "Do these make it some sort of weapon?"

The Sicarii's eyebrows rise as it watches the scanner shake in my tight grasp. "You really don't know," it says, its lips trembling as it tries to hold back a smile. "You're not a threat at all."

"You have no idea how much of a threat you're facing," growls Congers, wrenching his arm away from Race and raising his weapon.

The Sicarii gazes at him with icy contempt. "You have gathered your most formidable people within this crater, the only ones with any knowledge that could complicate our peaceful invasion. You have also gathered within these walls the only weapons that could interfere with our plans. You have taken so long to figure out that I was among you that I was able to destroy most of the defenses that could stop our scout force from flying in and taking what we want, killing all of you, and proceeding with our mission to clear the way for the rest of our species, which is already crossing the galaxy." The Sicarii chuckles, part pity, part hatred. "And now you're so obsessed with forcing me to give you the answers that are right in front of you that you're virtually guaranteeing your own deaths. We will burn this compound to the ground."

Race and I lock eyes as a wave of dread rolls through my body. "They're coming," I say in a choked voice. "It must have found a way to contact the rest of the scout force. We've been wasting time. It's only talking because it thinks they'll be able to neutralize all of us."

"At last, one of you has drawn an intelligent conclusion," the Sicarii mutters.

The room explodes in shouted commands and deliberate motion. "Radio the defense stations," snaps Angus to his guards. Congers already has his phone to his ear and is barking instructions. Race orders the guards to take the Sicarii to the storage room and lock it in.

"No," says Congers. "I'll take care of it." And with that, he raises his weapon and shoots the Ellie-Sicarii between the eyes.

"It took out three of the six stations," I say, lunging for the door and bolting into the hallway, the scanner still clutched in my sweaty fist. "The Archers will be needed to defend the compound."

Race and Graham catch up with me a second later as I burst into the atrium and head for the back. "Then we'd better pray that Manuel works fast," Race huffs.

"Tate, hold up!" my mother shouts as she darts from an elevator, waving a plastic bag in front of her. "I figured out what these are!"

I slow down and let the others run ahead. Mom reaches my side as we crash through the doors and head for the Archers. "Can you tell me now?"

She points at the scanner. "These should fit those ports." She touches the contents of the bag, which turn out to be three of the chips that spilled from the broken compartment of the H2 wreckage this morning.

"I thought they might. What do they do?"

"Each of the three responds to a different species' DNA, sending off a specific electromagnetic signal when it detects it. I tested them on Charles's neural tissue, and this one lit up."

"And the other two?"

"I tested them on two of the bodies in the morgue, one H2 and one human." She touches one of the chips. "Human." She touches another. "H2."

"But what do they do?"

"You'll have to stick them in the scanner to find out. I was told we have the Sicarii prisoner. We could test it on her and—"

"No time." I grab the bag from her without even slowing down. "The scout ships are coming. The Sicarii was trying to stall us. I should have figured it out when it was willing to explain so much, but—" *I was too desperate for answers.*

We come to a stop at the edge of the lot and look out at the bustle of activity around the five remaining Archers, one of which has a dented front end and broken hood cannon. The one the Sicarii hijacked must have been too damaged to repair quickly.

I look up at the sky, wondering from which direction the fight will come. Wondering if we'll stand a chance.

Wondering if, when we are face-to-face with the enemy, the scanner will be what my dad said it was: the key to our survival.

ПIПETEEП

PEOPLE ARE SCRAMBLING OVER THE ARCHERS, ALL
purposeful movement and teamwork, and my mom rushes
over to help, even though she's clearly favoring her injured
arm. Everybody's loading the custom artillery shells into the
cannons, oiling the autocannon rails, fastening the enormous
lenses into place. It's an act of pure faith. We still have no idea
what those lenses do, but they're right above the weapons console. It may help the gunner get a visual if the console screen
fails, but it also puts him or her in a very vulnerable position—
the lens is like a sign painted on the roof of the vehicle that
says "SHOOT HERE."

I still don't get it. And right now, I don't have time to figure
it out. While everyone else goes about their work, I sit on the
curb with the chips and the scanner. I handle each component
gingerly, because if they do actually weaponize the device, I

don't want to end up killing myself with it. I remove each component and lay it on the plastic bag. I match the shape to each port along the side of the scanner. Then I insert the H2 chip into the scanner. It slides in, proving the device was made to accept it. I then slide the Sicarii chip in, but as soon as I do, it ejects the H2 chip. When I push the H2 chip in, it ejects the Sicarii chip.

The scanner is meant to house one chip at a time, which reminds me of what the Ellie-Sicarii said about it—it had been impressive in its intensity *and specificity*. Since I only have one enemy at the moment, I pull the H2 chip from the scanner and tuck it back into the bag, along with the human chip, and keep the Sicarii chip installed. I turn on the device, aiming it away from me. It glows yellow, then blue as Kellan walks by, his muscular arms straining to heft a large box of ammo.

The scanner seems to be working normally. I put the bag containing the remaining chips in my pocket and head over to the Archers. Manuel has his head down. His olive skin is ashen. Kellan leans on the rear of the vehicle, his curly brown hair messy like he's been running his hands through it. "He was a good kid, man. And the only one left in his family. We're The Forty-Nine now," Kellan says quietly. "It feels wrong."

Manuel nods, clutching a screwdriver so tightly that his hand is shaking. "We'll end it here. When they come, we'll be ready."

He raises his head and looks out at the crowd that's moving

through the lot; the patriarchs and matriarchs of The Fifty are heading for the underground bunkers.

As they pass us by, I look around the crater, at the destroyed defense stations in the distance, at the five Archers that will have to make up for the loss. They look so small and powerless when I think of a bunch of Sicarii ships descending on us. "We need more firepower than this."

Race's gaze traces the interior of the Archer, sliding over the unique controls for the cannons and the lens hanging over it. "Maybe we have more than we think we do. We just haven't had time to figure it out."

By silent agreement, we climb into the vehicle, moving aside while Manuel makes sure the console is secure. Race and I eye the lens. It fits awkwardly over the hole cut into the vehicle's roof, into a maneuverable carriage that has its own shock-absorbing system to keep it from cracking if the Archer hits a bump. The two autocannons are mounted on rails on either side, directly above the gunner's pit, with its rotating chair and stick controls. As I imagine sitting beneath a giant piece of glass with those Sicarii ships flying overhead, I understand why Angus suggested we leave them out. Sure, the Archer is armored, but if one of the Sicarii lands a vertical hit on one of these lenses, the gunner below is going to be cut to ribbons or vaporized entirely. The driver, piloting from the reinforced cockpit, stands a slightly better chance of survival.

"If people die because of this . . ." I say, running my finger along the underside of the lens.

"Any ideas at all?" Race asks.

I shrug. "No good ones." Nothing worthy of my dad. If he were here, would he be disappointed in me? I know I am.

Race sighs. "We don't know when the attack will come. We need to select our combat teams."

He pushes past me and exits the Archer, standing on the sidewalk.

"This is a volunteer force," Race shouts, and everyone stops to listen. "We need five teams of two, and each of those teams needs to understand that this is a very dangerous mission. We will be defending the compound. We are greatly outnumbered. We're operating powerful weapons we don't fully understand. But the alternative is to allow the Sicarii to overrun the compound. They could take down the satellite shield. And if they do that, this planet will be theirs. The stakes could not be higher."

As he speaks, Angus and Congers approach. They've been controlling the procession headed down to the bunkers and communicating with the perimeter defense stations. Both look ready for war in their own way. Angus is all flame and ferocity, his massive frame tense and vibrating with violence. Congers, on the other hand, is absolutely still, ice to Angus's fire. They listen quietly and watch the assembled group in front of them.

"I'll go," says Graham. He stares at his dad as he steps forward. Race smiles and claps him on the shoulder, but Congers doesn't move. His eyes don't flicker with any emotion at all. Graham sags a little.

I'm about to open my mouth and join his combat team when Sung says loudly, "I'll ride with you. I know how to operate those guns." He stands next to his fellow Core agent, shoulder to shoulder, and Graham straightens. His expression flickers with gratitude. Congers looks away, his gaze focusing on the distant horizon.

Graham steps forward suddenly. "Dad," he says quietly.

Congers turns back to him. For the briefest moment, Congers's chin trembles, but then he regains his tight control. He places his hand on Graham's shoulder, squeezes, and then lets his son go.

Graham's eyes are painfully bright as his father walks away to stand next to Angus again.

"We have one team, then," says Race, looking at the two young agents with obvious pride.

"I'm definitely going," Manuel says loudly. "I want a chance to shoot one of those Sicarii out of the sky." He lopes over to the sidewalk and stands next to Graham and Sung.

Kellan joins him immediately. He looks at Angus, who nods. "I'll drive you, man," he says to Manuel. "We'll do it for Leo."

"We have a second team," Race announces.

Figuring I'd better claim my spot, I start to move forward, but Christina suddenly emerges from the crowd, her hair pulled back, her face pale. There's a smear of Leo's blood on her shirt.

The bottom drops out of my stomach. I assumed she was still with him, grieving but safe. Instead, she's here, offering up her life. Her storm-blue eyes are on me, so focused, so determined. I grit my teeth as she stops in front of me.

"We have a third—" begins Race.

"I can't," I say to him, and then I turn to Christina. "I can't. Please don't ask me to."

Everybody's watching, and I know that, but they fade away as she comes closer. "I'm good with those guns. You need me out there." She reaches out to put her hand on my chest, but I flinch away. "You said we'd do this together."

I can barely speak over the lump in my throat. "No," I whisper. "I can't do this if you're with me. I can't be on a team with you."

She looks over at the other two teams, shoulder to shoulder, and then her gaze returns to me, questioning and hurt. And I want to tell her how much I've felt for her and for exactly how long, how I'd break if something happened to her, how I'd fall apart completely if it went down *in front of me*. I've already had to watch Leo die. I can't do it again. But all that comes out is, "I'm sorry."

My mother appears at Christina's shoulder right as my girlfriend's eyes go shiny with anger and defiance. The sting of rejection is so plain on her face, her cheeks suffusing with pink. She's looking at me like she wants to knee me in the balls. She doesn't understand at all. I think my mom does, though. She links her arm with Christina's. "You and I can be a team. I'll drive and you shoot."

Awesome. One of the Archers will contain the two people I love most in the world. "We have our third team," Race says, his eyes on me like he expects me to object. But how can I? I already know my mom's a badass behind the wheel and that Christina is nearly unbeatable with those control sticks in her hands. But that means she'll be sitting beneath that lens . . .

The horror of the images in my head freezes me up, and at that moment, Rufus shoves his way through the crowd. "I'm going, too. No way am I going to miss out on the chance to help take down those alien bastards. I'll drive. Who's riding with me?"

People seem so stunned that a patriarch of The Fifty has volunteered for what sounds like a suicide mission that everyone goes still. And in that quiet, Congers very calmly says, "I will."

Angus puts his hand on Congers's arm. "You might be needed here, for your agents—"

Congers stares him down. "Can I trust you to command my agents with respect, like you treat your own?"

Angus lets him go. And in the way he's looking at Congers, I see these two men have formed some sort of odd bond over the past two days, as they've perhaps realized that the differences between them aren't so vast. "I will," Angus says.

Congers nods at him and goes to stand next to Rufus. He arches an eyebrow. "Is this going to work, Mr. Bishop?"

Rufus folds his arms over his chest, resting them on his protruding belly. He looks straight ahead, not at Congers, as he says, "Only if you can shoot those guns at the right target."

Congers suppresses a smile and nods. Now we have four teams.

I'm standing in the open space between the Archers and the crowd, still shaken by the idea of the two women I love facing this danger when all I want to do is shout at them to get into those underground bunkers and stay put. It's short-circuited me.

"Tate," Race says loudly. When my gaze snaps to his, he says, "I'll drive."

I stare at the guy I used to think was my worst enemy. The severe, serious look on his face reminds me to focus. It reminds me I'm not helpless—and that I still have work to do. I stride over and stand next to him. "And I'll shoot."

We choose our vehicles and get ready. We could have hours or minutes or days or seconds, but the way the Sicarii was acting, an attack is imminent, so we prepare accordingly. I try to shift my attention to what lies ahead, and avoid looking at Christina as she climbs into the back of her Archer and slides into the gunner's pit. A moment later, Mom leans into my vehicle and lays her warm hand on my cheek. "I'll take care of her," she says softly.

"Who'll take care of you?" I ask, my throat tight. "Your arm—"

"My arm will be fine." She moves her left shoulder carefully and gives me a tight smile. "And as for who'll take care of me: Christina will." Mom nudges my chin up. "She's a good match for you, Tate. Whatever happens, I want you to know that's what I believe."

I bend down and pull her into a hug. "Thanks. I hope she believes that, too."

"She does. That's precisely the reason she's so mad at you right now. And she'll only forgive you if you make it to the other side of this, safe," says my mother, pulling away.

"I can understand that."

She takes my face in her hands. "I'm proud of you. I'm *so* proud of you. And if your father were here, he'd be proud of you, too."

I swallow hard. "Don't say that to me yet."

"Then I'll say it to you later. Good luck." She turns on her heel and climbs into the back of the Archer she'll be driving, closing the rear door behind her.

"You made the right decision," says Race as he joins me at the back of our assigned vehicle. "About Christina."

"I think we both know it wasn't my decision." I glance at the locked door of her vehicle. She's in there, probably firing up her control panel, flexing her fingers, getting ready. "It was hers."

"That wasn't the decision I was talking about." He heads to the front while I climb into the rear and settle myself in the circular area of the gunner's pit, putting the scanner down next to me. I'm right beneath the lens. I peer up through it and see dark purple sky. The sun has just set, and now the Sicarii have the cover of darkness. It'll be harder to see them coming. Through the smooth expanse of glass above me, the moon is a pinprick of light in the distance, looking much farther away than it actually is. I guess the lenses are definitely not meant to aid with sightings of the enemy.

After I clip on the earpiece that will allow me to communicate with Race throughout whatever we're about to face, I reach up and poke at the lens, and it rattles within its carriage. There are funny hooks protruding down beneath it, but I have no idea what's supposed to be hanging from them. "Come on, Dad," I whisper to myself. "What were you thinking?"

Race's voice crackles in my earpiece, interrupting my thoughts. "In case I don't get to say it later, I'm glad we're on the same side."

I let out a huff of quiet laughter. "So am I. I just wish it could have happened a lot sooner." *Like before my dad was killed.*

"Me too," he says.

"Do you have kids?" I ask. For some reason, I really need to know.

He's quiet for a few long seconds. "I do, actually. A son. He lives with my ex-wife in DC. He's seven."

"See him much?"

Another pause. "Not often enough. My job—"

"Can I give you some advice?"

"Can I stop you?"

"Try harder," I say. "You're more important to him than you think." I busy myself looking at the circular view screen, letting my eyes adjust to the night vision. "That's all."

"Duly noted," he says quietly. "You know, Tate, I've—"

BOOM.

I stare down at my control panel in time to see an entire squad of scout ships zoom over the crater wall, their spiraling hatches opening to reveal the devastating glow within. The defense stations are firing their cannons, but every single shot misses, exploding on the grassy expanse of the crater floor or in the lake. My earpiece erupts with frantic cries that must be coming from Race's communications console in the cockpit, everyone screaming to get the Archers moving, to protect the main compound. From outside, I hear Angus shouting at people to get below. The Archer jolts as Race stomps on the gas. We lurch forward and fly across the lot to engage the enemy.

We're not ready. We're so not ready.

But we're all there is.

I slide my arms into the cuffs and take hold of the control sticks. Closing my eyes and trying to breathe slowly, I remind myself not to force it. To let my father's brilliant design do its work while I do mine. "How many are there?" I call out.

"I've counted twelve—no, thirteen," Race barks. "They'll

try to take out the remaining perimeter defense stations." He's somehow switched the radio to a two-way channel, because I hear nothing but him, nothing from the outside, and that's good. "Hang on."

I do, watching my screen for any chance to lock onto the Sicarii ships. But they move so fast, and they seem to know that the five vehicles streaking in different directions beneath them are an actual threat. The Ellie-Sicarii must have warned them. The ships don't hover or slow down, just streak overhead and fire. Explosions turn my screen white, and there are so many that it feels like a strobe to my eyes and brain, this hypnotic, dizzying horror. But I don't look away, because I remember that Sung said the eye-tracking feature of the screen was the way to achieve target lock. As Race careens toward one of the defense stations on the south lawn, my persistence pays off, because one of the ships swoops low and glides toward the station, which fires frantically at the approaching ship with little effect—it merely spins out of the way.

Until I fire my autocannon at it. The ship tilts on its side to avoid the impact, but the Fred Archer–designed artillery shell curves around and follows the movement, slamming into the underside of the obelisk and making it falter in the air.

The next shot brings it down, and Race makes an abrupt, victorious shout before swerving around the flaming husk of the ship. About a quarter mile away, another Archer lets loose a barrage of artillery as it races toward another defense station, which is taking fire from above. The Archer swerves as the scout ship above it fires, leaving a small crater in the soft earth near the vehicle. Whoever's driving that Archer takes evasive action again, making a sharp U-turn and heading back for the flaming wreckage of the scout ship I just downed.

Whether it's looking for cover in the smoke, or for the light from the flaming wreckage to interfere with the Sicarii targeting systems, I never get to find out. Because the ship above it fires again, landing a solid hit to the Archer's armored left side, and the vehicle flies into the air, pirouetting under the night sky before landing brutally hard.

"Are they okay?" calls Race as he brings our Archer around, headed for a spot between the two defense stations. "They're not responding to radio calls."

I peer at the monitors. No one's getting out of the vehicle. "The Archer seems okay, but I don't know about the people inside. We need to go get them."

Race doesn't argue. He makes the turn that sets us on a rescue mission in the middle of the battle. I'm firing on another Sicarii ship descending to take advantage of the unmoving Archer when movement on the ground catches my eye. But it's not coming from the wrecked combat vehicle. "There's a Sicarii survivor!" I shout.

It's a woman. She sprints away from the spaceship I shot down, seemingly unhurt. She's wearing a slick sort of flight suit, the material glinting in the flames of her destroyed ship, and she's headed straight for the damaged Archer, only a hundred yards away.

"Can you shoot that thing from here?" Race asks.

"Not unless we want to risk killing the people inside the Archer. Let me out." I grab the scanner, my only sidearm. At least, that's what I hope it is.

Race makes a frustrated noise over the radio. "I can't give the scout ships another stationary target."

"Then let me out and swing back for me." Because even as I watch, the Sicarii has reached the Archer and pulled some sort of wand device from its belt, which it's using to cut a hole in the back of the stalled vehicle. I have no idea what it plans to do if it gets through, but memories of what happened the last time a Sicarii commandeered an Archer pour adrenaline through me as Race lurches to a stop about twenty yards from where it's all going down. The Sicarii finishes cutting through the door, having created a foot-wide hole. It shoves at the metal, which falls inward.

Christina might be inside. She might be unconscious over her console, helpless and unaware.

I hurl open the Archer's rear door. The thunder of the battle is so loud that it vibrates inside my chest. As soon as I jump clear of the vehicle, Race roars away—just as another scout ship glides toward us. Without slowing, he fires at it with his hood cannon, insanely aggressive and ballsy, considering his big guns are lying still and quiet on the roof of his ride.

Knowing that he's holding the ship's attention, I turn my focus to the Sicarii, who's reaching through the hole in the rear door, trying to open it from the inside.

"Hey!" I shout.

Despite the roar of cannons all around us, she spins around at the sound of my voice. My stomach tightens. It's the lunch lady from my school, the one who was on TV. Helen Kuipers, who disappeared a few days ago. Or, it looks like her, because it's stolen her appearance. The Sicarii holds the tiny, lethal, laser cutting tool at its side as it strides toward me, calm and steady.

The driver of the stalled Archer may have been knocked silly by the blast, but as the Sicarii comes for me, he or she must regain control, because the Archer's engine roars, and it races back into the fight, leaving me and the Sicarii alone on the grass.

I look down at the scanner, with the Sicarii-specific chip glinting in its designated port. I switch it on, and its light turns my legs blue. The Sicarii's eyes narrow when it sees what I have in my hand. It halts abruptly, and its gaze meets mine, full of the same ancient, cold curiosity I saw in the Ellie-Sicarii's eyes. Then it turns on its heel and runs.

My heart jolts as I take off after it.

The lunch lady–Sicarii should probably have chosen a more athletic body before this fight started. It's heading for the elevator of the nearest defense station, but I'm eating up the ground between us with longer, faster strides. Triumph beating through my veins, I lift the scanner high and bathe the Sicarii's back in orange light, hoping it'll burst into flames or melt or vaporize.

I stop, waiting for vindication. The scanner is important. It has to be. It's the weapon the Sicarii don't want us to have. My dad said it was the key to our survival. He said . . .

The Sicarii pauses abruptly in its flight toward the elevator. It looks down at itself and turns to stare at me and the scanner.

"We thought you had figured it out," it says, lifting the laser cutting tool and aiming it at me. I tense, my muscles coiling to run, the horrible realization dawning: *It didn't work.* The scanner didn't—

A huge blast of white fire slams into the Sicarii from above, lighting the sky and turning it to ash where it stands.

TWENTY

I'M THROWN INTO THE AIR BY THE EXPLOSION AND
land in the grass, gasping, my ears ringing, blinking as bits of
dirt rain down. I rub my eyes and squint—there's a small crater
where the Sicarii was standing. I look at the sky. That didn't
come from a defense station. Or a scout ship.

It came from higher than that. Much higher.

The scanner *did* work.

Inserting that chip weaponized the device, all right. Now
it doesn't just scan—it *burns*. That bolt of hell came from one
of my dad's satellites. I'm sure of it. I nailed the Sicarii with its
beam, and less than ten seconds later, it was vaporized. If I can
use the scanner to paint a target on each of the Sicarii scout
ships, maybe the same will happen to them. I know the scanner penetrates solid barriers and detects what's behind them,
so this could actually work.

My head throbbing with each deep, devastating explosion on the field, the roar of Archer engines, and the low hum of the Sicarii ships, I grope for the scanner, praying it wasn't damaged when I went flying. I freeze when I see a blue flash on the lawn. The device is still on, lying several feet from me. I scramble over to it and clutch it to my chest. And then I look over my head, where the Sicarii ships are zooming and shooting. I turn the scanner's light toward the sky, but its beam is too weak to span the distance.

Seething with frustration, I look around the battlefield. One Archer is just a flaming tangle of parts in the middle of the clearing, one a smoking wreck near the crater wall, and three others are still rolling around the field, including the one with the hole in its door. Two are shooting, the dual guns on the top tracking and firing viciously, and the third's guns lie silent, though it seems to be playing decoy while the others fire away.

I watch them speeding and turning, and then I count the ships in the sky. There are eight still in the air, five on the ground. Two look like they made controlled landings but were destroyed by cannon fire from the defense stations. Unfortunately, those defense stations are aflame now, as one of the scout ships has focused its fire on the perimeter. We're still outnumbered, and the three remaining Archers won't be rolling much longer with those kinds of odds. The one with the hole in its rear door streaks by, the lens rattling in its carriage as the vehicle rumbles past.

"The lens," I whisper, watching the Archer with silent

guns pull an incredible turn and race toward one of its sister vehicles, then break off at a startling angle, drawing one of the scout ships away. That has to be Race. He's vulnerable out there because he doesn't have anyone sitting beneath that giant lens, controlling the guns. The lens . . . I look at the scanner in my hand, bathing my legs in blue light, and every single loose puzzle piece in my mind locks into place at once.

"The lens!" I shout, running flat out toward Race's Archer. "The lens!" I wave my arms.

Race slows his vehicle. He must have seen me. But so does a scout ship. Shimmering and spinning, it descends from the sky. Its round hatch of death begins to open.

Boom. It's hit with a blast from another Archer. The alien ship falters in the air, then silently moves after its attacker. The rear hatch of Race's vehicle pops open, and Race peers out. "Get in here now," he barks before lunging for the driver's compartment again.

I vault into the Archer as it starts to move. I stare up through the lens and see the pinpoint moon and stars. I hold the scanner up to it, with the lit side pressed to the convex surface. The curved glass focuses the light, turning it into a single, sharp beam that reaches high in the sky. "Race! I know how to take them down."

"Start shooting, Tate. That's the only way to take them down!" he roars as he guns the engine, and we race into the battle again.

"Then get us underneath every single one of those things before they can do any more damage!" I hold the scanner to the lens, but it's awkward—until I notice the hooks again. Of course. I swing them under the scanner, and they create a sort of harness so it hangs perfectly beneath the glass, easy for me to control and turn so the beam moves around.

Race has no idea what I'm doing back here, of course, but it doesn't matter. I watch the gunner's screen as the other two Archers fire and dodge, fire and dodge. Race probably knows exactly who they are, but I don't ask. The eight remaining ships close in and create two formations, preparing to take them out. I'm glad I don't know which Archer is which, or whether Christina and my mom are still rolling. I aim the scanner's beam at one of the ships, one at the end of the formation targeting an Archer that's zooming along the edge of the clearing, near where the lunch lady–Sicarii was cut down a few minutes ago. It's hard to keep the beam on the chosen scout ship. It stays yellow for several seconds, but then it flashes orange.

"I don't hear you shooting back there, Tate!" Race shouts.

"Trust me; you will." I start to count down from ten, praying that the satellite is reliable—

Boom. The sky lights up, and there's a tremendous explosion. Debris pelts our Archer, and Race makes a sudden turn to get out of the way as what remains of the scout ship comes down.

"What the hell was that?" calls Race. "Was that us?"

"It was the scanner and the satellite system!" I reply. "They're connected now. Get us close to another scout ship before they realize what we're doing!"

He doesn't waste time with more questions. He rolls us right beneath the four that are firing at one of the remaining Archers—the one with the hole in its door. The wicked blasts take huge chunks out of the ground as they land within feet of the vehicle, and I know it's only a matter of time before the thing takes a direct hit. I grit my teeth and aim, forcing the beam to linger on the hulls of first one, then the second, then the third. I know I've made a hit when the scanner beam turns from bland yellow to lurid orange, and I can't draw the light away until that happens, no matter how close the ships get to that Archer . . .

The Archer takes a hit square on its front. It bounces into the air like it weighs nothing and pirouettes, landing upside down. Race shouts a curse. "Can you make that . . . *whatever-that-was* happen again?" he yells.

"Give it a few seconds."

Race steers us toward the overturned Archer as its rear hatch opens and Manuel stumbles out, coughing and bleeding from a head wound. I unlatch our rear door, and Race lurches to a stop. Manuel claws his way into the back as a scout ship turns in the air and zooms toward us.

"Kellan?" I ask, offering my hand and yanking him deeper into the vehicle.

He shakes his head, his face contorting with sadness. "Gone."

With a pit in my stomach, I slam our rear door shut as Manuel collapses next to the gunner's pit. "That other ship is coming right for us! Why aren't you shooting?" he shouts.

"I am." I go back to aiming the beam at the scout ship, but there's a bright flash of light as an Archer shell hits it broadside. It wobbles in the air and veers out of sight.

Boom. Boom. Boom. Manuel squeezes his eyes shut as the explosions flash bright through the lens and turn his face orange-white-yellow-red. Three more scout ships down. "Was that you?" he yelps.

I nod. "That was me."

"Do they know it was you?"

"Not yet." There are a few seconds of delay as the scanner communicates to the satellite and as it latches onto its target and fires, and I think that's saved us—along with the fact that they thought the scanner *itself* was the weapon—they didn't expect the fire to come from above.

"Manuel! Can you take control of the guns?" calls Race.

Manuel blinks at the sound of Race's voice crackling over the radio. "Can I . . . yes! Sorry." He climbs awkwardly into the gunner's pit and straps in while I stand over him, my feet braced on either side of his console. "Dude, this is closer to your *huevos* than I ever wanted to be," he mutters as he opens the controls and peers at the viewing screen.

"Fire the damn guns!" Race's voice is full of enraged desperation as he lurches us into motion. "Tate, we need to take out the remaining four before they get the other Archer. They're closing in."

Manuel shakes his head as he watches our sister vehicle race ahead of us. "Your mom's a scary driver," he says as he slides his forearms into the cuffs and grasps the stick controls.

I glance down at his viewing screen to see the last remaining Archer apart from our own. Four scout ships pursue it across the clearing as it swerves around enormous potholes made by previous shots from the Sicarii weapons and past the hulking carcasses of destroyed Archers. "That's my mom?" I whisper. I watch as its two guns swirl in different directions, firing simultaneously at two ships.

That's my mom and Christina. With four ships descending on them. "Get us between them and those ships!"

"No, we can't risk losing the scanner," Race replies. "They're presenting a more immediate threat to the scout ships, and that's why they're being targeted. Let them do their part, and we'll follow behind."

Manuel curses as a Sicarii shot hits within a few feet of Mom's Archer. "I'll cover them," he says, getting to work.

The crater is littered with debris now, chunks of the scout ships and the Archers, gaping holes in the turf from the impact of the Sicarii guns. Race weaves through it, bouncing us this way and that as I try to get a bead on each of the remaining ships. Every time the beam turns orange, I call it out. *One. Two.* But one of the remaining pair comes straight for us, like it's finally realized we're the cause of the destruction. The others, including the two I just hit with the beam, abandon their pursuit of my mom and come for us as well.

"Hang on!" shouts Race. The Archer accelerates, crashing through a deep hole and—*crack.* I'm thrown on top of Manuel as we roar out of it. I look above me. The lens is split down the middle, spiderweb cracks fissuring off each side. I press the scanner to it. All we have is weak shards of yellow light. *Fuck.*

Boom. Boom. The flash is blinding as two more Sicarii ships are blasted out of the sky. "We lost our lens!" I yell. "I need an intact lens. There are two more scout ships that haven't been targeted!"

"Our lens shattered when we crashed," says Manuel. "And Graham and Sung were taken out with a direct hit to theirs."

I can't think about that now. I wish I didn't know it at all.

"Stay where you are, Tate!" orders Race. "We still have our guns!"

"Then use them! And radio my mom and tell her to come get me." I roll off poor Manuel and shove the rear hatch open again. The two Sicarii ships glide smoothly toward us across the field. "Go, as quick as you can," I say to Race, then glance at Manuel. "Shoot straight."

"Done," he says, giving me a worried look. And then he

slams the rear hatch, and I'm out in the open. Race loops the Archer in front of me as Manuel fires both guns at the oncoming aliens.

Then Race veers away suddenly—but there's an Archer coming straight at me. It swerves around me and keeps going, but slower. She can't risk stopping completely, not when a scout ship is still pursuing us. The rear hatch is open already, and Christina's blond hair catches the firelight as she holds out her hand to me. I sprint for my life as the ground-shaking *whomp-whomp* of the Sicarii guns hits close enough for me to feel the searing heat on my legs and back. I stretch my hand out and skim Christina's. The desperate, terrified look on her face hurts me, so I focus on her hand, her fingers. Mine tangle with hers, and she yanks, giving me enough leverage to leap onto the back of the Archer. I bang my shins on the hatch opening as I heave myself inside.

Christina's already turned back to her guns. She shoves her arms through the cuffs and bows her head over the view screen. "Race said you needed the lens," my mom calls out over the radio.

"I do, and I need you to get close to both ships." I press the scanner to the lens and secure it with the hooks.

"No!" Christina screams.

I look down to see that Race's Archer has taken a direct hit. Helplessness tears through me. "How bad?"

Christina leans forward, trying to decipher the scramble of images on the screen. With all the fiery debris, it's hard to make out exactly what's happening, so I look up through the lens at the starry sky. "It's on its side. They could have survived," she says.

She fires up at the two Sicarii ships, which spin and dart toward us. "Here they come, Mitra!"

"I see them," Mom shouts, veering toward the clearest section of the field, heading straight for the lake as Christina fires and I aim the beam of the scanner.

It flares orange.

Whomp. The Archer squeals and shakes as the Sicarii blast hits close by. Christina's arms jerk, and her hands and fingers move in a blur. She mumbles under her breath as she works, trying to aim as we move.

"Yes!" she cries as there's a huge explosion outside. "One left!"

"Do you know if it was the one I hit with the scanner's—"

Boom. Her cheer turns to a scream as we're tossed into the air, rolling end over end. I hit the lens and land on Christina, then grasp for the nearest harness as we take another hit and I feel the Archer take flight. We crash down hard, and I collide with the door that leads to the driver's compartment. Pain nearly making me black out, I blink furiously and try to focus. Christina's above me, arms dangling sideways toward me.

She's strapped into her harness in the gunner's pit. Her head lolls, and her fingers twitch. The Archer must be on its nose, its rear pointing at the sky.

Aching, barely able to breathe, I turn onto my side and pull the door to the driver's compartment open.

It's filling with water. We landed in the lake. And my mom is down there, strapped in. Drowning. I gulp a huge lungful of air and plunge into the cool, murky pool. It's all black, but I feel the softness of my mother's hair and grope for the latch to her harness. With clumsy fingers, I fiddle with it, fighting panic, reminding myself that the only way I'll get her out of this is by staying calm. I slide my hand down and find the latch, and then the harness loosens and she bobs up toward me. I yank at her, pulling her limp body against my chest. I grab the door frame and heave us up, shoving her face above the water's surface, which is now at least a foot above the driver's compartment door and rising. This whole vehicle will be filled soon. I lunge upward, nearly sucking in a mouthful of liquid as it pours down on my head. Christina's awake and out of her harness—with the scanner in her hand. Her feet are wedged against her controls. She's shoved the rear hatch open, and water's rushing in. "The back of the Archer's only an inch or so below the surface of the lake," she shrieks through the crash and roar of the water. "We can get out."

I wrap my arm around my mom's waist. Christina grabs

a fistful of my mom's shirt and pulls. Mom's bleeding from a gash in her cheek. Her nose is gushing. I jab the side of my fist into her solar plexus a few times, and she starts to cough, horrible, wracking spasms. "It's okay, Mom," I say. "I'm here."

I hold her tight and kick as hard as I can, half climbing, half floating up to the rear hatch, which is our roof now, our salvation. Christina's already halfway out, sitting on the rear of the vehicle and tugging my mom up. Her knees are next to my face as I get my mom to the surface of the lake. I look up at Christina, her expression tight with determination, right as an eerie light slides over it. She raises her head, and so do I.

The last remaining Sicarii ship hovers above us.

Its circular weapon hatch begins to open. And we're here, a stationary target. Christina looks down at me and gives me a sad smile. "I love you, Tate."

I gaze up at the instrument of our destruction. With everything inside me, I refuse to surrender now. Not yet. I lunge upward, yanking the scanner from her hand and throwing it at the ship, as hard as I can, a Hail Mary if ever there was one. It spirals end over end, its light flashing blue and red at us, back to yellow—and then to orange as its beam hits the enemy ship.

The scout ship gives off the telltale hum that tells us we're about to be obliterated.

"Get back in the Archer!" I shout, and shove my mom down under the water, yanking on Christina's legs and forcing her to do the same. I lunge for the rear door and swing it down over us with all my might as the bolt of white lightning from above strikes the Sicarii ship. I almost have the hatch closed as the wreckage rains down.

Something slams into me, and the door cracks on my head. It's all darkness and quiet after that.

TWENTY-ONE

MY DREAMS ARE MADE OF ICE. CHRISTINA LOOKS DOWN at me, her beautiful face lit by the eerie light of the scout ship, frozen in that sad smile. *I love you, Tate,* she says, over and over, and even though I'm cold and blind and paralyzed, I hear her. I feel it. I cling to those words.

"I love you, Tate," she whispers. "Wake up. Come back again."

The pressure of warm fingers on my skin. The tickle of breath on my neck. The soft brush of lips against my temple.

"Today's the day you come back for good." Her voice is in my ear. A shiver streaks along my spine, and goose bumps erupt.

Christina.

"I'm here. I'm right here. All you have to do is open your eyes."

So I try. And it hurts. The tiniest trickle of light beneath my closed eyelids feels like a splinter in my eyeball. "Can't."

"I'm naked."

My eyes pop open. I manage to see her smile—and the fact that she's clothed—before clamping them shut again. "Dirty trick," I mumble, my voice slurring.

Her fingers slide through my hair. "You had such a bad concussion."

"Tell me . . ." The last thing I remember was seeing the white bolt in the sky.

"You saved us from getting hit by burning wreckage when the Sicarii ship came down, but I barely got you and your mom out. Race and Congers made it to the water and helped me get you guys to shore."

"Congers survived?"

"He did." She takes my hand. "Rufus didn't, though."

"And my mom?"

"She's in the next room over. She had a lot of internal injuries from the crash. Dr. Ackerman removed her spleen and was able to stop the bleeding. She's recovering."

"Manuel?"

"Broken arm, but he's fine."

"Sung? Graham?"

"They didn't make it," she says in a choked whisper. "It was quick, though."

I wait for the ache in my chest to subside, then force my eyes open a crack. I'm in the infirmary. There's an IV line hanging by my bed. "What day is it?"

"It's been two days since the battle. You've been in and out, but Dr. Ackerman said you wouldn't remember much of that."

I focus on closing my own fingers, on the feel of her skin against mine. "Are you okay?"

"A lot of bruises and aches, but I'm totally okay."

I swallow. My mouth is so dry. "And are *we* okay?"

She leans forward, lips curving into a mischievous smile. "You've asked me that every time you wake up. And I'll repeat what I've said every time: I'm all right, and you're all right, and we're all right. I was really upset that you didn't want to be with me, but your mom . . . she said it was because I was important to you, not because you didn't think I was good enough. That helped."

"You're a badass," I say, smiling despite cracked lips. "But you're also one of the most important people in the world to me." My dad told Leo that each family had to decide what was most important. And as the patriarch of the Archers—I have. No idea what that means yet, but I'll take it one day at a time until I find out. "I love you." There. I've finally said it when she's awake.

She grins. "You've said that every time you regained consciousness, too. I think this was lucky number seven."

Figures. "Then you know I mean it."

Her lips touch mine. "Yep."

A shadow appears in the doorway and clears its throat.

Christina raises her head. "I'm hoping he's back for good," she says to it.

"Mind if I sit with him for a few?" It's Race.

"No." She turns back to me. "I'm going to go down to the cafeteria. I'll be back later."

I nod and watch her go. Race takes her place in the chair next to my bed. His arm is in a sling, and he's limping slightly. His face is bruised, and he looks exhausted, but not unhappy. I try to sit up, but it's a struggle. He hits a control and motors me up, so at least I'm not flat on my back. The movement makes me feel like I might barf, though.

"I checked the population counter," he tells me. "There are no more anomalies. We got all of them."

"Any sign of others on their way?"

"Not yet. But now that the network's active, we've notified our government contacts all over the world. There will be co-operation to bolster it quickly, so when the Sicarii do show up, we'll know long before they get close and be able to hold them out there until they . . . run out of telomerase and die of old age, I suppose. That Sicarii prisoner said they were now running through victims every few weeks. They can't stay in space forever. With your dad's plans and the remains of the wrecked H2 defense ship, we can strengthen the network and create a deadly, robust shield."

"What now?"

Race sits back. "Bill Congers and Angus McClaren are negotiating. But I believe things will be different from now on. We have a new understanding."

"No more secrets?"

He chuckles. "Oh, the secret will remain, for now at least. What good will it honestly do to reveal that two-thirds of the population are descendants of an alien species? No, I mean that The Fifty and the Core will be allies now. There will be no more aggression between us."

"What do the Bishops have to say about that? Their patriarch is dead."

"But in the end, he knew who his enemy was, and he was willing to give his life to save this planet. The Bishops have been notified of recent events, with the understanding that they will stay quiet if they want the money to keep flowing. They can live however they'd like, as far off the grid as they want to be—as long as they don't hurt others or try to reveal the existence of the H2. If they do, they'll be cut off."

I stare up at the ceiling. "So many people have died."

Race grips the side railing of my bed. "And if you hadn't figured out the lenses, every last one of us would have been wiped out. They could have cut our connection to the satellite shield and rendered it useless. But you prevented that."

"It was my dad. My dad's system."

Race looks me right in the eye. "It was you who made it

work. He didn't do that for you. He left you the pieces, and you put them together."

"I had plenty of help." If it hadn't been for Leo, I might still be trying to figure out the freaking password.

"But it wouldn't have happened if not for you."

"Exactly," I whisper. "If I hadn't stolen the scanner from my dad's lab, none of this would have happened."

His bloodshot gaze is steady on me. "That's absolutely true. Your decision to steal the scanner set everything into motion."

I swallow hard.

"And if you hadn't done it, the invasion would be on schedule, and the Sicarii might have thoroughly infiltrated both sides by now, easing their path to planetary domination and the death of everyone on Earth."

"What?"

"Tate, your father was aware of the anomalies and had created the defense system, but he didn't have all the information he needed, because the Core had the other pieces of the puzzle. Your actions, rash as they were, with all those terrible consequences, were still the thing that brought the two sides together, and that's the only thing that saved us."

"That's a pretty rosy interpretation of what I did."

"'Everything we do has a result. But that which is right and prudent does not always lead to good, nor the contrary to what is bad.'"

"Did you seriously just quote Goethe to me?"

He gives me a small smile. "Your father did a remarkable job with your education."

"I know," I say, feeling hollow. "I know."

He shifts in his seat, looking uncomfortable. "Listen, I didn't know Frederick Archer very well. On the few occasions I met him, we were on opposite sides of a deep divide. It is now very clear to me that he was a good man, and a brilliant one. Whether I pulled the trigger or not, I'm going to live with his death on my hands for the rest of my life, and that's what I deserve." He pauses, and I wait, my stomach tight. "So I don't have the right to say what I'm going to say, but I'm going to do it anyway." He clears his throat. "He would have been proud of you, Tate. You may have made mistakes, but you still honored his legacy and his name. He lives on through you."

I suck in a breath, despite the heavy weight on my chest. "Everyone thinks he was a terrorist."

"No. We have discredited that explanation of events. Bill made it a priority."

"*Bill* did?" I have trouble imagining why that would be important to Congers.

Race sighs. "Bill lost his only son in that battle, Tate. And they left a lot of things unspoken between them. I think he's trying to make up for that somehow. He won't talk about it to anyone, but he's taking Graham's death hard."

I close my eyes. I don't want to think about the people we lost. There are too many. It's overwhelming. "I think I need to rest," I whisper.

I wince as Race's chair scrapes against the floor. "Then I'll leave you to it," he says. "We'll talk when you're on your feet again. But, Tate?"

"Yeah?"

"Whatever happens from now on, I want you to know that I'm grateful to you. We all are."

The conference room is packed as I walk in, slowly, with Christina's hand in mine. Right now, I'm holding on to her as much for balance as for affection. I'm on my feet a lot more now, two days after I woke up "for good," as Christina describes it, but I've still been sleeping a lot.

It's time I start to help around here, though. Everybody's been cleaning up the factory, and the people who don't work here are getting ready to leave and return to their homes, their lives. This is the last thing we have to do before we say good-bye.

We have to say good-bye.

The massive circular table that usually sits in the center of the room is gone, replaced with row upon row of chairs. At the front of the room is a podium, surrounded by pictures. Brayton Alexander. Ellie Alexander. Aaron Bishop. Rufus Bishop. Graham Congers. Daniel Sung. Kellan Fisher. Leo Thomas. And so many others. The ones we lost, the heroes who fell. No separation between human and H2, no distinction.

We file past them, dozens of pictures, lined up in rows. Fingers reach out to stroke faces that we will never touch or see again. I stand for a long time in front of Leo's picture, which will soon be hanging in the hall of the patriarchs next to his father's. It's so wrong, and everything about it hurts.

"If it hadn't been for you, I wouldn't have figured it out," I say to him. "I'm going to miss you." For the rest of my life, I'll miss him. Christina leans her head on my shoulder and swipes a tear from her cheek.

All around me, others are mourning. Bill Congers's jaw is clenched as he fights his own lonely sorrow. Race stands beside him, his mouth tight. I wonder if he's thinking of his own son, if he'll do things differently, if he'll learn from me and my dad, from Congers and Graham. The mistakes we made and the opportunities we missed. I hope so.

As I turn to go to my seat, my mother is wheeled in by Dr. Ackerman. Her eyes are black, and she has a bandage over her nose and on the side of her face. She looks awful, but I grin as I break from the line to go to her. I so easily could have lost both my parents, but she's made it through. Yesterday she told me she was arranging a sabbatical from Princeton so she could be in the city with me during my senior year. I have no idea how that's going to go, but I'm thankful I have the chance to find out. "I didn't think you were allowed out of bed," I say as I lean down and kiss her cheek.

"I'm not," she says, arching an eyebrow and looking over her shoulder at the scowling Dr. Ackerman. "But this was important."

Angus strides in with one of the Core agents, carrying a large stack of portraits to position at the front of the room. Most of them are men I don't recognize, but after a moment I realize they're Core agents who lost their lives in our earlier battles. And then I see the last four set in line with the rest:

Peter McClaren.

George Fisher. My heart sinks as I realize his body must have been found.

Charles Willetts.

And my dad.

"These are the heroes whom we haven't yet mourned or celebrated," Angus declares, "and we thought it fitting that we do so now."

My father's stern, handsome face peers out at me. There's something defiant in those eyes, a keen, cool intelligence. I stare into them, wishing for the warmth I craved, that I still crave. My mother's hand slips into mine. "When you were born, he was so scared."

"What?"

"He told me that he knew he'd make mistakes. He wasn't sure he knew how to be a father. His own father had been so strict and so stern. But he loved you, Tate." Her face crumples. "He loved you more than he could say."

And that's what does it. So many people have said I'm like him. They've told me he would be proud of me. But this, from my mother, breaks me apart. After everything, all the mistakes he made, the mistakes I made, the distance between us that will only be bridged through memory and thought because I'll never hear his voice again . . .

I let go of her hand and approach the picture. Frederick Archer, my father, the man who figured it out, who put everything in place, who saved the world with a little help from his son. "You did it, Dad," I say to him quietly, under my breath, words for no one but him. "I couldn't have done this if you hadn't prepared me. I'd be dead if you hadn't done what you did."

I move closer. I don't know what I believe, whether he can hear me, but I hope he can. "I love you, too."

I step back. Nothing's changed. We're still grieving terrible losses, people whose sacrifices saved us but whose absence will haunt us always. We're preparing for an enemy of unknown number and strength, hoping what we have is enough to protect our planet. The Fifty and the Core have a lot to figure out. Things are complicated, and they'll stay that way for a long time.

But I'm proud of my dad, of what he did, and if he were here, he'd be proud of me, too.

And that much, at least, is simple.

ACKNOWLEDGMENTS

Many thanks to the incredible team at Penguin for helping and cheering us on. My gratitude goes to Stacey Barney, our editor, for being patient, thorough, and thoughtful. Thanks also go to Marisa Russell for coordinating publicity at Penguin, and also to the team at JKS Publicity, including Julie Schoerke, Samantha Lien, and Grace Wright, for doing everything from getting us interviews with *Publishers Weekly* to snagging me a cab at midnight on Bourbon Street.

A special thank-you goes to the team at New Leaf Literary, but I want to express my intense gratitude to Kathleen Ortiz and Joanna Volpe for providing support of every possible kind throughout this process. You guys set a high bar for agents. Like, up in the stratosphere.

To my friends who never wavered in your electronic (((hugs))) and encouragement—Brigid, Jaime, and Virginia most especially—I am in your debt. And Lydia, not even a mountain of shrimp toast could properly convey my adoration.

Thank you to my family for holding me together, and to my colleagues, especially Paul, for being willing to let me mix book talk with psychology talk.

And finally, to our readers, thank you for hanging with Tate and Christina during the most intense week of their lives. Whether you scan red or blue, I love you all. —Sarah Fine

———————————

Thanks to Melissa, my love and the CEO of our family.

My incredible co-author, Sarah Fine, who somehow juggles four full-time jobs at once!

Joanna Volpe, the Guinness World Record holder for the Greatest Agenting Moves in One Calendar Year.

The entire team at New Leaf Literary and Media, most notably Kathleen Ortiz, Jaida Temperly, and Jackie Lindert for their editorial prowess during the writing process!

Our incredible team at Penguin, including the marketing and publicity teams (Marisa Russell, Erin Berger, and Erin Gallagher); Tony Sahara, who designed our incredible covers; Cindy Howle, copy chief, who oversaw the production process; our copy editor, Wendy Dopkin; and Stacey Barney, who loved this series from day one and made it work through sheer will.

My mom, Nahid Ghaffari, who taught me to read practically before I could walk. My dad, Faraz Shahbazian, who loves books as much as anyone. My entire family and my friends for their support over all these years. —Walter Jury

WALTER JURY

was born in London, went to high school in Silicon Valley, worked in the infamous agency mailrooms of Hollywood, and currently resides just outside of Manhattan. *Burn* is his second book for teens. Under his real name, he is one of the movie producers of the Divergent series, amongst other films and television shows he is developing.

You can visit Walter Jury at walterjury.tumblr.com or on Twitter @WalterJury

Photo © Rebecca Skinner

SARAH FINE was

born on the West Coast, raised in the Midwest, and is now firmly entrenched on the East Coast. She's a clinical child psychologist and the author of the Guards of the Shadowlands series and *Of Metal and Wishes*.

You can visit Sarah Fine at sarahfinebooks.com or on Twitter @finesarah

"Nonstop, action-packed thrill ride." —Morgan Rhodes, author of the *New York Times* bestselling *Falling Kingdoms*

WALTER JURY | SARAH FINE

MY DAD IS ALMOST TO THE BACK DOOR, HIS CELL PHONE at his ear, his words staccato and commanding, talking so fast, I can't catch any of it. Christina is close behind him, pale as a ghost. I look over my shoulder to see all the kitchen workers staring at the door to the cafeteria. The cops are pounding on it, shouting, "Police! Open the door!" over and over again. But I've created just enough uncertainty to hold them in place for a few seconds.

I squat low by the heavy metal door to the outside, feeling the breeze at my back as Christina holds it open for me. I wrench the cap off the container in my hands. A few seconds later, I've laid a little vegetable-oil welcome mat for anyone who chases us out this way. Again, it will gain us only a few seconds, but I'm thinking we need every advantage we can get.

Christina takes off, and I weave through a set of Dumpsters and recycling containers, hot on her heels. She's fast as hell and agile, too, and she streaks into the open and sprints behind my father, who's several strides ahead of us, cell phone in one hand and the scanner in the other. He runs straight up the sidewalk. A few faces are pressed against the classroom windows, no doubt happy for the distraction. A black SUV skids around the corner, from the street at the front of the school, and accelerates toward us. For a second I think we've got another enemy, but my dad waves his arms at the vehicle.

He brought a getaway car?

His powerful strides don't slow as he looks over his shoulder, as if to gauge our distance from him. As soon as I see the expression on his face, I know the cops are closing in. I don't even turn around to look. Instead, I kick it into overdrive and close the distance between me and Christina. We're a few car lengths from the SUV, and whoever's inside has thrown the passenger-side door open. We're going to make it.

My father doesn't dive through the open door like I expect him to, though. He turns back and runs toward me as Christina sprints past him and ducks into the SUV. Before I have a chance to wonder why, I hear a series of echoing cracks and the windshield of the car next to me shatters. A voice back by the Dumpsters yells something, but I can't make it out. My dad is right behind me a second later, shielding me with his body. The police are firing at us like we're terrorists or criminals, like we're a threat, and I have no idea why. They're not supposed to shoot at unarmed civilians, right? Especially right next to a school?

My brain is a soupy fog of questions and fear as we stumble the last few feet toward the SUV while the world explodes around us. My dad flinches and falls against my back with his full weight, nearly knocking me over. The groan that rolls from his throat is pure, animal pain. He reaches around me and presses the scanner into my chest. "Take this," he says, sinking to one knee.

I turn toward him, the scanner dangling from my fist. The back of my father's pressed white shirt is blossoming with red.